BROKEN GATES

The P.J. STONE GATES TRILOGY

Book 2

AVA WIXX

First Edition: October 2025
Published in the United States of America by
Wicked Wixx Press.
The Wicked Wixx Press Logo is a trademark of
Wicked Wixx Press.
Originally published under the title
Broken Gates: 2013

Cover Art, Ava Wixx Logo, Wicked Wixx Logo, & Interior Book
Graphics by Lindsay Tiry of LT Arts
Trilogy Logo by Jordan P. Fremgen

Print ISBN: 978-1-955950-45-9
Kindle ISBN: 978-1-955950-46-6
EPUB ISBN: 978-1-955950-47-3

For more information visit: avawixx.com

Content Warning

Coerced sex, gun violence, attempted murder, murder, teenage dumbassery, and probably a few other things I forgot about because it's been over a decade since I wrote this book.

If you can't take the heat,
then don't tickle the dragon.

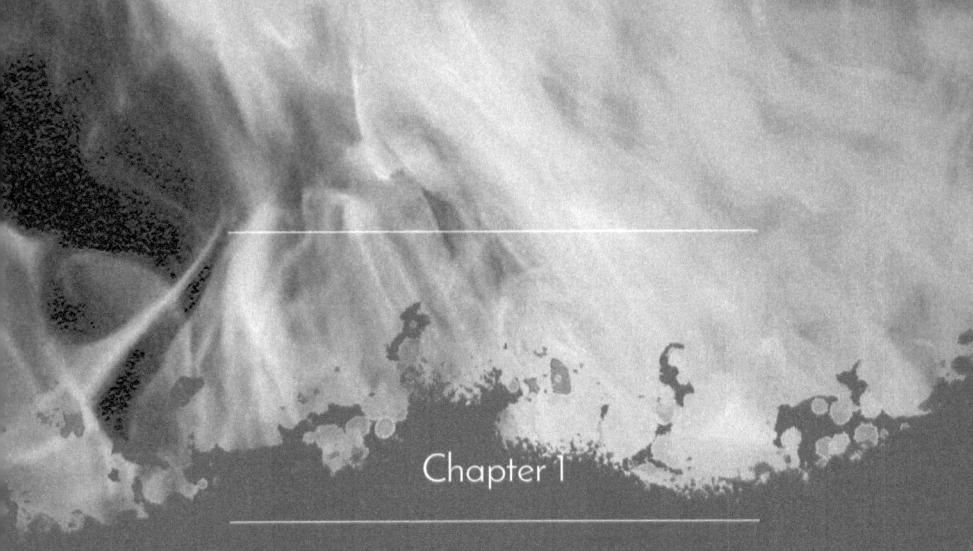

Chapter 1

We were at war.

And just like in every war there were casualties. Jenna, Jeremy, Bryn, and myself were the last of our kind... Speaker, Gatekeeper, Guardian, and Seer...respectively. Only a short time ago our kind had been thriving, our numbers many, but then the alien Riders had exterminated them.

Because of me.

If not for my visions, they'd still be alive. The revenge I yearned to mete out, I hoped, would help me to assuage my feelings of guilt. I just prayed that no one else would suffer because of me.

Too bad I forgot to pray for myself.

I sensed something was wrong only an instant before the bedroom door slammed open. But in life and death situations an instant can mean the difference between one or the other.

"Bryn!" I gasped, jolting up in bed with a start. My eyes flew to the doorway where a large threatening shape was backlit from the hallway lights. The man's face was illuminated for a brief moment as he pulled the trigger on a gun, the bullet exploding in our direction. I reacted without thinking, throwing myself over Bryn. A flash of white-hot searing pain ripped across my shoulder, just before a blinding light erupted in my head. Silence engulfed me, followed by a ringing in my ears. I gasped for breath, struggling to bring oxygen into my lungs. *Bryn, oh God Bryn. Please let him be okay. Please, God, let him be okay–*

Everything went black.

"I HAVE FORESEEN the outcome of both choices, and it leaves us with only one course of action. As much as it pains me, you must do what I ask of you."

I watched as an unfamiliar woman spoke to an unknown man kneeling in front of her. The man seemed to be in pain, if the way he clutched at her dress was any indication. The woman was tall and regal, with long white hair that hung halfway down her back. Despite her hair color, her pale face was young and completely unlined. The man kneeling in front of her had dark auburn hair burnished brighter by the flames in the nearby fireplace, his skin nearly as pale as hers. His build was massive, and

I found myself thinking that he could quite possibly dwarf even Khol in size.

"No, please. You're asking me to betray you." The man sank down closer to the ground, slumping into himself. His thick arms reached up to wrap around the women's legs as if she was the only thing keeping him anchored to this earth.

The woman's dainty hand lifted hesitantly, as if she would stroke his hair, but it fell back to her side before actually making contact. "If you do not do as I ask, *that* will be a betrayal to me." Her words were harsh, but there was no mistaking the anguish in her glowing golden eyes.

"Send another," the man said raggedly.

"It must be you. I can trust no other with this task."

The man abruptly stood, rising up to his full height. The woman seemed childlike in comparison to his size, and yet her presence overtook his, her power greater in some way. The two of them stared at each other for what seemed like an eternity, a battle of wills silently waging between them, until the man suddenly dropped to his knees again. "As you wish, my queen." With those as his parting words, he disappeared.

The woman froze in place, as if in shock, her features eerily blank. Suddenly she was in motion, throwing herself on the nearby bed, her small form crumpling in on itself as she sobbed hysterically. Her anguish was palpable, and almost too much for me to bear. Tears of my own pricked the corners of my eyes.

I took a step towards her, drawn in by curiosity. Why was I being shown this particular scene? It didn't have the same feel as my normal visions, and yet, I couldn't come up with any other explanation. *It has to be a vision.*

The woman lifted her head, gazing into the flames of the fire, her tear-streaked face blotchy and yet still beautiful. "Paige Joplin Stone, you are our first and last hope," she whispered.

My breath caught in my throat and I blinked rapidly, confusion washing over me. Was this a vision after all, or something more? And if it was a vision, was it from the past, present, or future? Who was this woman and how did she know about me? She and her companion were obviously both dragons, as evidenced by his disappearing act and her glowing eyes but—but he'd called her queen, and her hair was white. I knew of no dragon queens, or factions of white dragons. None of it made any sense.

"My little Seer." Khol's voice echoed inside my head, causing me to turn away from the enthralling scene before me.

"What are you doing here?" I asked, wondering if in fact, he was really here.

Khol's iridescent eyes blazed bright, casting an eerie green glow on everything before him. It was almost blinding. He reached out his hand, palm up, in a silent offering for me to take it. "Come back to us. You can't stay here any longer."

I tilted my head to study him. There was desperation

etched into every line on his face. "Where's here? Who's she?" I nodded in the direction of the once again sobbing woman.

"Please. We can't lose you," he rasped as if I hadn't said anything at all. *"I can't lose you."* The last part seemed to be said inside my mind, as if I was reading Khol's thoughts.

"I'm not going anywhere. No one's gonna lose me."

Khol's lips turned up into a grim smile, the skin around his eyes pinching. "That's where you're wrong, my little Seer. You're already here, which makes you lost, and you need to return to us. *To me."* His thoughts echoed in my head again.

"But—"

"Do you trust me?"

I eyed him warily for a moment, wondering why he would ask me such a question at a time like this. *Oh well, I suppose I can at least humor him.* "Yes, you know I do."

He offered me his hand again. "Then come with me, now."

I rolled my eyes but walked towards him anyways. I reached out my hand to intertwine my fingers with his, meeting his gaze. As I stared at him, everything washed out into a vivid green, blinding me.

"KHOL?" I mumbled, my throat scratchy and raw.

Why are my eyelids so heavy? It was if both of them were

weighted down with fifty pounds each. "Khol? What happened?"

A loud crash sounded, making me wince, followed by some scuffling noises. "I told you to stay the hell away from her," Bryn's familiar voice growled.

An answering growl reverberated off the walls, "I just saved her."

"I would have—was going to save her," Bryn snarled.

"I gave you a month," Khol snarled back.

"Hey," I grumbled. "No fighting." My eyelids finally shed their excess weight and I blinked them open to a much too bright room. "Bright lights," I muttered to myself, feeling like I imagined a Mogwai would. *Just call me Gizmo.*

"Oh, my God, you're awake." I barely had time to focus in on Jenna's elated face before she was on me, crushing me with a much too tight bear hug.

"Can't breathe," I sputtered.

"Oh, right, sorry," she said, releasing me. "Guys—she's awake. Not just mumbling anymore," Jenna called out without breaking visuals with me.

Khol and Bryn seemed to just appear at my bedside, both of them wearing almost identical expressions of surprise intermingled with joy. My gaze danced between everyone's faces as they stared down at me. I shifted under the scrutiny. "What happened?" I couldn't shake the feeling I was missing something pretty major.

Bryn dropped down beside me, taking me into his

arms, pressing his unshaven face into my hair. "Twice," — his voice cracked— "I've almost lost you twice now."

I peered over his shoulder to meet Khol's eyes with question. "You were shot," Khol said. His gaze flicked away as if he couldn't bear to look at me anymore. "I healed you the best I could. I couldn't do it properly with you being so close to death, and unconscious. You slipped into a coma…"

I gasped as the memory slammed home…

An image of a man's face being illuminated for a brief moment before a bullet exploded in our direction. Me reacting without thinking and throwing myself over Bryn. White-hot searing pain ripping across my shoulder, just before a blinding light erupted in my head. Silence engulfing me, followed by a ringing in my ears—gasping as I struggled to breath. Everything suddenly going dark.

"I remember," I whispered, my body numb. "I almost died." Yes, the words felt right when I said them out loud, even though Khol had just said as much himself.

"I wasn't worried. I knew these two big galoots wouldn't let you die." Jenna grinned, staring down at me through long, thick black bangs. *I guess the more things change, the more they stay the same.* Jenna hadn't dyed her hair some outrageous color but the deep black signaled that it wouldn't be long before she shirked the restrictions. We'd agreed in order to help her go incognito that she had to stick to shades of dye that appeared natural. I knew it was only a matter of time before she rebelled. Jenna wouldn't be Jenna if she didn't.

"I still don't understand why I only slipped into a coma if I was so close to death, and I couldn't be healed properly." I reached up around Bryn, who was still clinging to me, to gingerly explore my head with my fingertips. I heaved a sigh of relief when I found nothing but a whole healthy scalp of hair. *Phew. No bald spots.*

"It took all of my strength to heal your body," Khol rumbled, his voice on the verge of cracking. "But even then I almost failed. A part of you went somewhere else I—"

Bryn released me, turning to square off with Khol. "I would have found her. I—"

"*You* don't have the power. I gave you a month." Raw energy snapped out of Khol, rolling off of him in angry waves. "She could have been like that for years if I would have waited for you to figure it out."

"She's *my Anam Cara*," Bryn grated through clenched teeth.

"Are you even sure about that anymore?" Khol's words were like a slap to my face.

What does he mean by that exactly? My heart pounded against my ribs.

"What's that supposed to mean?" Bryn said, mirroring my inner thoughts.

"Your bond was shaky at best out here, and with her near-death experience—"

"Holy shit!" Jenna interjected. "It could have null and voided your *Anam Cara* bond Bryn, just like it did to Khol's before!"

I'd been bonded to Khol as his *Anam Cara* for what felt like five minutes before I'd attempted to take my own life. Being so close to death had broken the bond, and Khol being so filled with guilt, had finally let Bryn bond with me. Could all of that have been for nothing? Could my and Bryn's *Anam Cara* bond be broken now as well?

"Exactly," Khol confirmed.

Bryn's whole body seemed to deflate with the revelation, and a torrent of dark emotions swirled in his sea storm eyes as he looked at me. I awkwardly pulled myself from bed, lurching into him since I was still so weak. "Bryn. It doesn't matter, we'll fix it."

At least a dozen heartbeats passed before he spoke, "Maybe it happened for a reason."

My heart squeezed as if a boa constrictor was wrapped around my chest. I sucked in short, shallow breaths, struggling against nausea. "What—what are you saying?"

"Just what it sounds like," he said, no longer able to meet my eyes. "Maybe being mated to Khol would be the best thing for you." *This isn't really happening. I must be dreaming, or still in a coma. That's what it is—I'm having a horrible coma induced nightmare. None of this is real.* "He has the power to protect you when I can't."

"No, listen to me, none of that matters! I love *you*. I want *you*. Bryn—"

"No, *you* listen to *me*. It does matter. We can't even bond all the way, and having you walk around without a full bond is like painting a sign on your back asking other male dragons to force themselves on you. And—and—"

Bryn stammered, his fingers digging into my shoulders, and his eyes burning a bright dragon blue. "What if Khol hadn't been there when you were shot? You'd be dead."

My face crumpled, and fat tears began to run down my cheeks as I gulped for air. "Please—I love you." It was a miracle I managed to get even those words out.

Bryn's expression softened, his thumbs wiping at my tears, the motion so tender it only made my heart squeeze tighter. "I'm only doing this because of how much I love you, Peej. You tried to sacrifice your life for me once, now it's my turn to do it for you."

"No, I won't let you," I squeaked. *No...no...no...no...no...* That one word began to bounce around in my brain as I struggled not to panic. Bryn was just upset. He wouldn't really leave me. He told me he would fight for me as long as I wanted him. He promised. He told me *always.* I trusted him—in him.

"You don't get a say in this choice." Bryn dipped his head, taking quick possession of my mouth, sliding his tongue in to intertwine with mine. I clutched at his shoulders trying to pull him closer to me. He sank into our embrace, savoring me, but only for a moment before he jerked away completely.

I stepped into him, scrambling to hold on, but he slipped through my fingertips, disappearing into thin air. "No!" I screamed, knowing there was no way for me to follow him. Without his touch, I was left ice cold, and I dropped to the ground as my vision blurred like watercolors running off a page. "No!" I screamed again.

Khol's strong arms wrapped around me, pulling me into him, his chin pressing against the top of my head. His warmth and scent enveloped me, but instead of comfort I found only anger. I wrenched around to face him, pounding at his chest, my fists balled tightly. "This is your fault! You did this on purpose! All of it! You never meant to let him have me, did you?" I kept swinging, hollow thuds sounding each time my fists made contact. "Did you?" I screeched.

Khol didn't respond, and his silence was nearly deafening. Not that he could have said anything to change my mind. I blamed him for Bryn walking away. I wanted nothing more than to hurt him like he had wounded me. I reached out, clawing my nails down his face and neck. When I didn't find the relief I was looking for, I started ripping at his shirt. Once the flimsy material was out of the way, I tore at his muscular chest, wanting to rip his heart out of his body with my bare hands. Because— because that's what he'd done to me.

But Khol just stood there, taking everything I gave him, not even flinching.

"P.J., stop," I heard Jenna say, but her command had little effect on me. "She's gonna hurt herself," she then said to Khol.

"She'll be fine."

"She's making you bleed," Jenna argued.

"I will heal."

"I hate you!" I seethed.

Khol had become the focal point of all my anger.

Everything is his fault! I scratched, tore, and even bit, until I lost all sense of everything, and eventually collapsed in his arms.

He carried my limp body over to my bed, depositing me there, where I cried myself to sleep, wishing I could fall back into a temporary coma.

Chapter 2

I had no home. I belonged nowhere. I was a single leaf, separated from my tree and set adrift upon a wind of nothingness. By walking away from me, Bryn had painted my world the deepest black. There was no point in going on anymore. I wouldn't take my own life. I had only tried that once to spare Bryn an existence of torment, but I could simply stop living…cease to exist. Maybe if I just laid here long enough, I would simply disappear into the nothingness that had seemingly swallowed me.

"Peej," the heartbreakingly familiar voice rasped, just as the bed dipped. "You can't keep doing this to yourself." A large warm hand attempted to run through my ratty, tangled hair. It'd been days since I'd washed it, let alone brushed it. *So good luck with that…asshole.*

A flash pan of rage ignited within me. *How dare he break my heart into a million pieces and then seek to comfort me!* He told me he would always love me...always fight for me. Lies...all lies. "Don't touch me!" I croaked, even as my body craved nothing but more of his caresses. "You don't get to comfort me when I'm this way because of you."

"Peej," Bryn whispered, his voice cracking. "It's what's best for you. We were kidding ourselves before to think we could truly be together."

Jerking upright, I whirled around to face him, my dragon fire magic rousing just under the surface. "And who said you get to decide what's best for me? You don't get—"

My anger fizzled out as I took in his dejected expression and slumped shoulders. "I love you, Bryn. How can I live without you?" I reached out to touch him, and he snagged my fingers in his large hand, meeting my gaze. His eyes seemed a darker blue than normal, as if the light from the room couldn't be reflected in them—as if he had lost a little bit of his life essence somehow.

"You won't have to live without me, Peej." His eyes moved over me, coming to rest somewhere over my right shoulder. "I'm still your best friend. And that's never gonna change."

A weird strangled noise erupted from the back of my throat. "*Best friends?* Can you actually look at me now and tell me that you truly believe there was ever a time when that's all we were?" Of course, he technically wasn't, in fact, currently looking at me. Not directly. *Coward.*

Bryn remained silent as the seconds ticked by. What could he say? No matter what words he used to try and sooth me, to try and make things easier on me, we both would know they were a lie. "You almost died...again," he muttered, turning his entire body away from me. "And I didn't have the power to save you."

"You're the one who's killing me now!" Anguish twisted my gut as I crumpled back down on the bed. Bryn loomed over me, cupping the side of my jaw in his warm palm. I pressed my cheek into his callused skin, desperate for his attention. I greedily studied his face—the face of the man who I'd come to think of as home.

His black eyebrows were furrowed, standing out in stark contrast against his pale skin. The lines of his face seemed harsher than I remembered, as if some hardship had eroded away the soft edges of childhood. He'd changed so much over the last year... *We'd* changed so much over the last year, yet there was still one constant for me.

"I won't let you walk away from me," I whispered.

"You can't stop me," he replied softly, even as his thumb circled my cheek tenderly.

Wanna bet? I wound my fingers around the back of his neck, yanking him down to me. I slammed my lips into his, forcing a grunt from him as I aggressively slipped my tongue into his mouth. He only resisted for a moment before the stiffness in his body melted away to make room for another kind of tension between us.

Suddenly his hands were in motion, sliding down to explore my body, knowing exactly how to touch me. I sucked on his tongue, drinking down his heady flavor with desperation. Back when we had just crossed the line in our relationship, I wouldn't have known what I was missing if he had walked away, but now...now I would mourn the loss of his touch with every breath I took for the rest of my life. I couldn't bear the thought.

"Don't leave me, Bryn," I choked out on a moan. I shifted, sliding my hands under his shirt, my fingers curling into his warm flesh.

"I have to—" I plunged my tongue into his mouth again, not wanting to hear what he had to say. I would kiss him until he had no rational thought left and he could no longer resist giving me what I wanted.

I kissed, groped and fondled, somehow maneuvering Bryn onto his back. When I sat on top of him with my thighs astride his, I dipped down to continue kissing him as I worked on getting the both of us out of our clothes. He wrapped his hands around my waist, both trying to stop me from grinding against him and to press me harder into him at the same time.

My stomach twisted, gurgled, and then did a weird little flip-flop. I lurched sideways and proceeded to revisit the very little bit of food that I had eaten that day. When finished, I rolled off Bryn, groaning in utter mortification. *Talk about a mood killer.* It was just as well that Bryn was planning on leaving me because I doubted if I could ever look him in the eyes again. I flipped onto my side facing away from him and silently pleaded for any deity that might be listening to open up the floor so it could swallow me whole.

Bryn rubbed my back gently in slow soothing circles. "You okay?" His voice was still gruffer than normal, which made my stomach do another little flip-flop but for a completely different reason. *I guess throwing up didn't necessarily kill* my *mood.*

"I'm fine," I said in a clipped tone, not really sure how to react to Bryn in that moment. I mean, I both loved and hated him, while also both being turned on and humiliated. *Talk about being conflicted.*

"Hey," Jeremy called through the slightly ajar door. "I was just coming to get you guys for a meeting. Khol wants to catch P.J. up on everything she's missed..." His voice trailed off. I didn't want to know what he was thinking when he saw Bryn and my half-undressed state and the evidence of my unsettled gut. "But I guess I could tell him you guys are busy right now."

"No," Bryn said, the bed moving as he got up. "Just give us a few minutes." I remained silenced by my complete and utter humiliation.

"Yeah, okaaay," Jeremy replied, hesitantly. His retreating footsteps then sounded in the stone hallway. Silence enveloped the room, and for a few moments I actually wondered if Bryn had just gone and disappeared on me ala dragon style.

"Do you need anything?" Bryn asked, his deep voice cutting through the silence.

You, my mind supplied without thinking, but I kept that thought to myself. *Yeah, this isn't awkward or anything.* "No," I croaked.

"It's for the best, you know?" I fought the urge to stick my fingers in my ears to keep from hearing what else he had to say to me. *Mature, I know.* "We need to both try and move on."

His words sliced into my heart, tearing it in two, but from that pain stemmed fresh anger intermingled with jealously. Was there someone that he planned on moving on with? Was that what this was all about, and he was just trying to cushion the blow for me? I whipped my head around to face him, sure that my green eyes were glowing with rage, my embarrassment burned away by my hostility directed at him. "Who do you wanna move on with, Bryn?" I hissed. "Has that buyer's remorse finally set in? Or did you figure out when you were away that there were better options out there?"

Bryn's mouth dropped open and his eyes widened as he stared at me in shock, but my doubt at the authenticity of his reaction spurred me on. Bryn loved me, I had no doubt about that—but maybe he wanted someone else more. *More…* God, I was really starting to hate that word. "Nala," I ground out her name. "You've decided to choose her over me, and this whole situation is a lucky coincidence for you, isn't it?" Nala…the stupid black dragon bitch that wanted Bryn for herself. *I hate her.*

"No," he said, his jaw muscles twitching. "It's not like that. I don't want her. You know you're the only one for me."

He locked gazes with me, and my anger, just like that, folded up into itself. Maybe I just wanted a reason, something to get mad about, something to cover up my pain. It was the not knowing why he'd suddenly given up that was driving me insane. Surely, he couldn't just walk away if he still loved me as much as he claimed.

"Then, why?" I asked, my eyes roaming his face for clues. "No one ever said it would be easy, no one ever said—"

"No one ever said it would kill you."

I crawled across the bed on my knees, stopping right in front of him. "None of that is your fault, but if you leave me"—I reached up and caressed his face, his eyes sliding shut on contact—"that will be your fault. And that will be what kills me."

Bryn's jaw ticked with tension under my palm. A few heartbeats passed before he pulled away, leaving me cold from the loss of his heated skin. "I've made up my mind and nothing you can do or say will change it."

He stalked towards the door, pausing to look at me over his shoulder. His eyes seemed to hold the weight of the world in them, and for the first time ever, I found myself wondering if the events of the last year had buried the Bryn from my childhood for good. "A world without you in it isn't worth living in." His voice cracked and broke an octave lower. "But a world with you alive and well, even if I can't have you, is a world worth fighting for."

My mouth opened and shut a few times, like a fish trying to breathe out of water, but by the time I found my voice, he was already gone. I sank back down on the bed, the numbness I'd been feeling before returning in full force. *How can I go on without him?* For me, a world where I didn't get to have Bryn wasn't worth anything.

"Hey, you need any help getting to the meeting?" I looked up to meet Jeremy's concerned brown eyes.

"I thought you left," I mumbled.

Jeremy made his way farther into my room. "I did, but I came back to check on you. I was worried."

I chuckled darkly. "Or you saw an opportunity to swoop in and get me on the rebound from Bryn, you mean."

He frowned, shaking his head. "No, it's not like that anymore. I—well, I finally came to terms that you and me weren't ever gonna happen and I've moved on. You were right, maybe I never really loved you…just thought I did… but—" He looked away, flushing. "I have feelings for someone else now. And I think this is the real thing." He gave me a tentative smile. "I'm ready to accept that offer of friendship…for real this time. Or maybe I should say I can handle being a friend to you now."

I gave him a smile that threatened to crack my face. "I guess I can't keep anyone's interest, can I?" I meant it as a joke, but it came out sounding dark and bitter. I gulped, trying to swallow down the sour taste in my mouth. "That's not what I meant, what I meant was that—" Much to my shame, I burst into tears before I could salvage the situation.

"Whoa, whoa, whoa, don't cry! I know this is tough right now—with everything. I understand what you meant." He hunched over to encircle me within his arms and I pressed into him, crying on his shoulder...literally. As I sobbed into the soft cotton of his worn t-shirt I heard Jeremy clear his throat, and felt his muscles move restlessly against my cheek.

Pulling back enough to meet his gaze, I sniffled unabashedly as his gold-flecked eyes bore into mine. "We should probably get going. I'm sure everyone's waiting on us by now."

Using the back of my hand to swipe at the tears on my face, I nodded in affirmation. In the past, I would have wanted a few minutes to try to make myself look somewhat presentable, but not anymore. I felt like crap and didn't care if the whole universe knew I felt that way by way of my appearance. I snagged one of Bryn's oversized hoodie sweatshirts off the floor, pulling it over my head. I inhaled deeply, luxuriating in the small comfort his scent offered me. "I guess I'm ready to go," I mumbled.

Jeremy put his arm around my shoulder, guiding me along as I stumbled blindly beside him. We eventually reached our destination...the common room. I let Jeremy steer me to a chair, sitting me down like I wasn't in control of my own body, and I guess I kind of wasn't, emotionally speaking. I was vaguely aware of the sensation of eyes being on me, but I kept mine averted for fear of spotting the one pair I couldn't handle seeing so soon after their owner had just ripped my heart out... again.

"He's not here," Khol's rumbled, breaking the silence in the room. I lifted my head, meeting his penetrating green gaze with question. "Bryn. I think he's trying to give you some space."

My heart twisted inside my chest—that was the last thing I wanted from Bryn—and I hated the fact that Khol still seemed to be able to read my emotions after all this time. "Oh," was what I managed to choke out as a response. I let my eyes slide back down to the table despite the lack of Bryn's presence.

"There's a lot that you missed while you were... recovering," Khol said tactfully. "You need to be informed of the state of things."

I lifted my shoulders and shrugged. "Sure."

"We found out why the Riders are trying to kill off animals," Jenna piped up. "It was so obvious I can't believe I didn't see it right away. It's because animals can see what people have inside of them. We can use the animals to help us identify the Riders without having to use just you, P.J." She paused for dramatic effect. "And that's exactly what we've been doing."

At that I did raise my head to scan the room—not only were Jenna, Khol and Jeremy there, but also Macon, Drake, and a few dragons I didn't recognize. Two males with silver hair, and two males with gold hair... representatives of the silver and gold dragon factions, I realized. Before I'd fallen into the coma, we'd received news of each of the factions wishing to enter into talks about the alien Riders, but to see them actually here was...

well, kind of shocking. I did note that the black faction was not being represented, although I saw no real purpose for any of them being present for my so-called catching up meeting.

Surprisingly, for the first time since I'd awakened from my coma, I wondered about the circumstances of my shooting. "Who attacked us exactly? I mean I assume it was the Riders but—how did they find us…me?"

I could almost hear Khol's teeth grinding together from across the room. "We don't know how they found us, or how they managed to get past our security to hunt you down so quickly, but I can assure you nothing like that will happen again."

"Someone ratted us out!" Jenna exclaimed in a manner that let me know this wasn't the first time she was making that particular accusation.

"No, there must be some other explanation," Khol stated flatly. "None of our kind, no matter their situation, wishes to see this world destroyed by those things."

"My lord," Macon chimed in. "I mean no disrespect in disagreeing with you, but I as well can't seem to come up with any other explanation besides betrayal of the most egregious kind."

"What a surprise that you seem to share the opinion of the tiny Speaker who you're currently bedding," Drake said, a wry smile twisting his lips. "Your opinion means nothing because it is not of your own making."

"And you never have a thought that goes against our

lord's," Macon growled. "He'd do better with a second who could think for himself."

"Enough!" Khol bellowed. "There are many other issues to discuss besides things that we don't have the answers to."

I angled my gaze, scanning everyone's faces with suspicion. A shudder raced up my spine to think that maybe someone in this very room could have been responsible for me nearly dying and slipping into a coma. I shifted uneasily, pulling up the hood on Bryn's sweatshirt like a child who thought hiding under the covers was some kind of protection from the boogey man. Silly but effective, because once cloaked in the shadow of the much too large hood, I heaved a sigh of relief, Bryn's scent swirling around me in a comforting embrace.

"Fine. Let's get on with it then," one of the silver dragons demanded.

"As Jenna was saying," Khol started, all the while searching for my eyes that were hiding in the protection of Bryn's hoodie, "We've begun using the animals as our aids to track down the Riders. We haven't figured out how to remove them from their hosts yet, at least not without killing them, but we'll find the answer eventually."

I inhaled sharply. "So, you're just killing them?"

"What choice do we have?" Jeremy asked.

"But they're in so many people. Do you all even comprehend how many of those things came through the gates?" I swung my head around to look at Khol, even though from the expression on his face I could tell he still couldn't see my eyes in the hoodie. He frowned, probably picking up on my tumultuous emotions. "We can't just kill all of those people." My stomach clenched, and I doubled over to dry heave, luckily there was nothing left for me to throw up. Suddenly I was surrounded by Khol, Jeremy, and Jenna, all of them vying for my attention so they could help make me feel better. *Yeah, that's gonna work.*

"P.J., you need to take care of yourself, girl. This all can wait," Jenna said, pushing back my hoodie and gathering up my hair.

"I'll help you back to your room," Jeremy said at the same time as Jenna.

And Khol's deep voice interwove amongst the chatter my friends were throwing my way. "I'll take her to her room and make sure she gets what she needs…food, water, and maybe more healing."

"Stop!" I snapped. They were boxing me in, making me feel claustrophobic. *They need to back off.* "I'm fine. Can we just get this damn meeting over with, please?" I sat back up, the wave of nausea passing. I raised my chin with determination, meeting each of my friends' gazes.

"Very well," Khol conceded.

Following Khol's lead, everyone else settled back into their seats for what would turn out to be a very long meeting indeed.

Chapter 3

I missed a lot while I slumbered away a month of my life in a coma. Truthfully, it felt like I'd missed a much bigger chunk of time because the alien Riders had really been making good use of it. Maybe they knew somehow that I was temporarily out of commission and they were trying to take advantage of our side's lack of my visions. Although, I bet they hadn't counted on Jenna and her furry little squad of spies/assassins. I suppose humans, dragons, and aliens alike all underestimate the true threat a Speaker represents...especially a pissed off one with a taste for revenge.

Our little band of misfits—not so little anymore with the addition of the silver, black, and gold factions of dragons to our cause—had really been putting a major hurting on the Riders. Of course, as far as the media was concerned, there was some kind of crazed cult out there committing political assassinations. The Riders were starting to become desperate from what it seemed, tightening their grip on the government and any other place of power they could manage. There was a threat of martial law in the United States, and the equivalent in Europe, along with radical new laws being pushed through that severely limited the rights of the world's citizens. In a nutshell…things had reached DEFCON 1 at warp speed.

I leaned against the wall of the shower, letting the hot water beat down on my sore body. I was struggling to fully wrap my mind around everything I'd been told in the meeting, along with the fact that I would have to face all of it without Bryn. I mean it wasn't like he wouldn't be there fighting for our cause, but he wouldn't be *with* me, and therefore it wouldn't be the same. Nothing would be the same ever again.

With a heavy sigh I turned off the water, grabbing a towel to wrap around my middle. I wiped the steam away from the mirror, studying myself. The black dye I'd applied to my hair was completely washed away, along with any remnants of the henna I used to use, which left me with a shoulder length bob of bright strawberry blonde hair. Not only was it a horrendous shade of red, but it practically screamed baby dragon to anyone in the know. I wrapped a second towel around my offensive hair and left the bathroom, trudging slowly back to my room —the room Bryn and me used to share. He'd gathered up most of his things when I was in the meeting and moved to his own room across the compound. The better to avoid me with, apparently.

I was right outside my door when I was tugged out of my body by a vision. Struggling to keep myself from collapsing in the hallway, I lurched forward in an attempt to make it to my room, even as the ground come up to meet me.

I was in the same room from my coma-induced dream/vision, although this time around I knew with certainty that I was having a vision and not a dream. I still wasn't sure whether it was from the past, present, or future though. *Where are some ghosts to fill me in when I need them? Maybe they only come out to play around Christmas time?*

I focused in on the white-haired woman dragon that was sitting rigidly on the edge of the bed, her gaze blankly fixated on the fire burning nearby her. I got the sense she was waiting for someone, so I waited with her, so to speak. An undetermined amount of time passed, neither of us moving, when the same man from my last vision appeared in front of her. I noted in the back of my mind that I still hadn't actually seen his face.

He dropped down in front of her, his head bowed deeply, his voice coming out low and hoarse. "It is done. I have fulfilled the task you sent me to complete." The woman remained rigid, not acknowledging the man. He reached out to touch her, tilting his head up just enough so he could look up at her, but before he could make contact, she shirked away. The man cried out, the sound strangled and filled with anguish. "Please, my love, Mori…don't punish me for something you commanded me to do."

Her face crumpled, as if she would cry, but smoothed out again moments later. "My love," she whispered, her eyes still fixated on the flames of the fire, "I don't wish to punish you, but"—a single tear slid down her cheek—"I seem to be unable to control the feelings that twist inside of me when I think of the two of you together in bed."

"I begged for you to send another," the man rasped.

"And you know I could not," she replied, her tone chilling. "My visions are never wrong, you know that."

"So you will banish me from your touch, for doing something that you commanded…*my queen?*" The man spat out the last part with complete and utter disgust. A second later his tone changed. "Please," he begged, "don't do this. I was never unfaithful to you in my heart. Thinking of being in your arms again was the only thing that got me through the task."

"Did you whisper words of endearment to her? Did you tell her that you loved her?" Mori asked hollowly.

"It was the only way that I could convince her to give me—*us*—what we wanted. It's what you asked of me—"

"And yet I find myself hating you for doing what I asked of you," Mori's voice cracked. "I wish to welcome you back into my bed and my heart—but I fear the latter has been crushed by your actions—no matter that I set them into motion."

"No." The man inhaled sharply. "Please don't turn away

from me." He rose, going to her in a blur of speed, covering her with his large body. She gasped in surprise as she accepted his embrace with fervor...but only for a moment before she pushed at his chest, braking off his demanding kiss. "Mori, please..." the man rumbled, his hands clutching at her desperately.

"Oh, Dragos," she murmured tenderly, sliding out from under him. "I fear that you will be the death of me..."

I didn't hear the rest of what she said to him, nor did I hear what he said in turn, because a buzzing sound had begun in both of my ears. I stumbled back in shock. I knew that name. Red hair...red dragon...*Dragos*... The man standing before me was none other than my biological father. *Holy shit!*

The vision began to fade, and I felt myself being pulled back towards my body, but not before I heard Mori's voice as if it were in my head, "Paige Joplin Stone...you must come to me."

"Why? Who are you? Where are you?"

I got no answer as everything went dark.

"WAKE UP, MY LITTLE SEER." Khol's low rasp sounded against my pounding head.

I blinked open my eyes to meet Khol's illuminated green ones. "My father..." I started, unsure of what else to say. I never really had a desire to meet or find out more about my biological father. He'd abandoned my mom when she found out she was pregnant with me, and my dad, the only father I had ever known, had swooped in to take care of us. What else did I need to know? Of course, maybe I wouldn't have to say anything to Khol since he probably viewed my vision right along with me through our link. I hated that I didn't mind the link when it was convenient for me. It made me feel very hypocritical. *Probably because I am.*

Khol sat down beside me, pushing my damp hair out of my face. "Yes, I did share the vision along with you." He studied my face. "Are you over being angry with me? Or do you still incorrectly blame me for what happened with Bryn?"

"I haven't decided yet," I stated, raising my chin obstinately at him.

Khol's lips quirked up slightly at the corners, his eyes sparkling with amusement. I'd forgotten how attractive he actually was since most of the time I only had eyes for Bryn. Or maybe since I was no longer even partially bonded to Bryn, I was right back to where I started with my body craving Khol's again. I found myself, much to my chagrin, suddenly very aware that I was wearing a towel… and nothing more. "Well until you do," he said with a slight chuckle, "we will still need to work together on the task at hand."

"Which one?" After all, there were so many with the Riders working overtime to take over our world.

"The task you have been charged with from your vision, of course."

"Oh, so what...I'm supposed to just find this Mori? Why is she so important?" Besides the fact that she seemed to have some kind of tumultuous relationship with my biological father. *Hmmm... those kinds of relationships must run in the family.*

Khol's face turned serious, his eyes blazing brighter. "This Mori is the queen to us all, and she has been lost to us for many years now. No one is exactly sure what happened to her. Some say she slumbers, some say she journeyed to another world...and some say she was killed by Dragos in a fit of jealous rage."

"My father—I mean my biological father, could've killed the friggin' dragon queen?" I blanched. "But I thought there weren't any dragon kings or queens? And if she's dead, then how the hell am I supposed to find her?" I remembered asking Khol once why he thought I should be impressed that he was a dragon lord because a king would be better. He had then promptly informed me that there were no dragon kings. Didn't it stand to reason that meant there weren't any queens either?

Picking up on my emotions, or maybe my thoughts, because sometimes I still wondered if he could actually read my mind and he just wasn't telling me, Khol answered, "There has ever only been one queen, and she ruled us all—the red, the black, the gold, and the silver. She was all seeing and all knowing, at least that's what we all believed." He turned away from me, bowing his head as if in mourning.

My gut twisted. "Did—did you love her?" Because he

could have—if she died that would have freed him to love another one day—me.

"We all did in a sense, we all worshipped her," Khol murmured. He turned back to face me, running one of his long heated fingers down the side of my neck, eliciting a shiver from me. "But I've never loved another like I love you." Flames erupted in the depths of his irises. "I never knew it was even possible to love someone the way that I do you."

"Oh," I whispered.

Khol's hand slipped under my head to support my neck. Liquid desire ignited in my middle, my gaze trailing down to his full supple lips. *What would it be like to kiss him again after all this time?* So much had happened since the last time his lips had touched mine—and we'd already slept together once. It could be nice...*more than nice*...to give myself over to Khol. Lust heated my insides, and I didn't resist when he brought his lips down to mine, sweeping his tongue in to take full possession of mouth. My hands wound around the back of his neck as if on their own accord, and I tugged, wanting him closer.

Wait—what am I thinking? I can't do this. Or maybe that was the problem—I wasn't thinking. The one time I slept with him...or, more aptly, let him have sex with me to save Bryn's life, I'd felt like my heart had frozen inside of my chest. Even though my body seemed to be all right with being a free agent again, my heart would always belong to Bryn. *But what if Bryn never changes his mind? Khol would never walk away from you the way he did.*

No...I couldn't let Bryn's temporary rejection spur me on to do something stupid and rash. Because when Bryn changed his mind—emphasis on the *when* and not *if*—I couldn't have done something irreparable...like have sex with Khol and end up mated with him. *Damn these dragon hormones!* Now that I had fully tasted all the intimacies of being part of a mated dragon pair, the craving to have that again was almost irresistible. My body craved, and I wanted, but I couldn't let myself give into it.

"No, stop," I gasped into Khol's mouth, struggling to push him away.

He shifted to wrap his arms around me, pressing his face into my hair. "But you're right, my little Seer." His breath tickled my neck and I squeezed my eyes shut, willing myself not to pull him closer again. "A dragon's love is eternal, and I would never—*could* never walk away from you—because I already would have by now. Maybe Bryn is too human to love you the way you desire...the way you deserve."

"But what if I am dragon enough to love Bryn forever?" I hadn't thought about that before. What if Bryn wasn't dragon enough to love me forever? And what if I am? Was I doomed to love Bryn for the rest of my life and to maybe have him move on to love someone else? Maybe more than one someone else?

"I've explained this before." Khol kneaded my back, his fingers digging into my flesh sensually. "It's different for female dragons, that part of you isn't triggered until you've mated."

"But I *was* mated!"

"To both myself *and* Bryn. Even if some part of your prior matings linger…it still…" He pulled away far enough to look into my eyes again from mere inches away. I gulped nervously at the intensity in his green depths. "It still means *I* have a chance with you too. And I'm not going to miss any opportunity I might be presented by Bryn's stupidity."

His lips slamming back into mine, kissing away any retort I may have had. I moaned into his mouth as he pressed himself down into me on the bed. He tugged at the towel that offered me little protection from his roving hands. I had absolutely no idea what to do. Thoughts of doubt about Bryn kept circling in my head, and yet they looped back around to the fact that I couldn't give myself to Khol for fear of losing Bryn forever. But what if I already had? It was an endless circle that caused nothing but uncertainty.

A sharp intake of breath acted as a small dose of sanity for me and I pushed Khol away—only to meet the dark blue eyes of none other than Bryn. It was as if my thoughts alone had conjured him to witness my betrayal. *You can't betray someone if they left you at the curb like yesterday's trash.* A split second before Bryn's face clouded over into an unreadable mask, I saw the hurt that my actions had placed in his eyes. "Bryn!" I gasped. Khol stood, walking out of the room without another word, but I didn't miss the smug look on his face, and I'm sure Bryn didn't either.

Bryn's cool assessing gaze met mine, and my cheeks heated with shame. "I see that it's not gonna take you long before you're mated with him then. Good."

He might as well have slapped me. "*Good?* You can't mean that!" I struggled to breathe. "*He* kissed *me*, I want you—I love you! You know that! Bryn please!" I began to feel lightheaded from lack of oxygen, if only I could manage a couple deep breaths.

"We're not gonna have this discussion. I want you to move on, just like I'm gonna...with Nala."

My heart collapsed in my chest, and I couldn't pull air into my lungs. I floundered a few moments trying to process what he'd just said. "Bryn, no," I rasped when I finally found my voice. "Don't do this. I've known you since we were both five years old. I know you think by pushing my buttons, by using Nala, I'll get angry and mate with Khol... Just please...stop."

"So maybe I don't have any real feelings for her, and maybe what I said to you before was true." When he finally met my gaze again, there were so many dark emotions swimming in his sea storm eyes that I couldn't see the old Bryn—*my* Bryn—in them at all. "But I want you to mate with him, and if giving myself to Nala is the only way I can make that happen"—he bared his teeth at me in a mock smile—"then I'll do it. Make no mistake about that."

"Bryn." His name rolled over my tongue and out of my mouth in a hushed whisper, carrying with it a silent plea that I could somehow make him see what a huge mistake he was making.

"I was born to be your Guardian, and I swore to myself that I would do whatever it took to protect you, even if it meant protecting you from myself." He turned, taking a step towards the door. "I'm just not strong enough—not powerful enough—not good enough to be with you. I just wish I had accepted that from day one. It would have saved us both a lot of pain."

Khol chose that moment to return, strolling into my room with barely concealed smugness. Bryn and Khol locked gazes, the look that passed between them very male somehow, and then Bryn left without so much as another word to me. I stared after him, hating Khol freshly in that moment.

"We must make plans for your journey," Khol said coolly. He was a very wise dragon to not push me any more in that moment. *Maybe with age does come wisdom.* He knew I'd talk to him about the task I was assigned by the missing dragon queen, but little else.

"And where exactly am I going?" I grated.

"She will let us know where, when it's time."

"What's that supposed to mean?" I asked, my stomach sinking.

"It means we have a lot to talk about," Khol said as he closed my bedroom door behind him.

Chapter 4

"Knock, knock," Jenna said, walking right into my room and flopping on my bed.

"You know, saying *knock, knock* and then walking straight into someone's room is not the same thing as *actually* knocking and waiting for a reply." I scrunched up my nose at her, feigning annoyance, even though the truth was I missed her…a lot. It felt like forever since we'd had any real girl time, and chances of that changing anytime soon were unlikely

"Your door was open," she retorted, sticking her tongue out at me.

I rolled my eyes. "No," I said, stuffing the last of my clean laundry into my dresser. "It just wasn't locked."

"Same thing."

"Not really," I grumbled.

"So… you and Bryn are really over, huh?"

My muscles locked up, and I froze with my back to her, my heart tripling in time.

"Why, what do you know?" Had Bryn already mated with Nala? Wouldn't I somehow just *know*? It couldn't all be over like that...could it?

"Well, he did move out of your room, didn't he? And I've seen him skulking around all moody and broody. So —yeah—I connected the dots. You're not the only one that's known him forever."

My knees buckled with relief, and I slid to the ground. He hadn't mated with Nala, at least not yet. "Oh, thank God," I gasped on a sharp intake of breath. Until he did, I still had a chance, and I wouldn't believe otherwise. I scooted around so I could face Jenna, my back resting against my dresser. "Have you seen him hanging around with any female dragons...like Nala maybe?" I couldn't seem to control my morbid curiosity.

Jenna's laugh came out sounding like a sharp bark, and she eyed me with amusement from under her black fringe of bangs. "No, he's been avoiding all female dragons like the plague. Especially Nala. Is that what he told you? That he was gonna mate with someone else?"

I averted my eyes sheepishly. "Yeah, that's exactly what he told me. Right after he told me that he *wanted* me to mate with Khol."

Jenna groaned, slapping her hand against her forehead. "Men, I swear. If they weren't so useful in the bedroom, I don't think we would keep them around at all."

I couldn't help the smile that cracked my face. "Yeah, I guess." In an effort to think about something else—anything else—I was about to do the unthinkable: I was actually about to ask Jenna about her sex life. "How are you and Macon doing?" And that was all it took to send Jenna off on a male bashing tirade. She went on and on for no less than fifteen minutes, barely stopping to catch her breath. For most of it I tuned her out, until something she said caught my attention.

"And you know male dragons aren't any different than any other males out there. They get all weird and possessive, and they freak out if you even talk to a friend that happens to be a guy." She sighed loudly. "I just don't know what to do."

My lips curled up into a wry smile. "Yeah, uh-huh...so who is he?" Jenna batted her dark eyelashes rapidly, her large brown eyes appearing to be limpid pools of innocence. I knew better. "Don't give me that face. Just spill it."

She rolled onto her back, heaving another loud sigh. "I don't know what you're talking about."

"Reeeally? Are you actually gonna try and pull that crap with me? I may not be a Speaker, but I know *you*."

Jenna rolled over again so that she was facing me, perching her face on her hands. "I like Macon and all, maybe even more than *like* him, but we can never really be together. He's a dragon and well...I'm not. He can't mate with me."

"So? It's not like you can mate with anyone else either

—you're human." I rolled my eyes at her. The whole dragon-mating thing may have seemed like an awesome thing in the beginning but now…not so much.

"So? Let me explain this to you P.J.—*he can.* He can mate with someone. How do you think I would feel if he felt the pull of some female dragon's powers and because he can't mate with me went off and hooked up with her? That could happen, and no one can tell me otherwise."

"Yeah, okay, point taken. So this other guy isn't a dragon…" My mind started shuffling through the very few possibilities that could fit that bill at the moment. And then it hit me. *Holy Crap!* "Jeremy. It's Jeremy, isn't it?" *Wow.* I most definitely did *not* see that one coming.

"No!" Jenna snapped back much too quickly. She began studying my bedspread very intently. "And even if it was… I can't let Macon know until I've broken things off with him. He would kill…whoever."

Whoever my ass! I internally huffed. Jenna was always getting so indignant when I didn't spill all my inner most secrets to her, and yet she wouldn't even come out and tell me that some kind of secret relationship was blooming between her and Jeremy. "Fine, whatever. But I don't wanna hear another word…*ever*…about me keeping things from you." I stood, stalking to my closet. My heart stuttered when I spotted the empty left side where Bryn's clothes used to hang. *Why did I come over here again?*

"Don't be mad. I can't help it," Jenna groused.

Suddenly the air was filled with a delicious,

mouthwatering aroma. "What is that smell?" I lifted my head, sniffing. *Hmmm...so good. Seriously, what is that?* I stumbled out of my room, following the scent like one of those cartoon characters led by their noses. It didn't take me long to find the source of the delectable aroma—it was coming from a plate that Jeremy was carrying past my room. I snatched it from him, revealing a steak and some other sides on it. Without any further thought, I attacked the food like a ravenous wild animal. I didn't pause to use utensils, or to apologize for stealing Jeremy's meal, I just proceeded to stuff my face with my bare hands, polishing everything off in less than five minutes. When I was finished, as I licked at my bloodied fingers, I glanced up to see Jenna and Jeremy both staring at me.

Jeremy shifted uncomfortably. "Does Bryn know?"

"Know what?" I asked, my stomach clenching unpleasantly. I rubbed my belly, frowning as a sudden wave of nausea hit me. "Oh my God, I think I'm gonna be sick again." I scrambled towards the bathroom, luckily making it just in time to throw up in the sink. I was angling for the toilet, but oh well, at least it wasn't the floor.

Both Jenna and Jeremy crowded into the bathroom seconds behind me. Jenna gathered up my hair, but it seemed like my nausea had passed just as quickly as it hit. I rinsed my mouth out with some mouthwash and turned to face my friends with embarrassment. *I really hate getting sick in front of people.* "Sorry guys. I think I must be coming down with something, or maybe it's left over ickiness from the coma."

Jeremy studied me for a minute, his brows furrowed. He finally seemed to come to some conclusion, shock washing across his face. "You don't know, do you?"

"Know what?" Both Jenna and me asked at the same time.

"That you're..." He paused, glancing around before pushing the bathroom door shut behind us, which clicked closed ominously. "That you're pregnant," he whispered.

"I'm not pregnant!" I squeaked, a chill running up my spine.

"Of course you're not," Jenna said reassuringly, while she shot Jeremy a nasty glare. "Why would you upset her by saying something like that?"

"Because it's true," Jeremy responded, eyeing us both warily like we might attack him at any moment.

"And you would know that becau—?" Jenna clamped her mouth shut mid sentence, turning to deliver me a stricken look.

A feeling of complete and utter dread settling over me. "What?"

"Jenna just remembered how I could know. I even knew when you were a virgin, P.J., remember? Just from reading your energies." His eyes darted around the room and he cleared his throat. "That's how I know you're pregnant."

"No, that's not possible..." Something very pertinent

occurred to me. In all of the madness that had happened before with Khol claiming me, me trying to take my own life, me mating with Bryn...I might have missed a few of my birth control pills. And then something else occurred to me. "What if it's not Bryn's?" Khol and I had been together once, but that's all it took sometimes.

"You're not far enough along," Jeremy replied. "It's definitely Bryn's."

Oh God... I was pregnant with Bryn's child and he just broke things off with me. *What am I gonna do?* "Don't tell him," I croaked. "Don't tell anyone."

"He deserves to know," Jeremy stated firmly.

"No, he doesn't," I said between clenched teeth. Gripping the sides of the sink, I met my own eyes in the reflection of the mirror. "He walked away from me, and I'm not gonna be one of those pathetic girls who uses a pregnancy to force her ex to get back with her." I flicked my gaze to both Jenna and Jeremy's in the mirror. "He either wants me or he doesn't." Silence enveloped the bathroom and I gulped down the bile that rose up in my throat. "Promise me," I whispered. "Just promise me," I then demanded.

"I promise," Jenna immediately responded, but Jeremy remained silent.

"Jeremy, please. Be my friend like you said you were gonna be." I turned to look him directly in the eyes but he turned his head. "Please," I rasped.

"Jeremy, just promise her," Jenna growled.

"I can't," he mumbled. "I just can't. He has the right to know."

Desperate for a way to at least stall him from telling Bryn, I grasped at straws. "At least wait. Give me some time. Let what's gonna play out, play out."

"But it could make a difference in what he decides."

"Exactly!" I exclaimed, utterly exasperated. "And I don't want it to! I need for him to decide about me without this influencing him!"

"So you would risk him and you mating to other dragons when you could prevent it—"

"It's not that simple," I interjected. "I want him to be with me for me and no other reason. I love him too much for anything less. I would always wonder if he was only with me because of the child." Most girls if faced with my situation would use the pregnancy to win Bryn back, and I couldn't exactly fault the logic. But, what if finding out I was pregnant with his child had the opposite effect? He was already willing to let me mate with Khol because he thought he wasn't strong enough to protect me, how would he feel if he knew it wouldn't just be me he was protecting anymore?

Jeremy shifted uncomfortably under my and Jenna's stares. "Fine." He finally caved. "I won't go and just tell him, but if he asks—"

"Why would he ask?" Jenna snapped. "Now you're just being ridiculous."

"I'll take it," I said, exhaling with relief. It wasn't exactly what I wanted, but it was close enough, at least for the time being. Besides Jenna was right, I doubted Bryn would ever ask anyone in passing if I was pregnant, especially Jeremy. "Now"—I turned towards the door on shaky legs —"I need to go lie down for a while or something. This is all just—too much."

"We'll help you," Jenna said, putting false cheer into her voice. I could tell she was just as much in shock as I was. I was the responsible one after all. Well, at least I used to be. I always thought that if one of us got pregnant, it would be her.

When the door creaked open, Khol was standing on the other side with a wild look in his eyes. He reached out, snatching me up in his arms before I could even blink. The next thing I knew we were in another room. His room. "I guess you know?" I mumbled. Of course he would have picked up the information through our connection. *Duh.*

He set me down on his bed gingerly as if I might break. "It could be mine."

I rolled my eyes. *Men.* "No, it can't. Jeremy, who happens to be an energy reader extraordinaire, says that I'm not far enough along for it to possibly be yours."

"The gestation period of a dragon is different than a human's."

I squeezed my eyes together tightly. "Of course it is." And of course, Jeremy wouldn't know that, just like I wouldn't.

"You being half dragon, and me being full-blooded, if it was mine, the pregnancy would progress more slowly despite you being part human because the child would be mostly dragon. I would imagine if it were Bryn's, then the pregnancy would happen more along the human timeline."

"So what you're telling me," I said with my eyes still closed, "is that the child I'm carrying could be either of yours?"

"Yes," Khol grunted. I could tell he wasn't any more pleased with the situation than I was.

"Maybe I just shouldn't have it," I whispered more to myself than him.

A low guttural growl bounced off the walls, making me cringe as I squinched my eyes closed even tighter. *I don't wanna deal with this.* "You will not end your pregnancy no matter who the father is."

My eyes snapped open, anger boiling my blood. Who was he to tell me what to do with *my* body? "Why not?" I glared into his angry glowing eyes. "It's *my* body and *my* choice."

He leaned into me, taking me by the shoulders, another growl erupting from his chest. "It could be *my* child, and therefore *I* have a say."

"No—you don't. Especially if it's yours. What happened between us, even though I technically accepted it…it was about as close to rape without actually being rape as it could be." It was a tad more complicated than that, but I wanted to hurt him, and that was a sure fire way to do it.

"Please," he rasped, his expression softening to show the pain that was really fueling his anger. "I will take care of you...and the child...no matter who the father is. I will love you and the baby until the end of time." I'd never seen Khol appear so vulnerable before. He was showing me plain as day how much he wanted me, and my child for his own. I knew in that moment that he would do exactly what he promised, unlike Bryn, and he would never walk away from me. Maybe the best choice for me, and my child, would be mating with Khol. He would be strong enough to protect us, to keep us completely safe. *Wait...what am I thinking?* Were my hormones already making me lose control of my sanity? *Maybe that's what happened before too?*

"Your dragon instincts are taking over in order to protect your child. That part of you knows what would be best for you..." Khol reached out his large warm hand, placing it on my stomach. "And for the child."

I brought my much smaller hand up to rest on top of his. "Khol—thank you. I don't know what else to say. But I'm not that girl. A part of me wants to be—but I would end up hating myself if I made my decision based solely on what's easier for me." I paused to try and gather my thoughts better. Everything was happening so fast, as per usual in my world.

"I thought everything was settled. We've been down this road before, kind of, with the whole you and me and Bryn thing. It actually feels a little déjà vu-ish. I can't keep going in circles." But how would I stop? Maybe—*I don't know*—maybe it was time to let fate decide once and for all.

A plan slowly started to form in my mind, and honestly I didn't see any other option that I could live with. "I'm gonna let fate decide." I lifted my face up so I could meet Khol's eyes. "Whoever's child I'm carrying...I'll mate with him."

Khol's jaw ticked with tension. "And if Bryn has already mated with another, or refuses you because of his stubbornness?"

Would he? Would Bryn refuse his child and me if that ended up being the case? I just couldn't imagine him doing that to me, but then again I never imagined him actually walking away from me either. "I'll cross that bridge when I get to it." I grimaced. *Almost twenty and pregnant... Way to go, P.J.!* "Is there a way to tell this early?" I was sadly uneducated when it came to paternity stuff. Of course never in a million years did I ever think I'd end up having a *"who's your daddy?"* moment.

"No, not without risking the health of the child." Khol cupped my face in his hand tenderly, his illuminated green eyes glowing with hope. "But does that mean that you've decided to keep it?"

I bit my lip as I studied him. "Yeah, I guess it does." *Huh. I'm gonna be a mom. I—me—P.J. Stone—am—gonna be... a mom. I'm gonna be a mommy.* I knew it would happen eventually, but—but— Panic bloomed in my chest, worming its way through my nervous system. "I can't be a mom," I choked out, gasping for air. *Why is it suddenly so hot in here?* And why did it feel like I had an elephant sitting on my chest? I reached out, digging my nails into Khol's arm. "I can't—" But I couldn't finish the sentence, my lungs wouldn't let me.

Khol laid me down on his bed, pushing my now sweaty hair out of my face as I continued to struggle for oxygen. "Shhh… my little Seer. I will take care of you." He dipped his head down to brush his lips against mine and it was as if they contained the oxygen my body was craving. I took in a shaky breath as my eyes fluttered shut. "That's right," Khol murmured in a cajoling tone. "Rest. You need to rest."

"But what about our plans to find the dragon queen. What about…?"

Khol's lips brushed against my forehead, his sweet caress warming me, and quieting my worries. "You rest now, and afterwards we can go to our queen." *We*—he wasn't planning on going with me before, but I guess he'd changed his mind, or me being knocked up had changed his mind for him. "No matter what, I'll be by your side. You won't go through this alone." It was the last thing I heard before I fell into a fitful sleep.

I WOKE up alone in Khol's bed. I lay there a few minutes trying to wrap my mind around the fact that I was actually pregnant. My hand slid down to touch my belly. It was as flat as ever. Did that mean the gestation period was moving slower like a dragon's because Khol was the father or had the child just been conceived more recently? How long would I have to wait to find out who my baby's daddy was? *Maybe I should go on Maury Povich to find out?*

I rolled out of bed and lumbered over to the door, wanting nothing more than a nice hot shower and some breakfast. *Pancakes—no waffles—no scrambled eggs and bacon —wait—I don't even like scrambled eggs and bacon, or maybe I do now. Or maybe the baby does?* The baby certainly seemed to have a predilection for meat. Did that mean it was mostly dragon?

I was so caught up in thoughts about breakfast and the baby that I ran head first into Bryn's chest. "Oh..." His delectable scent stole the rest of the words from my mouth. I wanted to press my face into his warm skin and just inhale. Bryn's eyes flashed an intense dragon blue as they skimmed down to briefly rest upon my stomach before they made their way back up to my face. My head swam at the realization. *He knows.*

"Peej," he said gruffly. "I was just on my way to see you. Why are you out of bed?" He lifted his hand up to touch me, stopping short as if he suddenly thought better of it.

"Wh—who told you?"

"Khol."

I squeezed my eyes shut, unable to look at him. "Of course he did." I never thought to tell Khol not to inform Bryn of my circumstances.

"So you really were planning on not telling me?" he

snapped, his voice cracking. I cringed at the accusation, especially because it was true.

I slowly opened my eyes but I still couldn't manage to meet his, so I let my gaze settle on the floor in between us. "I didn't want it to affect your decision about me—about us."

"Whether you like it or not, it makes a difference if you're carrying my child," Bryn ground out.

Sudden tears splashed down my face, my lower lip trembling uncontrollably. "I just wanted you to pick me for me—not because I might be pregnant with your child."

Bryn tilted my chin up towards him with his index finger, and the instant our eyes met, I wanted nothing more than to throw myself into his arms. *You will stay put. You will not be so pathetic.* "Peej, I never stopped wanting you, and I never will. All those things I said to you about loving you—I will—always. But that's not what all of this is about. I just wanna protect you—make sure you're safe. Khol is your best option for that, but if you are carrying my kid"—he ground his teeth together—"then he's not raising *my* kid."

I slid my gaze away from him again. "And if it's not yours?"

Bryn's hand dropped away from me. "Then it's obvious. You mate with Khol."

Had Khol told him about my plan too? "So you're gonna go along with me mating with whoever's child this is?" I rubbed my stomach absentmindedly.

"Yes." He nodded slowly as if he was trying to convince

himself. "Khol and me have already discussed the arrangements. We're both gonna take care of you until the day we all get our answer and then—"

"And then I'll mate with one of you."

Bryn nodded again, his lips pressing together in a thin line, and his Adam's apple dancing up and down in his throat nervously. "I don't want this to be weird. I'm sorry about what I did before—you have to know that. You have to know I love you, Peej. Nothing could ever change that. I—"

"Bryn," I interrupted. "I've known you almost all of my life. I know you better than I think I even know myself sometimes and yet..." My face crumpled, but I continued on. "I never thought you'd walk away from me the way you did. If—if it turns out to be yours..." I rubbed my belly again. "How do I know you won't walk away again at some point because you're feeling insecure or something?"

His lips parted in surprise, his dark blue eyes muting out almost all of the reflected light in them. "You think I would leave you and my kid?" I let him see all the hurt in my eyes that he had placed there, and as his face clouded over...that's when I knew he finally understood what he had truly done to me...*to us.* He'd broken us in some way, taking away the only thing that I'd been sure about since this whole mess started...him. "Peej—" he started.

I shook my head. "No, now isn't the time. I have to get ready to search for—"

"The dragon queen, yeah, I know. Khol filled me in on

that part too. We're both going with you now." My mouth dropped open ready to catch any nearby flies. "Like I said, we're both gonna take care of you until we all get our answer."

"Oh." *Well, isn't this new development a nice little plot twist in the story of my life?* Me going on a quest, of sorts, with both of the guys who could be the father of my child. *Fabulous. Absolutely fabulous.*

Chapter 5

I t's one thing to want someone, to desire to be with them, but it's an entirely different thing to actually *need* them. I never wanted to need anyone ever again. I had a desire to be a stronger version of myself so I could be ready for whatever my new life could throw at me, and truth be told, I'd been deluding myself.

I thought I had become tougher, stronger, but in actuality I'd just been leaning on Bryn more and more. And when he decided to walk away from me, I broke into a million pieces. I had to learn how to rely on myself, and only myself, if I had any hope of truly becoming the person I strived to be.

I needed to grow up and stop clinging to the insecure habits of a child, because…well…I was going to have a child, so I couldn't be one anymore. It was time to get off the carousel from hell that I'd been circling on and to develop myself into an actual functioning adult. If Bryn and Khol thought that I was going to make 'taking care of me' a piece of cake, then they had another thing coming. I would no longer lean on the shoulder of any man for support. What was that saying? *Oh yeah. I am woman hear me roar! Rowr!* I chuckled to myself as I roared like a lioness in my head. *Hmmm... maybe the pregnancy hormones are making me a little off.*

"What's so amusing?" Khol's voice cut into my inner musings.

I couldn't help the smile that spread across my face. "Nothing that you would appreciate." Nope, he definitely wouldn't appreciate what had just been tickling my funny bone.

"Why don't you try me?" Khol said, a glint of amusement in his eyes.

I eyed him suspiciously. Sometimes I swore that he could read my mind and he just wasn't telling me. But then again, what would he find amusing about what I'd just been thinking? Unless he was under the testosterone driven impression I was deluding myself and that I needed him and Bryn. Or did he find me amusing like you find your new kitten when she tries to puff up and act all intimidating but all she manages to be is super cute? "No, I don't think I will," I snapped.

Khol grinned. "Have it your way, kitten."

Ugh... how does he get under my skin so easily? Did he just read my mind, or did he get the kitten thing from my emotions? I narrowed my eyes at him. "Why don't you just leave me alone?" I ground out through clenched teeth.

Khol's face drew into serious lines, signaling the subject was closed as far as he was concerned. "It's time."

"Oh." My mind was reeling. "What should I bring with me? Anything specific? Why didn't I think to ask you before?" A jolt of adrenaline coursed through my system, and I started pacing the small space in my room.

"You have nothing to worry about, my little Seer. We shouldn't be gone long." Khol took my hand in his, tugging me towards the door. The fact that he was taking every opportunity to touch me since the bond with Bryn had been broken wasn't going unnoticed. I hated that his touches both comforted and excited me, making me crave more from him. *More*…that word had come back to haunt me tenfold in the past year. But I wouldn't cave. I wouldn't let myself *need* a man's touch ever again. *And yet…damn I certainly want it right now.*

I trudged along after Khol, mentally chastising myself the entire way for always letting my stupid hormones run my life. We came to an abrupt halt in a clearing out in the woods. Bryn, Jeremy, Jenna, and Macon were already there, waiting for us. I drank in the sight of Bryn greedily, moving over the hard lines of his body from bottom to top. His eyes flared dragon blue when his gaze snagged on my and Khol's intertwined hands.

Not wanting to hurt Bryn, I automatically tried to tug my hand free, but Khol tightened his grip possessively. It was then the two of them locked eyes, and I swear testosterone filled the air. So that was going to be the way of it? So much for their agreed truce until we found out who the father of my child was. Or maybe the truce was keeping them from actual physical blows like it had come down to in the past. But I wasn't going to let myself get caught up in any of it again. I would stick to my plan, letting fate decide my course of action. Until then it was hands off for both of them.

"You're not all going with us now, are you?" I asked as I finally freed my hand from Khol's grasp, causing his lips to turn down slightly at the corners, and Bryn's to tip up. Ugh...men.

"No." Jenna's lip stuck out in a demonstrative pout. "Khol says it might draw too much attention to you if we all go. As if the two of them aren't gonna draw plenty of stares." She waved her hands first in Bryn's direction and then Khol's.

I laughed. She kind of had a point. Both Bryn and Khol, even if they looked nothing alike, shared the drop dead gorgeous gene. "So why are you all here then?"

Jeremy cleared his throat. "I need to open the gate for you guys."

My eyebrows shot up in surprise. I hadn't been aware that we were going to be doing any traveling of that kind. Khol had simply explained to me that the queen would let us know through some kind of sign when we would begin our journey. Khol had also informed me that I needed to be ready to go at anytime, to which I hadn't been as evidenced by my lack of being packed status. He said that in the old days, the days when the dragon queen had reined supreme, that was how it had been done. If she wished to see me then it only made sense that we would follow suit because that's what she would be expecting.

I'd been under the impression we would receive the sign, or rather, Khol would since he knew what to look for, and we'd simply travel to wherever she had deigned it appropriate for us to meet with her. Although Khol had alluded to the possibility it could be a bit more complicated than that, I had chosen to oversimplify the situation, it seemed. Maybe we would be *searching* for her after all. My stomach dropped into my feet. Why did this whole thing suddenly have the feel of some kind of quest from the days of yore? I just wasn't the quest kind of girl. I had a feeling it would be bad for my complexion.

"So where are you opening the gate to?" I asked hesitantly, not sure if I really wanted to know. *As if I won't know shortly anyways.*

"Well, I'm just kind of opening it," Jeremy said, a note of confusion in his voice.

Khol stepped forward, capturing my gaze with his. "She will bring us to where we are supposed to be. We must trust in her—in the dragon ways."

"You've got to be kidding me!" Jenna exclaimed. "You guys can't just step into a gate without any sense of where you're going! You guys could—"

"Get lost," I finished her sentence, gulping. My eyes widened as I stared at Khol, his gaze imploring me to trust him, but that wasn't the problem. I did trust him, just not some dragon queen who I'd never actually met. "I know.

But I trust Khol. He wouldn't let anything happen to me or…" I raised my hand to my stomach. "Or my baby."

"P.J., you can't go." Jenna stared at me with an intensity that seemed to say she was under the impression she had suddenly become a *Jedi* and could will me not to go with her mind alone.

I considered the option of refusing to go, but I had too many questions and the queen seemed to hold all the answers. "I have to." I had no other choice, just like with a lot of other things in my life.

Khol took my left hand in his, stepping forward with me in tow, while Bryn grasped my right hand tightly, trailing along with us. I was suddenly overheated touching both Khol and Bryn at the same time, and my overly hormone addled brain conjured up images of the three of us together in a much different scenario. One that I pushed away as quickly as it sprang to life because it wasn't actually something I would ever consider in reality. But the effects of my momentary fantasy still had me wishing for a cold shower and a little bit of space from the two men at my side. *How am I ever gonna get through this with them?*

"Begin," Khol commanded to Jeremy in a tone that was meant to halt any more protests from Jenna. Too bad Jenna didn't get the memo.

"Jeremy, don't," Jenna snapped, before whipping her head around to plead with Macon next. "Macon, please, don't let him take her into the gate like that."

Macon smiled tightly at her and then glanced up at

Khol. "It's the way of the dragon," he said flatly. "Something that I don't expect you to understand." His tone held an undercurrent of emotion that pointed at a double meaning to his words. *Uh-oh, looks like Jenna's been voicing her discontent about the mating situation to him too.*

Jenna's face flushed with anger. Not a good sign. "Not everything is about the way of the dragon. Everything can't be explained away using that stupid excuse."

Macon's eyes grew brighter with his own escalating anger. "It's not an excuse, it's just the way things are."

They squared off with each other in silent battle, none of us privy to what was really going on between them. "It's over," Jenna said, raggedly. "I can't deal with all of this dragon bullshit anymore."

"Your best friends are both half dragon, do you plan on turning your back on them too?" Macon snarled, but there was no mistaking the hurt in his eyes.

"I'm not sleeping with them! And besides look at the mess being part dragon got them into! I don't wanna end up like them!" *Ouch. How about telling us how you really feel?*

"Do you think you're fooling me? I know you have an interest in someone else. Don't hide behind the dragon excuse," Macon growled.

"You don't know anything! You—"

"Enough," Khol hissed, his hand gripping mine tighter. "This isn't the time or place for the two of you to air out your problems." He turned back to Jeremy, his jaw twitching in annoyance. "Begin. Now."

Jeremy nodded nervously, his wide brown eyes averted

away from Jenna and Macon. I almost wanted to laugh, if he thought that was going to keep him out of the argument. Macon seemed to already have a clue about what was going on with Jenna, and if he hadn't figured it out already, it wouldn't take him long to find out Jenna's new object of affection was Jeremy.

Energy crackled, causing all the fine hairs on my body to stand up. Suddenly my attention was riveted by what Jeremy was doing. I'd never actually seen a Gatekeeper open a gate before. Sure I'd been taught what to expect but nothing compared to actually seeing it with your own eyes.

Jeremy's hands moved in quick sweeping motions, and he rocked back and forth and side to side as if doing some kind of weird dance steps, but he did them with such confidence and grace that I was in utter awe of him. The whole thing was oddly beautiful. Slowly the gate appeared before us, and much like I'd seen in my visions, it looked as if a piece of sky had been ripped into the side of the forest. Different shades of purple and blue with flecks of night shown in a pulsating, changing state. I gaped, unable to put into words the true nature of what I was witnessing.

Jeremy stepped aside as Khol tugged me forward, and I pulled Bryn with me, the three of us like a little train. An errant thought popped up about why the queen would require us to make this kind of travel when Khol couldn't open the gate. In fact, as far as I knew, no dragon could travel the way we were about to, so how could it be tradition? Fear spiked through me. *What if we're making a huge mistake?* But it was too late, I was already crossing the barrier of the gate, ice racing along my skin. I inhaled the crisp air sharply, trying to focus my eyes on what I was seeing...or rather not seeing. The colors from the outside of the gate had given way to complete and utter darkness. If not for still being able to feel Khol and Bryn's hands clutched in each of mine, I would have panicked.

"Keep going," Khol's voice sounded in my head. "Let her guide us to where we need to be."

So I did the only thing I could think of to do: I focused my thoughts on the image of the dragon queen and began repeating her name in my head over and over again.

Mori...Mori...Mori...Mori...Mori...

"DAMNIT!" I sat up with a start. "Why do I keep passing out, or getting knocked out or whatever?! I swear I've spent more time unconscious in the last year than not!"

"Where are we?" Bryn's groggy voice rumbled in response to my rant.

Blinking the fuzz from my eyes, I focused in on Bryn's prone figure lying next to me in an unfamiliar bed. I won't lie, it kind of made me feel better to know that I wasn't the only one who'd been knocked out this round. "We're in the Smokey Mountains," Khol said, sounding not at all like he'd lost the battle with consciousness anytime recently, much to my dismay.

I turned towards his voice and saw that his massive back was angled towards us as he stared out a ginormous window. It took up almost the whole wall of the room we were in. "How do you know?" I asked.

"I, as I'm sure you've already figured out, did not succumb to the magic inside the gates and remained awake where as the two of you didn't."

I glared at his back, which seemed to mock me, I swear. "How long have we been out?" I asked, choosing to ignore my feelings of annoyance.

"A few hours." He finally turned so that I could see his face and he regarded me as if his mind was still partially somewhere else. I was just about to ask him if he'd seen the queen or knew where we needed to go when he dipped down on one knee beside the bed, offering me a letter. "This is for you."

I eyed the letter suspiciously for a moment before snatching it from Khol's outstretched hand. The plain white envelope with my entire name scrolled across it in elegant script was kind of giving me the creeps. After a few more seconds of staring at it, I finally decided I was being ridiculous. With short jerky motions I tore into the envelope to produce a single piece of white paper about the size of an index card. In the same handwriting as was found on the front of the envelope were two lines of text...

Let him go.

Don't leave the cabin for any reason.

"What does it say?" Khol asked. Like he couldn't just

pull it out of my mind somehow, or at least get the gist of it. *He is so patronizing sometimes.*

I responded while still staring at the note. "Where did you get this?"

"So, I'm guessing you saved her...again," Bryn snapped with irritation, causing me to whip around just as he pulled himself out of bed, staggering a bit before righting himself.

"I'm stronger than you are...older," Khol stated with irritation of his own. And I guess I couldn't really blame him, we'd been down this road one too many times lately.

Bryn's face darkened as he gazed at me. "Maybe we should skip this whole waiting to see who the father is and you should just go ahead and mate with him." He punched the wall in frustration. "Who was I kidding, anyways? He'd keep the both of you safer even if it is mine."

"Bryn—" I started, but he was already stalking towards the door. His moodiness and childishness directed at Khol had gone way beyond ridiculous. I was tired of having to worry about how he would react to everything. Anger short-circuited my brain and I yelled at him without thinking. "Fine, just walk away! If you were half as good at the dragon stuff as you are at doing that then you'd be the most powerful dragon of all time!" Bryn stopped short, every muscle in his body going rigid.

I should have stopped there, but I couldn't seem to help myself. I wanted to hurt him. "I hope it's not yours!" As soon as the words were out of my mouth, I wished I could stuff them back in somehow. *Oh God, no. I don't mean it.* In fact, I wanted nothing more than for Bryn to be the father of my child. No matter how upset at Bryn I got, I knew he was truly the only one for me. He was my home, and I wanted my baby to belong there too.

Bryn made some kind of indecipherable gutteral noise, before continuing on his way. I jumped to my feet to give him chase, but Khol grabbed my arm, stopping me short. "Let him go."

I tried frantically to free myself from Khol's iron grip. "You have no right to tell me what to do," I snarled.

"Not me, it's what the note told you to do."

I dropped my tear filled eyes down to the tiny piece of white paper that I was still clutching in my hand, sucking in a shaky breath. "That's not possible." How the hell had someone known to leave a note for me about something that hadn't even happened yet?

"You're not thinking clearly. You of all people know how possible such a thing is—you being a Seer."

Right. I wasn't thinking clearly. The whole pregnancy thing coupled with Bryn being an utter idiot had fried my brain. *Of course* I knew the dragon queen was some kind of Seer, otherwise I wouldn't be here. "But I can't just let him go. Who knows what he'll do when he's like this." I bit my lip and unleashed puppy dog eyes at Khol. "Will you—"

"No. I won't—" he started, already knowing what I was going to ask.

"Please," I whispered, tears spilling down my cheeks, leaving salty trails in their wake. "Please go talk to him."

Khol reached out to cup my face tenderly, even as he gritted his teeth in aggravation. "Your tears are my biggest weakness," he said gruffly. He stared at me for several more moments, his thumb swiping at my tears, before he turned to seek out Bryn.

Satisfied with the knowledge that Khol would bring Bryn back to me, I sank down on the bed and studied the note I'd been left. The first part of *let him go* had already come to pass, but what about the second part? How long would I have to remain in this cabin? I had a sinking feeling I wasn't going to like the answer.

What am I gonna do about the whole Bryn and Khol situation? By letting fate decide the outcome of who I would mate with, was I really being cruel to both of them? I was determined not to need either one of them, but I was kidding myself if I thought I wouldn't *want* either one of them.

I stared out the window, thinking, until the sun dipped below the horizon and the stars crested the night sky.

Where the hell are Bryn and Khol?

Chapter 6

"**P**aige Joplin Stone, awake now, for we have much to talk about and a very short time to do it in."

"Huh?" I mumbled, reaching up to rub my eyes with the backs of my hands. Then realization hit me. "The queen!" I tumbled out of bed. But—but something wasn't quite right. The queen stood before me, exactly as she had looked in my visions, except she appeared almost transparent.

"Be careful. You wouldn't want to injure the little one growing inside of you," she said, tenderness in her tone.

"What's wrong with you?" I blurted, and then flushed with embarrassment. One simply shouldn't ask a queen what was wrong with her, at least I would imagine because I'd never met one before, human or otherwise. "I'm sorry. I—"

She brushed my comment aside with a wave of her

dainty, yet almost transparent hand. "Surprisingly, you remind me much of myself at your age. Or rather, I should say it might surprise you, because of course it's no surprise to me." Her lips curled and I found myself studying her more closely. It was the first time I'd seen her smile, and there was something very familiar about it, if only I could put my finger on what it was. She stepped towards me, distracting me from my current train of thought, and focused down on my stomach. Her gaze glazed over for a moment before she looked back up to meet my eyes. "He will be beautiful."

My heart skipped a beat. "You can see him? Can you also see who the father is?" If she could tell me—

"Yes, I can see who the father is, but I won't tell you."

"Why not?" I demanded in a shrill voice. "If you know—"

"Because it will change the path for all of you and I cannot let that happen. Too much is at risk already. Just know he will be perfectly healthy."

A boy. I'm having a boy. An image of Bryn when he was a child flashed in my mind, his black hair tousled and hanging in front his bright blue eyes that always seemed to glitter with mischief—his patented smile, complete with dimples, inviting me to join in on the fun. My heart clenched. I wanted it to be his so desperately. "Why am I here?" I asked, trying to dislodge the image of the Bryn that had first captured my attention when I was still a child myself.

"First I will answer your question of what is wrong

with me." Amusement twinkled in her eyes. "I'm not really here. At least my body isn't. This is the only way I could come to you."

"But if you could leave your body, then why make me travel to you? Why not come to me if it's so important?" I was about to bombard her with more questions but then I stopped myself. She was the friggin' dragon queen after all, not just some random dragon. I could at least *try* to show her some respect—be a little polite.

"I want you to be at ease with me," she said in a very Khol-like manner, in which I mean it was as if she had plucked the thoughts right out of my mind and answered them. But then again if Khol could do it, then I'm sure the dragon queen could do it as well. I exhaled a huge breath as she continued on. "I'm very near death—I have been for some time now, and I only linger to finish the tasks I have set into motion." I nodded my head unable to find a response. She was dying, or near death...the same thing in my book. What is someone supposed to say to that? "My body is near here, protected by Dragos, who awaits my death to follow me into the afterlife."

That got a response out of me. "My biological father is near here? Does he wanna meet me?" The real question was: did I want to meet him? And what did she mean by follow her into the afterlife?

The queen's face tensed and she turned away from me so I couldn't see her eyes. "No, he has no interest in meeting you. Although he would never harm you—he blames you for the deterioration of our relationship and ultimately my death, and therefore his death as well."

After seeing what I had in my visions I could understand why he blamed me for the deterioration of their relationship, I suppose, but her death? And his? "I don't understand."

"Dragos knows the outcome of my visit here, but not the reasons. As for his death…he is my mate and he does not wish to go on without me. It's even doubtful if he could. Mates such as us sometimes follow each other into death because our bond is so strong."

I inhaled sharply. Was she implying something that would happen today—with me—would ultimately cause her to meet her demise? And my biological father too? He was my birth father and even though I was unsure about my feelings for him, I didn't want him to die.

"I couldn't let him know the truth. It would have ruined everything." She began pacing the small area in front of the huge window. "There were so many pieces and one wrong step could have meant the end of this world. It still can. I looked at it from every angle, fought to find another way. There just wasn't…isn't. I sacrificed so much, letting him be with another, it ruined us despite our love, and I still have one thing left to do." She brought her illuminated golden eyes up to mine abruptly. "I must give my powers, and therefore my life, to you…my daughter."

"What?" I backed up until my knees caught the edge of the bed and I tumbled onto it before sitting up so I could look at her again. "You're not my mother." But her smile, her face..."Everyone always said how much I looked like my mom," I whispered.

"That's why she was chosen."

"What? No." My mind was reeling. And yet her words, deep down, felt right to me somehow.

"Dragos impregnated who you thought was your mother so that the switch would be believable. No one, not even him, knew what I planned to do. He still believes you to be his half-human daughter—if he knew..." She shook her head as if trying to dislodge some thought from her mind. "He must never be allowed to know differently. Not that he has much time left, but I foresaw that my child...you...if I kept you—you would have been killed in your tiny crib when you were only five days old. Instead, the other child was murdered in your place, and you were left to grow up untargeted by those who wished to strip the dragons of their future queen."

A wave of dizziness slammed into me. *I had a half-sister and she'd been killed in my place. Oh yeah, and I'm apparently the future dragon queen. Can you say brain overload?*

"I gave you up so I could protect you."

I sucked in one shaky breath after another. "Why are you telling all of this to me now?"

"Did you really think that you could be so strong as a half breed? Your powers took longer to develop as a dragon, that's why you received your first vision so late. It's also why your powers call so strongly to ones such as Khol. He only believes you to be half human because of your emotions, he does not understand that being raised by humans, even a full-blooded dragon would not see the world as most dragons do. The way we are is more nurture than nature, but he does not believe that. Most dragons don't. You've only just begun to experience what you can do. You need to know these things because it is time."

"And Bryn? How is it that another dragon grew up so close to me?"

"I made sure he was there. He needed to be. I can't tell you anymore about him without risking a change in the future."

"But if I'm full-blooded dragon then why can't Bryn and me mate bond completely? And—" *Holy Shit!* "And does that mean I'll be able to shift into a dragon?" The thought actually terrified me. I'd been relieved when Khol had explained to me that half-breeds couldn't take on the second form of a dragon. In fact, it hadn't gone unnoticed by me that Khol and the others had never shown me their other form. Khol must have picked up on my fear of it. Maybe I was afraid because deep down I had known what I really was and didn't want to accept it.

"You're not strong enough to mate bond with someone like Bryn yet."

"*Yet*—that means one day I could. That means one day I could fully be mated with Bryn." My heart leapt in my chest with joy. There had always been the question about *if* Bryn and me would ever be able to fully bond with each other, even after we'd both come into our full set of powers. Now the question was answered, and it felt like I'd just won the lottery.

"If he's the father of your child, you mean," the queen said, raining on my parade. "Because isn't that what you decided?"

I dropped my head to study my feet. *Huh. I kind of need a pedicure.* "Yeah, it is." But could I really go through with mating with Khol when I could truly and completely bond with Bryn? Hopefully I would never have to answer that.

"With my powers added to yours, you will be the ultimate weapon to extinguish those dirty little creatures that have been threatening our world," she hissed with disdain. "I'm just sorry I never got to know you, my daughter...or my future grandson. And I'm sorry that so much will rest on your shoulders alone. Things will get a lot worse before they get better."

Um...but wait. "If I'm full-blooded dragon, then the child could possibly be full-blooded as well—if Khol is the father."

"Yes, but that information still won't reveal the father to you any sooner than it's meant to be revealed." Her expression hardened. "Now focus, daughter. Khol and Bryn will be back soon and there are still a few things we need to deal with."

"Okay," I squeaked, hating how young I sounded.

"You must know that these creatures can only get a hold in people that already have a darkness in them. There are very few that are pure enough to fight them off. Once inside, after a time, they bond so completely with the human that the human no longer remembers it being any other way. They don't know the alien is in them, but the alien has full awareness. The human rationalizes the actions the alien forces it to make. I tell you this because there is a way to remove the aliens from the humans, but they will still target you when they are gone, the fake motives for their actions will still be firmly planted in their minds. You'll never be able to go back to your normal life if that's the course of action you wish to take. Or..." She paused, studying me intently. "You could just continue to kill them like your friends have been doing."

"No," I gasped. "Killing them isn't an option, at least as far as I'm concerned."

A slight smile tugged at her lips and she nodded once with approval. Apparently I had passed the test. "Good. Then there is only one thing left for me to do." She strode over to stand in front of me and then placed her palms against my temples. Heat bloomed from where her nearly transparent skin touched mine, and quickly spread throughout my body.

"Wait!" I cried out. "I still have so many questions. You can't do this yet!" *How is she doing any of this if she isn't physically here? Talk about power.*

"The answers will be shown to you when the time is right. You will have the guidance to take control of all of your powers new and old when you need to." The heat turned to fire, burning its way through me, changing me in ways I didn't know if I was prepared for. "I am sorry about your hair," I heard her say. "Of course I am partial to the new color, but I know how much you'll hate it."

"What are you talking about?" I mumbled. "What about my hair?"

But then a bright light engulfed me, and my eyes fluttered shut.

SO MANY QUESTIONS...I had so many questions. They were all swirling around in my mind as I regained consciousness. Was I really a full-blooded dragon? Then why couldn't I do the whole disappearing act that even Bryn had already managed to master? How could I have grown up with the people I thought were my parents, and never known I wasn't human? Why when I had been behind the boundaries of Khol's lair had I not been able to have visions? We'd thought it was because my Seer magic was blocked and my dragon magic had taken control...but if I was truly a full-blooded dragon that would mean my visions came from my dragon magic. So why had I been affected the same way that Bryn had? Maybe the magic my people possessed and the dragons possessed weren't as different as we had all originally thought. But I couldn't really say they were my people anymore. My people, or species to be more specific, was dragon. How was I supposed to ever get used to that—to knowing I wasn't even part human? I certainly still *felt* human.

"Peej!" Bryn called with alarm. "What the hell

happened to her?" I felt warm strong arms scoop me up and press me into a rock hard chest...Bryn's chest. His enticing scent washed over me and I snuggled into him, inhaling with delight. I was home.

"Amazing," Khol murmured. "I didn't know. She hid it from all of us." It was in that moment I knew Khol understood who I was, what had been done to me—everything.

"Don't just stand there, heal her. That's what you're good for after all," Bryn growled.

"She doesn't need healing. She's perfect," Khol stated with reverence.

"Peej? Can you hear me? Peej?"

I was completely conscious and fully capable of responding to Bryn, but I didn't want to deal with reality just yet. I simply wanted to remain burrowed in his arms, where I felt safe and content. There, pressed up against him, I could pretend that nothing had changed between us. I didn't want to open my eyes and face the very real reality that I could lose him forever.

"There's no reason to keep clutching her to you like a rag doll," Khol ground out. "Place her back down on the bed. She's fine." *Uh-oh...the jig is up.* Khol must have sensed I just wanted Bryn to hold me and obviously he wasn't a fan of my plan.

"Bryn?" I murmured, pretending that I was just waking up.

"But then again, maybe I should give her some of my healing energy, just to be on the safe side," Khol spoke up, not letting Bryn get a chance to respond to me. "Give her to me," Khol ordered, and surprisingly Bryn obeyed.

I opened my eyes just in time to meet Khol's deep green gaze instead of the sea storm eyes I'd been hoping for. "What are you doing?" I hissed between clenched teeth.

Khol's eyes twinkled. "Why, healing you, of course, since you didn't seem able to regain consciousness quickly enough, pointing at the fact that you might indeed be injured."

I glared up at him angrily, but his expression told me if I called him out, then he'd do the same in return. *Ugh. I hate how he seems to know every thought in my mind! Not fair!* "Stop it," I grated.

"Stop what? I only seek to make you comfortable, my little queen." His hot, fevered lips met mine in a crushing blow, pushing all thoughts except for his caress instantaneously from my mind. His magic rolled over me like a tidal wave threatening to drown me. Held in his arms, basking in his power, with his kiss promising things that I couldn't quite fathom, I found myself wondering, again, what it would be like to give myself to Khol completely.

"That's enough!" Bryn's angry voice broke through my reverie, causing my entire body to flush with embarrassment.

I made sure to not look at either Bryn or Khol when I was put back down on the bed. I cleared my throat, swallowing in an effort to combat my nerves. "I'm feeling much better now. Thank you Khol." And that's when I swore I heard Jenna's voice in my mind. *"I know something he could do for you that would make you feel* much *better."* *Shut up! Shut up! Shut up!* I thought vehemently at the imaginary Jenna voice. I couldn't even find peace in my own head anymore.

Feeling angry, mostly at myself, I stood and stalked over to the bathroom, intent on seeing why the queen had apologized about my hair. I wouldn't allow myself to think about the fact that me having her powers, even though I didn't feel any different, probably meant that both she and Dragos were already dead. And I most certainly wouldn't allow myself to think about the fact that I had been lucky enough to have two sets of parents in my lifetime and now they were both dead.

I flicked on the lights in the bathroom, gasping in horror at what was reflected back at me in the mirror. "Oh. My. God." I reached up to touch the white glossy hair that was now in place of the strawberry blonde that had once adorned my head. Who would have thought that I would ever want that god-awful shade back? That's when I noticed that the eyes studying my new ghastly shade of hair were no longer green, but the same gold the queen's had been…and they were glowing. My mouth fell open as I stared, completely stricken, at the stranger in the mirror who seemed to match me in mood and horror. "I need—" My voice came out shaky and high-pitched. "I need—" I tried again.

Khol appeared behind me, meeting my glowing eyes

with his own illuminated pair. "What do you need, my little queen?"

Not once, but twice he'd now referred to me as *my little queen* instead of *my little Seer*, which had been his term of endearment prior to our little jaunt to the mountains. And I didn't want to be anyone's queen, let alone deal with the intimacy his nickname pointed at. Had Khol and me become closer than I'd realized over the last couple of months because I felt so comfortable around him? I hated to admit that there was no one I trusted more than him at the moment, not even Bryn after he'd broken my trust by walking away from our relationship. But I wasn't a queen, not really, and… "Don't call me that!" I erupted. "And I need some hair dye, damnit! I can't go around in public like this! It looks ridiculous!"

"You can't dye it," Khol said evenly.

"Don't tell me that I can't dye it! It's my hair and I'll do whatever the hell I want with it!" Where did he get off thinking he could tell me first what to do about the baby who was growing in *my* body, and then tell me what to do about *my* hair? *I have to draw the line somewhere.*

Khol's face contorted into the familiar expression of aggravation mixed with wariness that he seemed to reserve specifically for me. "No, I mean, you can't… literally. It's the magic that has changed the color, and it's the magic that will prevent any hair dye from taking root."

"Bullshit!" I hissed. "Just watch me!"

"It's a waste of your time," Khol retorted in a monotone voice. I don't know if he was trying to be calm to talk me off the ledge, so to speak, but it was having the opposite effect.

"Bryn!" I yelled. Whirling around I saw his bulky form hunched over on the bed, his face in his hands. "What's wrong?" I made my way swiftly to his side, dropping down on my knees beside him so I could look up into his face. *Well, I will once I get his hands out of the way.* After a few rough tugs, his hands fell away, and he gazed at me with tears glistening in his eyes. "Bryn?" I asked on shaky breath. What could possibly cause him to tear up, because Bryn wasn't exactly the type of guy who welled up easily. In fact, I didn't think I'd ever seen him look so remorseful.

He reached out, wrapping a piece of my hair around his index finger. Slowly, while still staring at me, he brought his other hand to gently cup my cheek with his thumb resting near my left eye. "It doesn't feel like you anymore. It's as if my Peej is gone."

"Don't be ridiculous." I tried to smile but my face felt too tight. "I dyed my hair before and you were okay with it. This won't be any different."

His sea storm eyes sparked with dragon blue, making them appear fathomless. "It's not because of your hair." He circled his thumb by my left eye causing my lashes to flutter involuntarily. "Or even your eyes." His grip tightened in my hair and on my face, but not enough to hurt. "It's just all of it—when I look at you—you're not the Peej I grew up with anymore."

"Of course I am. I'll always be her." But was I really? Was I ever her to begin with? Or was she just an illusion I created for myself out of the information I thought to be true about me?

"No." He shook his head slowly while still staring at me. "She was lost to me before I ever really had her."

"What are you saying?" Was he trying to tell me that he didn't love me anymore? That too much had changed? My heart picked up speed as I waited for him to respond.

"I'm saying that if I thought you were too good for me before well…" His voice broke off and he stood abruptly. "I don't know if I can stick with what we agreed to anymore."

"You have to," I whispered. "You just have to." It was the only chance I had to truly be with him and he couldn't take that away from me. I wouldn't let him. "I'll order you. I'm queen now, and you're half dragon. I'll order you to stick to the plan." I wasn't sure if I could do that, but being queen had to come with some kind of perks.

I expected a fight, the usual Bryn pigheaded stubbornness, but what I got was worse. So much worse. "If that's what you want." He then turned to stare out the window, his next words a low rumble. "I am your willing servant."

"*Servant?* What? No! That's not what I want. Bryn, don't do this to me!" My voice was starting to climb octaves and a wave of unfamiliar power washed over me. The heat coursing through my veins fueled my anger. But Bryn didn't respond, he just kept staring out the cabin window like I hadn't even said anything. "Don't do this to me!" I screeched again.

Finally Bryn spoke, "I'll meet you guys back at the compound." And just like that he was gone.

Khol had remained circumspectly quiet up until now, but when Bryn disappeared, he apparently decided he needed to intervene. He grabbed both of my shoulders, shaking me enough to get my attention, but not enough to cause me alarm. His green eyes flashed with anger as he stared down at me. "I've let this go on for long enough. It's time for you to grow up. Not only are you going to be a mother, but also the second ever dragon queen. It's time for you to start thinking about something other than Bryn. You're a woman, fully grown. And he's behaving every bit the baby dragon I've accused him of being. He doesn't deserve you if he isn't even willing to attempt to fight for you." His nostrils flared in and out as his chest heaved with emotion. "I'm right here. I'll never leave you. I'll never walk away. And my words are more than just words, haven't I shown you that time and time again?"

What I wanted to say was that I didn't care—that I loved Bryn and always would no matter the consequences but—but I knew I would only prove his point about me needing to grow up. Which would mean maybe the rest of what he said was right too. And the truth was, somewhere along the line I had started caring about what Khol thought of me. "We're sticking to the plan," I croaked. "So there's no point in talking about it anymore."

Khol's jaw ticked with tension, the planes in his face smoothing out, and his eyes cooling to reflect no emotion.

"You will have to lead our people. It's the legacy that Mori, your true mother, left for you."

My lower lip trembled as I stared into his aloof eyes. "I can't. I don't have it in me to be a queen of anything. I'm not strong enough. I wish I was, but I'm not…clearly."

He wrapped his arms around me, surrounding me in his heat, a comfort that I allowed myself to accept, although reluctantly. "She wouldn't have given you the crown if she didn't know you were capable. You might not feel strong now, but I'll help you. I'll be your strength until you can find it in yourself to stand on your own."

"Why?" I asked, my voice muffled by his embrace. "Why are you always helping me when…?" I didn't want to say the rest, but I didn't have to because I knew Khol would understand. He always understood. Why was he always helping me when I was in love with Bryn? Why was he always what I needed most, when I needed it, despite the fact that I so rarely showed him the gratitude that he deserved? I didn't deserve Khol's devotion, and yet he gave it unconditionally.

"Because a dragon's love is eternal…and unconditional. Denying you what you need when I know I can provide it would be like denying myself the air I need to breathe."

"But I don't wanna need anyone ever again." I mouthed the sentiments that I had been thinking barely a day ago.

"A noble notion indeed, but an unrealistic one. We all need others for something, whether it be the food we eat, or the shelter we dwell in. We—"

"You don't need anyone," I blurted out, interrupting him. "You could probably do everything for yourself, if you wanted."

Khol exhaled a long breath ending on a sigh. His arms tightened around me. "I need you."

"Me?"

"Yes. I need you to give me a reason to keep on going. I've already been alive much longer than you can currently comprehend, and that is why I grew weary. That is why I slept. That is why I withdrew from this world, taking my people with me." He began running his hands through my hair, his power tickling my senses, and I relaxed into him even more. "But from the first moment I felt your power calling to me—I awoke with a purpose—a purpose that morphed into a labor of love. Everything I do, everything I am is for you. If not for you, this world could have been destroyed and it would have passed beyond my notice. You brought me back to life, my little queen."

Khol was everything a girl like me could ask for: caring, strong, smart, handsome, and even funny sometimes. *And* he was head over heels in love with me. More than that, he loved me probably deeper than I could comprehend. I pulled away from him just far enough so that I could gaze up into his eyes. They were no longer cool and aloof, but filled with the vulnerability that a man wears after confessing the true depth of his emotions to the woman he loves. And that woman was me.

"Khol—" I started, but my throat closed up. I bit my lip,

hating the fact that I was wondering what it would be like to let him claim me. Being mated to a man like Khol would definitely not be the worst thing in the world. Maybe one day I would even grow to love him in the way he wanted. After all, being a dragon put time firmly on our side. I then began to wonder what would happen if I gave him a willing kiss? Just one. And what would happen if that kiss led to more? Would I eventually forget what it was like to feel Bryn's body holding mine, and only crave Khol's? Could I abandon Bryn the way he seemingly abandoned me?

Standing on my tiptoes, I reached for Khol's lips with mine, and when they met, he pulled me to him as if he might never let go. I let my tongue explore his mouth, the taste and feel of him unfamiliar, and yet not unpleasant, just different than Bryn. Khol let me control the pace of our kiss, even though I could feel the tension in his body urging him to take control. Suddenly heat sparked between us, blanking my mind. With Khol's muscled form pressed so tightly against me, his powers rolling through my body, it was unavoidable not to get carried away. I deepened our kiss, digging my fingers into Khol's heated flesh. I wanted to crawl into him, and since that was an impossibility, I settled for grinding myself against him instead. Khol's answering growl of approval only seemed to spur my body's desires on further, and with my true loss of control, Khol's tenuous grip on his snapped. We fell back onto the bed, which was conveniently close, and he covered my body with his.

"Let me make love to you," Khol growled against the bare skin of my chest.

When had that happened?

"Let me erase the bad memory of the first time we were together"—his voice cracked as his warm hands deftly dipped below the waistband of my jeans—"and what followed...with me worshipping your body and laying claim to you the way I should have from the beginning."

The mere mention of our first time together conjured the memories of my heart turning to ice in my chest even as he delivered me physical pleasure. He hadn't raped me, but he blackmailed his way into my bed by threatening Bryn's life. Shortly afterward I tried to end my own life to save Bryn's. Khol caused all of that to happen and yet...I had forgiven him...truly. Or maybe I saw the Khol that was currently trying to push his long fingers past the barrier of my panties, as a different man than the one who had done those things to me. And maybe he well and truly was, just like Bryn had accused me of not being the same P.J. he had once known, maybe Khol wasn't the same either. Maybe none of us were the same.

But I wasn't ready to let Bryn go, and I wasn't ready to pull away from Khol's touch either. I had absolutely no idea what to do. "Khol—" His name turned into a moan as his fingers finally accomplished their goal. "Khol...wait."

"Just let me do this just for you. Let me take away some of your pain." Khol's gruff voice seemed to tickle things on the inside of me and I shuddered. "Your hormones are out of control, I can feel it, let me take some of the edge off."

I couldn't deny the extreme lusty feelings that my pregnancy hormones seemed to constantly stoke. And no longer having a regular sex partner really seemed to be doing a number on my brain, and by number I mean turning it to mush. A thought dawned on me. "You made it so my morning sickness is gone." Funny, how I hadn't really thought about its absence until now.

He tugged at my pants and soon I lay before him with only one small scrap of silk keeping me from being naked. "Yes, and I could do so much more for you if you let me."

Biting my lip, I met his fire backlit eyes with uncertainty. "But you won't try to take it farther than I want? You won't try to claim me when I can't think straight?" Which I was dangerously close to already. "I don't trust myself with you." It had to be said, even if I hated admitting it to him and myself.

A small smile tipped up the corners of his supple mouth. "Then trust in me, my little queen. My pants will stay on. I swear it. I will only touch and kiss you, nothing else. I will never claim you again unless you beg me for it."

What the hell am I doing? But I wanted it, so badly. *I swear I will never make fun of Jenna again for being a slave to her hormones.*

"Okay," I murmured, knowing I most certainly would come to regret the decision that my pregnant brain coupled with Bryn's fresh rejection was making for me. Khol was offering me both pleasure and acceptance, the two things that I needed more than anything in that moment.

The word had barely escaped my lips when Khol ripped my underwear from my body. I shivered under his rapt gaze, fighting to keep from blushing as his rough palms skimmed down my body only to push up underneath me, lifting my core towards him.

"What are you doing?" My voice shook with nerves as he dipped his head to hover where his fingers had been minutes before. "You said touching and kissing only."

His eyes, completely filled with flames now, met mine as they looked up the line of my body. "I didn't say *where* I would kiss you."

Understanding skittered through my mind, pushing past the shock his words caused. I hadn't considered...I just assumed he would continue to use his fingers. "Oh God!" I screamed when he kissed me long and deep in a way that I'd never experienced before. Bryn had wanted to do this for me, but I had been shy, despite everything else we'd done. And boy was that a mistake. I definitely didn't know what I was missing.

Khol's head moving between my legs was erotic in a way I never would have imagined. His shoulder length hair had fallen out of the gumband securing it at the nape of his neck, and the silky strands tickled my thighs while he focused on giving me pleasure. The man definitely knew what he was doing, of course he'd had plenty of time to perfect his technique on who knew how many partners, a fact I really didn't want to contemplate.

Clutching at the bed sheets and finding that not enough, I arched up and dug my nails into Khol's shoulders, which caused a low growl of approval to erupt from deep in his chest. I fell back onto the bed, my muscles coiling tight, my heels digging into his muscular back, and then his power rammed into me, heightening everything I was feeling times twenty. *Too much. It's just too much.* I shattered into a million pieces of pleasure all the while screaming Khol's name until my voice gave out, followed by my body. Spots danced before my eyes, leaving me half blind.

"That was—that was—" My brain was too jumbled to find the right words.

"I'm not done yet," Khol growled, dipping his head to start in on me again.

"No!" I screamed in alarm, meaning it and yet not.

Could somebody die from pleasure? I was pretty sure I was about to find out.

WAS it possible to love more than one person at the same time? I always thought it was just a convenient notion that authors of novels and screen plays used to amp up intrigue in their stories. I could remember more than a few times while reading a book or watching a movie, I had laughed and rolled my eyes at the heroine for finding herself in such a situation. And yet…there I was…in love with both Bryn and Khol…at the same time.

I couldn't pretend anymore that when Bryn and me were semi-mated, my feelings for Khol hadn't changed. Under those circumstances, those emotions had been allowed to bloom without me feeling threatened by the very man that cultivated them. I hadn't realized it was happening until the bond between Bryn and me had been severed completely. Then my attraction to Khol could no longer be overlooked because those feelings ran so much deeper than the superficial ones they had been when we first met.

Khol wasn't a cruel, conniving dragon like I had originally thought, but just a man who hadn't known how to love me because he'd never loved anyone before. He'd been driven by his dragon instincts on how to claim me, but when push came to shove, he had sacrificed his happiness for mine. Now that there was another chance to be with me, unlike Bryn, Khol was doing everything in his power to capture my heart...and it was working. I never would have let him touch me the way he just had if things were the same between us.

"Khol?" I whispered. He pushed sweaty hair out of my face as I curled into his side. He still wore his pants, as promised, and I still wore nothing, but at the moment I was too languid to care.

"Yes, my little queen?" He couldn't hide the smile in his voice, and I for once wouldn't begrudge him his arrogance. The man deserved every little bit that he felt about himself.

"I just wanted to tell you...that...well..." *Should I tell him how I feel?* Could I? The nature of our relationship had suddenly shifted and I didn't quite know how to handle it.

"Shhh... my little queen, as per usual, I already know what you're feeling. Don't trouble yourself to tell me." *Yep, he is definitely one smug dragon.*

"Oh, well then you know that this doesn't really change anything. I still love Bryn...too." I hated having to talk about it, but it was only fair. Although I knew this conversation would be much easier than the one I would have to have with Bryn.

Or do I have to tell Bryn at all?

Khol's body tensed against mine. "Yes, I don't need to be reminded of your feelings for him now though. Soon enough we will all have to return to reality."

Sitting up abruptly, I scowled down at him, my cheeks heating when I met his eyes. They held secrets now, ones that only lovers truly shared. "I'm sorry. It's just that I feel so—so confused. About all of this."

Khol's gaze flicked away from mine. "Will you tell him then? In the sense of fairness, about the intimacies we shared?" Had he picked up on the fact that I was thinking about not telling Bryn?

"No," I blurted out, deciding on the spot. "I'm not gonna tell him, just like I never told you about the things that Bryn and me did together behind closed doors."

His glowing green eyes flicked back to me, anger simmering within them. "But I *knew*. Of course I knew. With me being so closely connected to your emotions, how could I not?" He sat up, threading his fingers into my hair at the base of my neck. "So I ask you again, will *you* tell him, or will *I* have to?"

"Why would you do that? What purpose would it serve?"

Khol bared his teeth at me in a mock smile, a growl erupting from his chest. "It would serve the purpose of you being able to see if he'll pull away from you even more. If the fact that I am your lover now too scares him away, then his love isn't pure...not like mine."

"No sane guy would be happy to find out what happened between us! Of course it's gonna bother him! You can't tell me it doesn't bother you to know what Bryn and I have done together!"

"Yes, it *bothers* me," he hissed. "And it should bother him if he truly loves you, which he does, in his own way, but it shouldn't run him off. When a male dragon loves, he loves unconditionally, and if you came to me after being with a thousand men, I would love you just the same. My love for you will never change, fade, or die."

"He's not fully dragon!" I screeched in frustration.

Khol tugged me closer to him with the hand that was still threaded within my hair. "But you and I are. And someone like you—a full-blooded dragon—will never be satisfied unless you are loved completely. The way you deserve. I had my doubts before, even when I thought you were half human. You will crave *more* than he can give you."

Yes...more. My body seemed to call out, fresh lust igniting in me, my eyes dropping to his lush lips on their own accord. What would happen if I initiated a kiss for the second time this evening? I hadn't exactly minded the results the first kiss had yielded. But Khol pushed me away, standing before I could make my move. "Put your clothes back on...what's left of them. It's time for us to return."

"But the note said—"

"That time has passed."

"How do you know?"

"I just do."

I hastened to pull my clothes back on, eager to get back to the compound and away from our fight. No good could come from it, either we'd end up saying things we didn't mean, or I would end up letting him claim me despite my determination to stick to my plan.

Even still, I couldn't help but wonder... Was Khol right? Did it matter that I was a dragon and Bryn wasn't? Maybe I wanted things from Bryn that his genetic makeup made impossible for him to give me. I'd always thought that love conquered all. And I still believed that to be true. But perhaps the question wasn't *would* love conquer all, but rather *whose*?

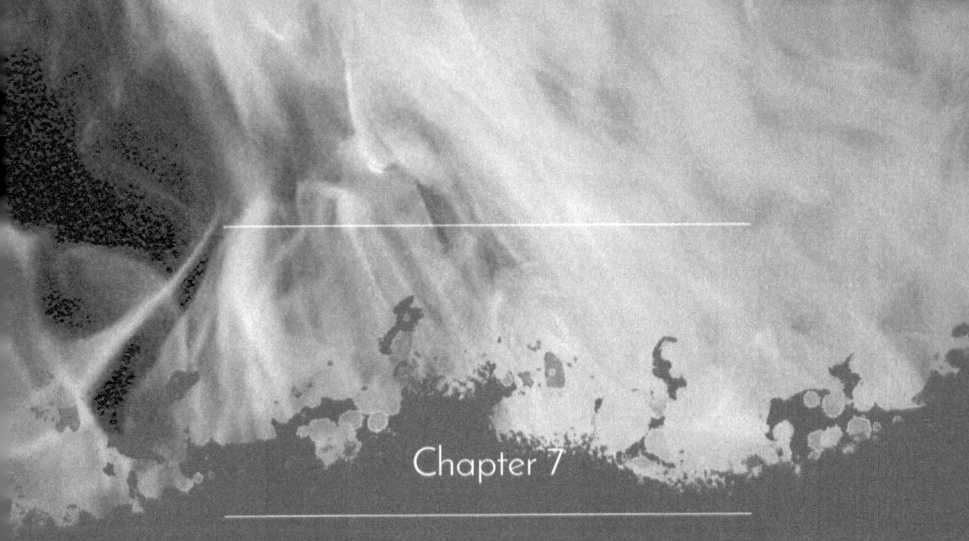

Chapter 7

"My liege," the short, stocky balding man said as he hunched over into a bow in front of his master. "I have news."

"Well," his master snapped, "stop sniveling on the ground in front of me and spit it out."

The man shakily pulled himself up to his full height of about 5'5", attempting to meet his master's eyes. "There are whispers..."

"Spit it out," his master interjected with anger. "Whispers of what?"

"Whispers that their queen has risen."

"No!" his master bellowed, slamming his meaty fist into his desk. "Their queen has been gone for decades, presumed dead." A hush fell over the large room that seemed to tick on for hours; finally the master spoke again. "What of our contact?"

The short man started shaking uncontrollably at the

question. "D-dead," he stammered. "The dragon sent only his head back, apparently—apparently—"

"Apparently what?"

"Apparently he felt very put out about the fact the girl was injured. The boy was to be our only target."

"The girl must die," his master growled, his human façade threatening to slip. "Find another way."

"Yes, my liege." The man made a hasty retreat towards the door.

"And Terrance," his master called. "No more excuses. I've grown to like this planet and all it has to offer. I'm not about to let the dragons and one silly little Seer put a stop to my plans."

The man nodded as he left, not wanting to linger for fear of having to bear the brunt of his master's anger. He'd gotten off light this time, but he had no misgivings about what would happen if he failed a second time.

The girl had to die at any cost.

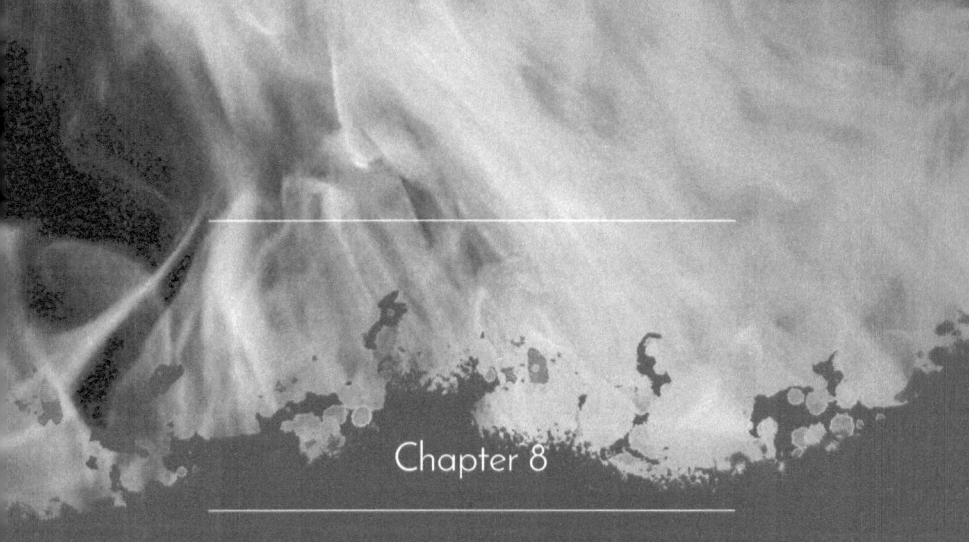

Chapter 8

Khol ushered me back to the compound and deposited me in his room with the order to stay put until he came to get me. He muttered something about announcing me to the dragons, which I could only take one way…that he wanted to declare me their queen. I wasn't really sure how I felt about that, being that I was a little wrapped up in the current deteriorating state of my love life.

I internally cringed as I considered the fact that I let Khol give me his intimate kiss when I was still involved with Bryn. My body undeniably craved both of them, and my heart loved both of them as well, but that didn't mean that gave me the right to be cavalier about sex with them. If it wouldn't have resulted in me being mated to Khol, I probably would have begged him to make love to me earlier. *Maybe I shouldn't have been so hard on Jenna all these years.*

A knock preceded Khol's door swinging open, and I glanced up from my pensive perch on the edge of his bed as Jeremy strode into the room. He smiled, relief washing over his face. "Hey, Khol told me you were back. I'm so glad everything turned out okay."

"*Okay.* Yeah, whatever." If okay meant that my dear old queen mummy had turned my whole world upside down in a matter of minutes, then yeah, everything was okay.

His smile faltered as he studied me. "What happened?"

"Where's Jenna?" I grumbled. "I really think she's the one I need to talk to right about now."

His jaw clenched as he scowled. "She's with Macon, fighting."

"But I thought she broke it off with him? I mean that's the way it seemed to me."

"He doesn't wanna let her go." Jeremy started pacing. "And I can't really blame him."

"Oh, I see." Although I didn't. Well, not really. I mean if Jenna didn't want to be with Macon anymore, he should just let her go, you can't make someone stay with you. *Shit.* Wasn't that exactly what I was doing with Bryn? I shook my head with uncertainty. No, it was different with Bryn and me because Bryn actually loved me. Jenna wanted someone else. *Totally different. End of story.* "Does he know about you two yet?"

Jeremy came to sit beside me on the bed. "No, there isn't any *us* yet. Not really." He then flopped back on the bed with a huge sigh. "I think she still wants to be with him."

"Don't be ridiculous. Besides him being a dragon and her being human puts a lot of obstacles between them. Obstacles that Jenna doesn't seem very inclined to wanna deal with."

Jeremy's eyes slid shut as he tucked hands behind his head. "I don't wanna be her second choice just because it's too hard to be with him. You of all people should understand that."

"Yeah, I do." My thoughts turned to my baby and how I didn't want Bryn to know that I was pregnant so it wouldn't affect his choices regarding our relationship. But Khol had let that cat out of the bag, and now everything was so tangled up that I was beginning to wonder if I'd ever get them unknotted. My hand rose involuntarily to my stomach. The motion comforted me for some reason. "Maybe she's just a little confused right now, but that doesn't mean you're her second choice. It is possible to have strong feelings for more than one person at the same time, maybe even love two people at the same time."

"Speaking from experience?" Jeremy asked, casually. A little too casually. I turned to look at him, realizing he was now staring at me with question in his eyes. I glanced away quickly, biting my lip. Why did I feel like such a horrible person for loving both Bryn and Khol? "You can talk to me. We're supposed to be friends now, remember?"

I gnawed on my lower lip for a few seconds before exhaling a huge breath. I studied the far wall, unable to meet Jeremy's gaze for fear of breaking down if I spotted pity or some other soft emotion in his eyes. "Does that make me a horrible person?" A lump formed in my throat, and I swallowed thickly. "I'm pregnant, and I don't know which one of them is the father. I love them both, despite everything that's happened, I do, I really do. And—and I don't know how to handle it." I paused, swallowing a few more times. "Do you think I'm—I don't know fickle or—a … a slut?" As soon as I let myself utter the words out loud, it was like I'd opened the floodgates and rivers of salt water gushed down my cheeks.

"What? You can't be serious?"

It was then Jenna decided to make her entrance, and a dramatic one it was indeed. She flung Khol's door open with such force it slammed against the wall behind it, swinging back to hit her in the shoulder. She staggered more from the surprise of it but toppled over nonetheless, landing on her ass. She looked over at me, blowing her bangs out of her face with a puff of exasperated breath. "What'd I miss?"

Jeremy hurried over to help Jenna to her feet. As soon as hand came into contact with the bare skin of her arm, a huge smile spread across her face. He blinked down at her as if dazed. I had the sudden urge to look away, like I was witnessing something intimate meant to be kept behind closed doors. *Yeah, No us yet, my ass Jeremy.* I'd never seen Jenna give a guy a look of true adoration like the one she was currently giving him. Lust yes, but this was definitely something completely different.

Like a light switched off, Jenna turned her focus from Jeremy to me, narrowing her eyes. "That's not really a good look for you, you know? I mean if you were going to do something drastic with your hair, I would have thought you'd have the sense to consult with me first."

How did I almost forget? Of course my new aversion to mirrors probably helped, not to mention that Jeremy hadn't said anything.

"And what's up with your eyes?" Jenna's face pinched as if my appearance physically pained her, and who knew, maybe it did. Although it was probably more likely she was just upset that she thought I went and had a major makeover without her help.

Touching my hair self-consciously, fresh tears spilled down my face. "I know, it's awful," I hiccupped.

Jenna moved to stand directly in front of me, studying me with her self-proclaimed discerning eyes. "This is why you should have come to me, grasshopper." Her lips twitched up into a smile. "But no worries, your sensei is here now."

"You don't understand. I didn't do this to myself." I motioned frantically at my white hair. "She did—the queen."

"Huh. Well, she might be a queen of something but it's definitely not of colorists."

Ugh. What did I have to do to get her to understand?

Thankfully Jeremy seemed to be quicker on the uptake at the moment. "It's not dyed, Jenna." His eyes widened almost imperceptibly as he studied me as well. "Her energy is different…way different. I can almost see the traces of the magic that did that to her hair. It's permanent."

"That bitch!" Jenna hissed. "She magically fried your hair? What the hell happened when you met with her?" And as if the words took a minute to seep into her consciousness, she whipped her head around towards Jeremy. "What do you mean it's permanent? Like P.J.'s hair is like this forever?"

"That's usually what permanent means," Jeremy retorted dryly.

A mask of pity settled over her features as she turned back towards me. "Oh, well, that's okay. The bright side is that you can pick any color you wanna dye it. You'll have to do it more often to avoid getting white roots, but old people do it all the time so—"

I ground my teeth together. "No, it's un-dyable! I'm stuck being a white-haired freak for the rest of my very long dragon life!"

"At least you're only half dragon so you won't—"

A strangled sound escaped from me as I flung myself face down on Khol's bed. "Just stop, Jenna! Stop!" I screamed into the comforter. "Next maybe you'd like to bring up the fact that I don't know who the father of my baby is!"

The bed shifted, a signal that Jenna had taken up residence next to me. A moment later more movement meant Jeremy had joined her. "What happened when you met with her?" Jenna demanded, as if I was the one antagonizing her. *Typical.*

"I'll tell you what happened," I grumbled, rolling on my side away from her. "She turned my already screwed up life on its head. I don't even know where to begin."

"How about with why the hell she fried your hair?"

I had to talk about all the new revelations and existing problems that made up my current life state, I simply couldn't hold everything in anymore. "I'm one hundred percent dragon. That's the first thing." The silence that clung to our little group told me I'd actually managed to shock both Jenna and Jeremy...a feat not to be taken lightly. "The second is that the queen is—was actually my biological mother. She passed on her magic to me, which did this to my hair." I tugged angrily on a few affronting white strands. "And this to my eyes." I waved my hand in front of my face demonstratively. "By passing on her magic to me, I'm to be the next dragon queen, but it also killed her and my father, even longer story, because of what she did. Bryn now has hightailed it for the hills because he thinks he's *especially* not good enough for me now, and I hooked up with Khol because I realized I love him too. But I still love Bryn and so I've discovered that not only am I pregnant with a child who I don't know who the father is, but I'm the future, or current dragon queen, I'm really not sure, who is in love with two men at the same time, and—and—apparently I'm slutty now too!" I gasped for air having spit out everything without stopping to breathe or pause once, but it was all out there now.

"You are not slutty," Jenna scoffed. "Who said you were? If anyone in this room is, it's me."

"Jenna—" Jeremy started.

"Please, Jeremy, don't try to argue that I'm not. I own my actions. Just because…things are developing between us…well, it doesn't change my past or who I am."

"But—"

"No buts about it. We're gonna have to agree to disagree then. Although, I'm sure we can both agree that P.J. is not slutty in any sense of the word. Who the hell told you that anyways?" Jenna asked again.

"Me. I told me that I'm slutty. I hooked up with Khol and I'm still involved with Bryn. I just—"

"Oh, for Christ's sake. It has to be the pregnancy hormones that are making you act all crazy. You were a virgin until after you turned nineteen years old. You've been with two guys. *Two guys.* I know it upsets you because you're a romantic headcase but—but you're going to bond with one of them, which means you will have been with only two guys your entire life. *Your entire life.* Sleeping with two guys doesn't make you slutty, P.J." She paused, chuckling to herself. "Unless, you were with both of them at the same time, then maybe I'd be willing to reconsider calling you slutty."

I snorted despite myself. "Of course, I wasn't with both of them at once. You know I'd never do something like that." *Fantasies of such a scenario don't count.*

Her voice took on a far away dreamy tone. "Can you imagine being with Bryn and Khol at the same time?"

"No!" Jeremy and me exclaimed at the same time.

"Talk about ecstasy overload," Jenna finished up as if Jeremy and me hadn't just yelled at her to stop. "Anyways..." She seemed to internally shake herself. And it was a good thing too, because I couldn't help but feel just a tad violent towards her for mentally imagining a threesome on herself with the two men *I* was in love with. "You're not slutty, P.J. Besides we are sex positive here. Why are we even discussing this? Ugh. "

She blinked at me a few times, a fresh smile creeping over her face. "Wait. When you say *hooked* up with Khol, I'm assuming we're talking about more than kissing or you wouldn't be feeling so guilty. So...spill it. What happened?" She leaned towards me with an eager expression, which caused me to stuff my face back down into Khol's comforter.

"I don't wanna talk about it."

"Oh, but you're going to," Jenna said, a hard edge to her voice. "I'm not leaving until you do." And I knew she wasn't bluffing. She'd sit there and pester me until I told her exactly what happened between Khol and me.

My face heated as memories of his intimate kiss skittered across my mind. "Maybe it's genetic," I mumbled to myself.

"What is?" Jenna asked.

"Me and my slutty behavior."

"For the last time, you are not slutty. And even if you

were, again, we are sex positive here—we embrace the slut," Jenna practically growled. "You're just trying to avoid talking about what happened between you and Khol. You're not fooling me."

I sighed. "Maybe I am, but that doesn't change the truth. Khol told me once that dragon females were nearly insatiable when it comes to...well, you know. So maybe I just can't help it."

"Or you just happen to want Khol and Bryn. If you were a genetic slut then you would have been putting out years ago. Now, time to spill what happened between you and Khol. No more subject changes." Jenna resumed her eager stare.

"Fine," I grated. "Khol and me...well I let Khol...he—"

"Just say it!" Jenna demanded. "What? What? What? He what?"

"Well he..." I wasn't sure if I could actually say it out loud. "He...kissed me—"

"And!" Jenna leaned forward on the bed, reminding me very much of a vulture waiting to scavenge a carcass.

"It wasn't a regular kiss..." My whole body heated, my heart racing as I again thought of what I'd let Khol do to me.

"Oh my God! Just spit it out already!"

I squeezed my eyes shut. "He kissed me...well..." I pointed down towards the general vicinity of my middle, opening my eyes to meet Jenna's confused brown pools. "Down there," I hissed. *Come on Speaker—get there faster.*

A grin stretched her cheeks ridiculously wide as

comprehension washed over her. "Holy shit! You let Khol go down on you?" She bounced up and down on the bed and I resumed my ostrich head in the sand position… a.k.a. my face stuffed into Khol's comforter.

"You did!" Jenna exclaimed with excitement. "Did you like it? I mean was it good? I need details!"

"I think I'm gonna head out now," Jeremy said. "I got some—stuff to do. I'll see you guys later." He scuffled out of the room, grumbling under his breath.

Neither Jenna or me acknowledged Jeremy's leaving, but as soon as the door clicked shut signaling he was gone, Jenna exploded into girly excitement. "Details! I need details! EEEEEE! I can't believe you let him do that to you! I'm so proud! Oh wait…did you reciprocate? Come on P.J.! I need details! All the details!"

I rolled onto my back, staring at the ceiling. "Yeah, it was good. Beyond good. I've never felt anything like it. Plus, with his magic…yeah…like I said, I've never felt anything like it." I worried my bottom lip between my teeth. "And no, I didn't reciprocate."

"Let me get this straight." Jenna's eyes widened to resemble tiny saucers. "He went down on you, and he didn't even expect you to do it back?"

"He said he just wanted to help me take the edge off. You know, because of the extra hormones I've got going on with my pregnancy."

Jenna flopped back onto the bed beside me with a huge sigh. "He's got it bad for you. No joke. If that isn't love then I don't know what is. Plus, all the other stuff he's always doing for you, but he's still a guy, you know. You're so lucky." She exhaled a loud demonstrative sigh.

"Macon loves you, and so does Jeremy."

"Yeah well, Macon acts like reciprocation is his God given right. I used to think it was kind of hot how he took all the control and everything, but now I mostly think it's annoying."

"Jeremy wouldn't do that." I'd always liked Jeremy and I couldn't pass up the opportunity to put in a good word for him. "Jeremy really cares about you, you know."

"Yeah, yeah, yeah." Jenna waved her hand in the air. "I don't wanna talk about it. I wanna talk about what you're gonna do about everything that's going on with you."

I scowled in her direction. Typical Jenna. She didn't want to talk about stuff she wasn't ready to, but she was always forcing me to divulge information before I was ready. "I don't know what I'm gonna do." I crossed my arms over my chest.

"Well, I'll tell you one thing you need to do... Pick some new colors for your wardrobe because what you've got now is so gonna clash with your new hair." She tapped her chin. "And you're gonna need some new eye makeup. Hey, if Storm from X-Men can look hot with white hair, then you can too. We'll make it work."

I giggled when I mentally pictured Jenna trying to dress me up in various superhero type costumes. "I'm not a superhero, Jenna. Just—"

She rolled to face me at the same time I rolled to face her. "A queen." We both burst into laughter.

"Who would have ever thought our lives would be so complicated?" I said, grasping at my side because I was laughing so hard. It was all so funny because it all…wasn't.

"Certainly not me," she barked out. "I used to be worried we'd miss out on all the adventures. And"—she clutched at her side too—"I used to worry you'd die a virgin. Ha! Look at you now!"

"Hey! Not funny!" But I couldn't help but laugh harder. It felt good to let go of some of the tension. It made me feel like some of the weight had been lifted off of my shoulders…even if it was only temporary.

A prickling of power slid across my skin causing goose bumps to erupt along my flesh. I sucked in a ragged breath a split second before Khol appeared a few feet in front of the bed. "That's new," I muttered, locking eyes with him.

"Oh hey, Khol," Jenna said. "We were just talking about you." She giggled. "All good stuff, I promise. But I have a few questions for you…"

"Jenna, stop!" God only knew what kind of questions she had for Khol.

She turned to me with an over exaggerated pout. "Fine, then." Her eyes sparkled with mischief. "I'll leave you two alone, for now. Just one question first…"

"Get out Jenna!" I yelled. "I'll talk to you later." I gave her my best stern face, which actually seemed to work.

"All right," she said in a singsong voice. "I'll see you two later." She skipped from the room with delight.

I turned to address Khol, my face heating with embarrassment. "Sorry about that. I—"

Khol grinned, his eyes tender as he stared at me. "It makes me happy to see you smiling again, my little queen." He dropped down on his knees in front of me. "I only wish that I had been the one to lighten your mood." He cupped my face in his large warm hands, his eyes flaring brighter.

The vision slammed into me, forcing the air from my lungs as I struggled to breathe. Unlike some of the visions I've had in the past, it was almost as if I was watching two TV screens at the same time. I could still see Khol as clear as day in front of me, but I also saw a second scene unfolding that dragged my attention towards it.

"Fight for her if you love her," Khol growled, stepping into the space directly in front of Bryn.

"I thought you'd be happy if I walked away." Bryn slumped into himself, defeat etched into every line on his face. "You're the better man...or rather dragon. You win."

Khol grabbed Bryn by the front of his shirt, his eyes erupting into flames. "I will win this battle fair and square, not because you simply gave up," Khol spat with distain, as if giving up was the worst thing anyone could ever do.

"We'll wait to see who the father is, like we agreed. That's all I can promise." Bryn wasn't even struggling against Khol. He seemed utterly and completely broken.

"You and I both know she won't be able to stick to that, she always has and always will follow her heart. She'll try, but she is after all a female dragon." Khol's lips turned up at the corners in a cruel smile. "She's already wavering in her decision. I plan to take advantage of any opportunity she'll give me. I'll claim

her before the child is born, if her will slips for even a moment, I'll claim her."

"Why are you telling me this?" Bryn growled, his eyes flaring dragon blue for the briefest of moments.

"Because I love her, and I know she would never forgive me a second time if I tried to rip you away from her. I need to make sure she feels you had a fair chance. But I can't fight my instincts. I will claim her."

"I know you love her, maybe even as much as I do. But that's why I'm walking away, because I can't protect her. I love her too much to see her suffer because of my selfishness."

"This will be the only warning you get," Khol stated, forcefully. "Do not upset her needlessly when it's too late for the two of you. There's no going back this time, once she's mine... she's mine."

Bryn pulled free of Khol's grasp, baring his teeth at him. "Message received and noted. Now leave me the hell alone."

The vision faded away slowly and I found myself staring into Khol's eyes. "What did you see, my little queen?"

"You don't know?" I breathed.

"No. The vision was closed to me for some reason. Tell me what you saw."

"It was just Bryn and you talking...about me. You told him to fight for me—you told him—"

"The queen's powers are beginning to show themselves in you. I know of which conversation you're referring to because it only just occurred, before I came to visit you here." Khol pushed the hair on the left side of my face behind my ear. "But it was not meant for you to witness."

"Yeah, I kind of got that," I said dryly. "So you plan on seducing me away from Bryn to break our bargain?"

Khol hesitated for a moment before responding, "Yes. I've made no secret about my desire to claim you...the right way this time."

I tried to be mad at Khol as I stared into his strong chiseled face, meeting his fire-consumed eyes. I tried to be mad at him as I ran my fingertips over his high cheekbones, bringing the fingers of my hand to caress his firm and yet supple lips. I tried to be mad at him as he gripped my hair at the base of my neck, tugging gently as he sucked one of my fingers into his mouth, reminding me of other things his oh so talented mouth could do. And I tried to be mad at him as his free hand slipped up to pull me closer to him, eliciting a moan from me.

"I can't trust you not to cheat in order to make me yours," I murmured.

"No, you can't." He nibbled on my fingertips before letting my hand drop away so he could claim my lips. I clutched at him, unsure of whether to push him away or pull him closer. My body craved his touch, and yet my mind screamed at me to punish him for his actions.

"Let's end this now." He kissed a scorching path down the side of my neck and I finally decided that pulling him closer was the best course of action at the moment. "Let me claim you so that none of us suffer any longer. You saw for yourself, he won't fight for you."

"It could be Bryn's child," I said, trying not to lose control under Khol's heated lips.

"He still doesn't want to fight for you, and I don't care who the father is. I will love it like it is mine…either way."

"I know," was all I could manage to say.

My brain was short-circuiting on lust. Khol continued his way down my body, nibbling, kissing and suckling. He paused to tug at my pants and alarm bells sounded in my head. I knew he was intending to wear me down slowly, another few rounds of what he'd done to me before and I'd be begging for him to make love to me, consequences be damned. *I have to do whatever I can to prevent that scenario from happening.*

"Wait…stop!" I cried out, desperate. "Let me—"

Let me what? Then my thoughts tumbled over what Jenna had asked earlier. "Let me…reciprocate." Khol stopped short, his heated gaze resting heavily upon me. "Please, I want to." I pushed up from my prone position, dipping down on my knees in front of him. As I unzipped his pants, I felt Khol's body thrum with tension. He seemed almost reluctant to let me repay his favor from earlier, or maybe he saw my aversion tactic for what it was.

Khol caught my head in both of his hands, forcing my gaze up. "Are you sure you want to do this?" His voice was strained, breaking an octave lower than normal.

Turning inward, I asked myself if I really wanted to do for Khol, something that I'd only ever done for Bryn, and only a handful of times at that. But the answering clench of my stomach followed by a rush of heat in my middle was the only answer I needed.

"I'm sure," I rasped.

My true feelings were a surprise, but I didn't doubt the truth of them. I liked the idea of taking control of the almighty Khol—of me having power over him in that kind of intimate way.

I smirked up at him. "Now just sit back and relax."

Khol enthusiastically obeyed.

Chapter 9

"**N**o. Just stop. I let you curl my hair but you're not attacking me with hairspray again. The last time I let you at me with that stuff I had to deep condition...twice...before I could even get a brush through it." I scowled at Jenna, who was currently brandishing the biggest can of hairspray I'd ever seen.

Her brows furrowed together with annoyance. "Just a little bit, or your hair's gonna fall and my effort will be completely wasted."

Scrambling away from her, I waved my hands around my head to keep her from spraying at me on the run. "I said no!"

"Come on, P.J., I don't see what the big deal is!" She vaulted after me, pushing down the aerosol button on the top of the can, letting loose a stream of spray in my direction.

"The big deal is that my hair is already white, if you

spray it until it could withstand a tsunami then I'm gonna look like a little old lady!" I crouched as Jenna shot another stream of hairspray at me.

"Don't be ridiculous, you're almost twenty not ninety, and without make-up you still look like you're twelve, so just let me make you pretty for this stupid announcement thing!"

"No means no Jenna!" I screeched, whirling around to grab the can from her. I still managed to get shot in the face. "Oh come on!" I coughed. "Plus, you're killing the environment with this shit! Seriously … who uses aerosol cans anymore?" Another round of coughs seized my chest.

A prickling of power across my skin signaling Khol's emanate arrival made me stop and straighten up. I still hadn't figured out what was going on with me being able to sense Khol's arrival before he actually appeared, or how I could tell it was him, but I had a feeling it had something to do with my still new to me powers. I hadn't had the opportunity to test out if I could sense it with anybody but him yet, but I was sure I wouldn't have to wait long.

"Khol," I breathed as he appeared a few feet in front of me. The smile he gave me made me weak in the knees, and I knew the answering one I wore probably made me look like I was a little drunk. And maybe in some ways I was. *Drunk on Khol.* "I'm not ready yet," I murmured, trying to ignore the little flip-flop that my stomach did as memories of what we'd done together, of how he had let me explore him with my mouth with leisure, rose unbidden to my mind.

"My little queen," he practically purred, and I had to fight the urge to fan myself.

"Jenna, hey...um...can you give us a couple minutes?" I said without breaking eye contact with Khol.

I wanted a few minutes alone with him after what happened between us. We hadn't really gotten a chance to talk. In fact, right after I'd finished...my job...Drake had called him away on some sort of dragon business. At the time I was kind of relieved because I was pretty sure I was about five seconds away from doing something stupid with him, but now I was regretting the lost intimacy that being with him afterwards would have surely offered me.

"Yeah, I guess," Jenna pouted. "But don't do anything to mess up your hair." She left the room grumbling under her breath about not being appreciated enough.

"I brought you something," Khol said, a twinkle in his eyes. He produced a small rectangular shaped box from behind him.

"What is it?" I asked.

"You'll just have to open it to find out."

"Yeah, okay." I made my way over to him, hesitantly taking the box from his outstretched hand.

I wasn't used to getting gifts from men, especially men who'd seen me naked. *Except for Bryn.* I quickly pushed the thought aside, ignoring the weird pressure in my earlobes from the small sapphire studs that Bryn had given me for my birthday almost a year ago. The black velvet box creaked its protest as I opened it, and I inhaled sharply at what was inside. Nestled on more black velvet was an enormous red stone surrounded by a dragon with outstretched wings. The dragon itself was intricately made, every small detail etched into the shiny silver metal with care. It was a pendant that I'd never seen the like of, and I was pretty sure I never would again. *Fire and Water*, I thought numbly, *ruby and sapphire*. Khol was a fire dragon, and Bryn a water dragon. The symbolism was too obvious to be ignored, but I decided to do just that. "That isn't real, is it?"

Khol snorted. "As if I would gift you with a fake ruby. And that's not silver, but white gold." I didn't miss the pride in Khol's voice as he informed me of the very expensive gift I was clutching in my hands. "I thought the queen of us all should have some suitable jewelry to adorn herself with. You will wear it, won't you?"

"Of course I will." I usually wasn't much of a jewelry girl, but for some reason the necklace just seemed to call to me, and the thought of not wearing such a beautiful thing suddenly seemed ridiculous.

"Then let me put it on you." Khol took the necklace from my hands, and made his way behind me. I lifted my hair so he could have better access, and he placed the cool metal against my skin, fastening it. He then kissed the back of my neck before I dropped my hair back into place. I shivered belatedly from the combination.

I reached up to caress the pendant. It was already heating from the contact with my skin. "Thank you," I whispered.

"My father gave it to me." I sucked in a breath as his

words tickled my bare shoulder. "He told me to give it one day to the one I love…my *Anam Cara*."

"Oh. Khol, no—"

"I know you're not my *Anam Cara*…but no matter what happens, you will always be the one that I love." His voice had grown ragged and he pulled me back into him, wrapping his arms around me. "Wear it for me…please."

What could I say to that, really? "Okay."

His hand skimmed up the side of my body, coming to rest over the pendant, which was conveniently close to my cleavage. "I have more gifts for you, my little queen," he rasped, his voice a low intimate growl. I merely nodded as my eyes slid shut, his enticing scent spiraling around me. It wasn't as familiar and comforting as Bryn's had become to me, but it was on the fast track to being its rival.

"Drake," Khol called, and a feeling of power, definitely with a different flavor than Khol's, ran over my skin. Drake appeared a moment later in front of us holding a large clothing box and a smaller shoebox.

Khol took the boxes from Drake, who shot me a smug smile before dipping down in a low bow before me. "My queen. It warms the cockles of my heart to see you have decided to cast the baby dragon aside to be with my lord. A wise decision indeed."

I opened my mouth to protest but Khol beat me to the punchline. "That's enough, Drake. No one asked for your commentary. Leave us."

Drake dipped lower, his voice almost a whisper, "My

apologies, my lord, it won't happen again." And with that he took his leave.

Khol met my eyes and held them with his intense gaze. "Don't read too much into what Drake says, he of course sees things the way he wants them to be."

I bit my lower lip, swallowing down the angry words I was about to say. "Yeah, I know. Just as long as all of us are on the same page." But I wasn't really sure *any* of us were on the same page.

"Now open your gifts," Khol said as he set them on the bed.

I obligingly took the lid off the clothing box first and gasped my surprise. "It's beautiful." I giggled with delight. Inside was the most amazing crimson silk dress I'd ever seen. It matched the ruby in my new necklace perfectly. I didn't bother asking Khol if he'd planned it that way because I knew he did. I pulled the dress out, running my hands over the luxurious material. "I guess this is for tonight, too?"

"Yes. I wanted you to look your new role, and you deserve to be dressed in nothing less than the finest silks and jewelry in the world, whether you were a queen or not. Try it on, I want to make sure it fits."

"Okay," I said excitedly.

It was kind of shallow, especially with everything else that was going on, but I'd never owned such a beautiful dress. Maybe I could blame it on the dragon acquisitiveness that had to be part of my nature since I was in fact one hundred percent dragon. *Yep, totally good rationalization.* "You're really putting the hardcore press on me, aren't you?" I asked, laughing.

But Khol's eyes were completely serious when he answered, "Yes. I've made no secret about the fact that I want you for my own. Now that I know you're fully dragon, I also know what buttons to push to help grow your affections towards me. My tactics were different when I thought you to be half human."

Choosing to ignore his mini confession session, I simply wanted to put the dress on so I could feel the soft material against my skin. "Turn around," I commanded. "So I can—"

"But I have already seen you naked," Khol protested.

My voice went up an octave. "That's different. You're a guy—you don't understand. Just turn around."

He grumbled under his breath but did what I asked of him. As soon as I double-checked to make sure he wasn't peeking, I slipped out of my jeans and sweater and into the crimson dream. I realized that it wasn't the type of dress that I could wear a bra with, or my normal boy shorts cut underwear, so I made quick work of removing those garments as well. If the skirt on the dress hadn't been so long and flowy I might have felt odd, but in the dress with nothing underneath I felt like some siren from the 40s or 50s. All I needed was one of those long cigarette holders...or was that the 20s?

"You look absolutely stunning," Khol rumbled, his voice warm and seductive. I couldn't even be bothered by the fact that I hadn't told him he could turn around yet.

I walked over to the bed to open what I was already sure were a matching pair of shoes, and I wasn't disappointed. They were a low-heeled set of elegant slippers that actually appeared to exude comfort. I slipped them on, turning to deliver Khol a dazzling smile. "Thank you. It's all so amazing." *Nothing like a little retail pick-me-up to brighten a girl's mood.*

Khol came to me in a blur of speed, wrapping his arms around me and tipping my face up towards his. "Believe me, the pleasure is all mine." He brushed his lips against mine at first softly before he deepened our kiss. I was suddenly *very* aware that I had nothing on underneath my dress.

"You're just lucky I didn't do her make-up yet," Jenna's petulant voice cut into my Khol induced fog.

He reluctantly pulled away from me, his heated gaze causing my skin to heat under its intensity. "I'll leave the two of you, for now. Call for me when you're ready."

The question was would I ever be ready? For Khol that is? I was so out of my league with him, and he was playing by a set of rules that I'd barely been introduced to.

"Wow," Jenna said, surveying my new outfit, compliments of Khol. "Who would have thought any straight man could dress a woman so well." She nodded her head in approval. "That dragon knows what he's doing." A wicked grin spread across her face. "In more ways than one."

"Shut up and finish helping me get ready. I don't need your running commentary," I said, a small smile threatening to break out on my face. Khol had really stepped up his game lately, in and out of the bedroom.

I went to stand in front of the bathroom mirror again, surprised by the image that was reflected back at me. I hardly recognized myself. The red of the dress combined with my white hair, and large dragon pendant, made me appear completely non-human, but then again I guess I wasn't…human that is. My hair had mostly grown out of the long-angled bob it had been cut into and it hung in loose curls just past my shoulders. The gold of my eyes picked up the red of my dress, making them seem more of an amber shade. I would definitely be believable as a dragon queen if I did say so myself, and the new look was even starting to grow on me…a little.

"That's one hell of a rock. I'm guessing it's real?" Jenna eyed the ruby centerpiece of my dragon pendant. "Does it mean something special? I mean is it like royal jewelry or something?"

I ran my hand over the necklace idly as Jenna began applying my make-up. "No, it's just a gift from Khol. But I do think it's appropriate, with the dragon and all."

"*Just* a gift." She snorted. "I wish someone would give me something like that. But yeah, it seems to fit you perfectly."

Her words suddenly made me want to tear the pendant from my neck. Everything about it seemed to declare me changed and different, because the fact that it fit me perfectly now…well I knew something like it would never have been me before. I inhaled and exhaled a few times to keep from doing something stupid.

Calm down. I am different. No point in trying to deny it anymore, it was time I just accepted that fact and stopped fighting it. "You almost done?" I asked, fidgeting impatiently.

"Almost, now keep still before I poke you in the eye."

After a few more applications of this and that, Jenna announced my transformation complete. As I stood, I caught the hem of my dress on the back of my shoe and to keep myself from falling, I grabbed Jenna's wrist…and was rewarded with being thrown into another vision.

"Hey Khol," Jenna said, sashaying through the open door of his bedroom. In the back of my mind I noted that Jenna's hair was rainbow colored, so this had to be another vision from the past. And from the general appearance of Khol's bedroom, it seemed like this vision took place when we had been in the dragon realm in Khol's lair.

"What is it that you require, little Speaker?" Khol didn't even turn to look at her as she walked farther into the room.

"Well, it's not really just what I require, but maybe what you require too." She ran her fingertips down his back and around as she moved to stand in front of him, then down his chest as she gazed sultrily up at him. There was no question what she wanted. She rose onto her tiptoes, attempting to wrap her arms around his neck, but Khol was too tall for her, so she settled her hands on his chest again.

"So what do you say?" She batted her eyelashes at him, smiling.

"I'm in love with another, which you already know." Khol shackled her wrists in his hands, taking a step back from her.

Jenna rolled her eyes. "Who is currently doing the nasty with her new mate, and that isn't you in case you haven't noticed." She wriggled one hand free from him, running it down his front, pausing with her fingers on his waistband. "I just thought I could comfort you is all."

A low growl escaped from Khol's throat. "I will never seek comfort from you."

Jenna frowned, dropping her hand away from him. "It's not like she's gonna care. She's with Bryn. She loves Bryn. In fact, she tried to off herself after you were with her. I'm thinking that pretty much means you don't have a shot in hell with her."

"Get out," Khol hissed, his voice barely human. "Get out before I throw you out!"

Alarm registered on Jenna's face and she scurried for the door, shutting it quickly behind her. As soon as she was gone, Khol started pacing back and forth, a wild look in his eyes. He then stalked into the bathroom, halting in front of the very same bathtub where I had attempted to end my life. The tub was clean, no trace of my blood anywhere to be seen. Khol stared at the empty tub for a few more minutes before he dropped to his knees clutching at the sides. An inhuman roar wretched from his chest as he ripped the tub from the ground, throwing it against the large mirror on the opposite wall. The sound of shattering glass and ceramic echoed in my ears. He then continued his rampage, obliterating almost every square inch of the bathroom.

When he was finished, he stood surveying his work, his breathing ragged. "Drake," he called out hoarsely.

The large dragon appeared a second later, dropping down into a deep bow. "My lord."

"Take care of this," Khol said with no emotion. "And speak of it to no one."

"That, of course, is a given, my lord," Drake responded in the same emotionless tone. He then shifted and stood facing Khol with question and worry intermingled on his face. "If I may be so bold to ask, why did you not merely kill him?"

Khol picked up a piece of the broken tub, studying it for a moment before answering, "She would never have forgiven me. I know that now."

"But she would be yours."

"Not completely. Not in the way that I truly desire her to be." Khol's face contorted into a mask of pain for the briefest of moments before becoming emotionless again.

"I do not understand, my lord. It is the way of the dragon."

"But it is not the way of love." Khol clenched and unclenched his fists. "And I fear love makes me grow weak." He whirled around, disappearing.

Drake remained motionless staring at the spot where Khol had just been. "I fear that too, my lord," he whispered to himself.

I looked up at Jenna, letting go of her wrist. So many emotions were swirling around in me at once. I was shocked at witnessing a side of Khol that he'd never let me see before, a side that made me love him just a little bit more than I had a few moments ago. Then there was an irrational anger at Jenna for her attempt at trying to seduce him. I knew logically that I'd been with Bryn, and that Jenna would have seen nothing wrong by going after Khol who I had no real claims on—but the dragon in me roared at the horrible offense.

"You tried to seduce Khol," I growled at her. "And you never said anything."

"Uhh…duh! Why wouldn't I try to seduce him? He's smoking hot, and I wasn't serious with Macon yet, and—besides you were with Bryn!" She cried out the last part with outrage. "I didn't do anything wrong!"

"If you didn't think you did anything wrong, then why did you never say anything?" My dragon fire magic rose up from underneath the surface and I fought to keep it under control. Abruptly, my mind conjured up an image of what Khol and I had done together, but with Jenna in my place. I think my blood actually began to boil.

"Why didn't you tell me?" I screamed.

"You were with Bryn!" Jenna screamed back, as she moved towards the door.

Khol appeared just in the nick of time as flames shot out of my palms in the general direction of Jenna. Khol grabbed my hands, siphoning off my energy, but I still heard Jenna yelp in terror even though I knew the flames hadn't touched her.

I heard Macon's voice as he entered the fray. "What the hell is going on?"

"She tried to burn me!" Jenna cried out.

"That's because you tried to fuck Khol!" I growled between clenched teeth.

"You were with Bryn!"

"My lord?" Macon said, his voice shaky.

"Nothing happened," Khol responded in a flat tone. "Take her out of here." He paused, seeming to think better of what he said. "Do not punish her, it was before the two of you were seriously involved."

"Don't punish her my ass!" I hissed, struggling inside the iron bars that were Khol's arms. "If you don't, I will!" But Macon and Jenna were already gone, and the adrenaline rush that had been fueling me suddenly dissipated into waves of dizziness.

"Hush," Khol crooned, kissing the top of my head. "You must learn to keep your dragon temper under control. You may end up hurting someone you do not wish to one day."

"But she tried to seduce you," was my lame attempt at an excuse even though the rational side of me was already beginning to chastise my behavior towards Jenna. She was right. I had no right to be angry with her for what she did. I'd been with Bryn at the time and had no claims on Khol. So why did I still feel so betrayed by her? "You don't seem all that upset," I groused at Khol. Yes, he had advised me that I would regret hurting Jenna, but he didn't seem angry at all by my outburst...not really.

"I'm sure I don't have to explain to you why." I could hear the smile in his voice.

No, he didn't have to explain why he was so pleased, not really. He was completely digging the fact that I had gotten all crazy jealous over him. "Why didn't you hook up with her? It's not like you didn't know I was with Bryn."

Khol turned me in his arms, brushing his warm lips over mine. "Let's not talk about it."

"But I wanna know." I fought the lust that his soft kisses where inflaming in me. He didn't answer, and merely tightened his arms around me. "I said I wanna know."

And just like that another vision slammed into me.

Khol was sprawled out on his bed, a tortured pensive expression on his face when a soft knock on his door caught his attention. "Yes," he growled.

The door opened slowly and a tall beautiful woman, with long curly red hair stepped through the door hesitantly. I'd never laid eyes on her, but the minute she spoke, I knew who she was. "My lord." She curtsied low. "Drake has sent me to you." It was Shannon—the female dragon that Khol had once used to try and forget me. The memory of him kicking her out of his room so he could heal me played across my mind briefly.

Khol stood, glowering at her. "I didn't ask him to send you."

She smiled at him, flirtiously. "Maybe you should give me a chance before sending me away."

"I don't want what you're offering—at least not from you." Khol's eyes sparked with anger.

Shannon approached him with more confidence. "No, but I can help ease your pain. Help you forget her, for I am dragon after all." She came to stand in front of him, dropping the dress that she had been wearing, showing that she had nothing on underneath. When Khol didn't say anything, she obviously took it as a step in the right direction, so she sat on the edge of the bed, leaning back in blatant offering.

In a blur of motion, Khol snatched her up by the arms, pinning her to the wall. "Not on the bed," he commanded, his voice dipping to sound inhuman. She stood on her tiptoes and tried to kiss him, his response was to flip her around, pushing her face first into the wall.

"Yes, you don't have to be gentle with me—"

"Don't speak," Khol snarled. He unbuckled his pants with one hand while still holding Shannon up against the wall with the other. He closed his eyes and slid into her. She moaned her delight, which only seemed to annoy Khol more. "I said not to speak—not even a sound."

I was completely and utterly taken aback. I'd known the aftermath of Shannon and Khol's coupling, but I'd at least thought he'd been somewhat decent to her while they were together. Boy was I wrong. With his eyes firmly shut he moved in and out of her sensually. He even let go of her wrists to wrap her hair around his fist. Things from that point on seemed to go pretty smoothly until Khol broke his silence with a moaned profession of love...for me.

I was suddenly staring into Khol's illuminated green eyes, the live version, the vision fading as fast as it had come. My heart clenched at the realization of what I'd just witnessed. I asked to know why Khol hadn't hooked up with Jenna, and my new powers, in a roundabout way, had shown me. He used Shannon, and apparently even pretended she was me, or at least tried. He didn't want to do that to Jenna, my friend.

"Khol—" I started.

"I wish you wouldn't have seen that," Khol's voice was somber. "I was not at my best then...right after it happened."

"I had no idea." Apparently about a lot of things. One of which was how deeply Khol had loved me even in the beginning. Would it have made a difference then? No. But now was an entirely different story.

I reached around him, pulling at the gumband that was holding his hair back, and entangled my hands in his long auburn hair. I studied him as he studied me. He was so otherworldly in his dragon beauty. He could have been the inspiration for romance novel covers everywhere, but he was the real thing...and mine...if I really wanted him for keeps. He'd never forsaken me, not truly, not even when he thought I was mated to Bryn for good.

"I love you," I said just before I brought my lips up to take control of his. I thought about giving myself to him right then and there, to ending the dilemma of who I would be mated to once and for all, but then uncertainty began to snake its way up my spine and into my heart. I loved Bryn too. He'd been the most important person in my life since the age of five. Was I really willing to throw that all away for someone I hadn't even known for an entire year yet? *Bryn threw you away, not the other way around*, a very helpful, or not so helpful voice, depending on how I looked at it, whispered in my head.

Khol broke our kiss, pulling away. "Not now—not like this—not until you're sure."

"But I thought you told Bryn you would take advantage if my will slipped, even for a second. *It's slipping.*" I stared at him with meaning, partly wondering if the dropping the dress trick that Shannon had employed would work for me.

"I meant it when I said it." He placed his hands on the straps of my dress, obviously guessing what I was thinking. "But now that I might actually be able to have you the way I want you, with no doubts"—he cupped my face in both of his large warm hands, staring into my eyes with flames igniting in his irises—"I want that. More than you can imagine." I just stared at him and swallowed, not knowing what to say, and trying to *not* listen to what my body was telling me to do. Which pretty much entailed destroying all clothes that were keeping us apart at the moment. "I'll let Drake know you're ready for the announcement to be made. Do any last minute things. You have five minutes." And then he pulled a Khol and popped out of existence.

Great. Things just kept getting more and more complicated. What other kinds of drama would my new powers bring to me? *It's probably better not to ask.*

Chapter 10

Shifting from foot to foot nervously, I glanced at Khol briefly while I waited for him to announce me. *Let's get this over with already!* We traveled to his lair, a place we hadn't been for some time, because apparently the compound didn't have any rooms big enough or appropriate for the proclamation that I was the next dragon queen. Of course, the actual journey had been almost instantaneous since Khol had just popped me right over with his dragon powers. Which again left me wondering why I didn't seem to have the ability to transport myself. It was the coolest dragon power I'd seen so far, and I wanted it.

"Is this all really necessary?" I whispered to Khol. "It feels beyond ridiculous."

He delivered me a patronizing smile, making me want to swipe it off his face, with my fist. "Yes, it's important to make yourself known. To gain the loyalty of all the factions. This is the easiest way to go about it."

"But who says they're all just gonna bow down to me? Not much has changed except for my hair and eye color. And the last time I checked, I wasn't getting much respect around here."

"Your hair and eye color is undeniable proof of your powers, none can dispute them. And with your powers comes the mantel of queen." He took my hand and interlaced our fingers. "I know you don't feel it yet, but you will one day be what your true mother was to all of us, and you will be adored beyond all measure."

"Yeah, you're right. I don't feel very all-knowing and adored beyond measure right now," I grumbled.

Khol dipped his head, skimming his soft supple lips against my temple. "I already adore you beyond all measure." His words caused my stomach to do a little flip-flop. *I'm gonna have to have a chat with my traitorous body a little bit later.*

Khol suddenly straightened up, placing my hand over his forearm, moving towards the huge oak door in front of us. "It's time," he said.

"But I didn't hear anything. How do you know?" In fact, it just occurred to me that I hadn't heard anything, not even people, or I guess dragons talking.

"There's a sound proofing spell on this room. Drake informed me through telepathy that it was time," Khol stated matter-of-factly, as he continued moving me forward.

"Oh," I mumbled as my witty response. *Telepathy, huh? Maybe Khol can't read my mind after all. Maybe I just accidently think things at him really loud. Hmmm...*

Digging my fingers into his arm, I followed close beside him, my nerves beginning to ratchet up. At least I didn't have to worry about my morning sickness deciding to make an appearance, so I could also announce that I was pregnant in front of a bunch of dragons I didn't know. Khol paused to peer down at me, his eyes trying to assure me that everything would be okay. He then pulled the door open.

The noise from the room hit me like a physical force and I had to concentrate not to stagger back. Khol wasn't kidding about the soundproofing spell. But as soon as I stepped into the room with Khol, it all abruptly stopped, as if the spell had fallen back around everyone again. I swear if someone had dropped a pin, I would have heard it. Keeping my chin up and gaze forward, I avoided the burning gazes of everyone around me.

And then, someone called out, "Look at her hair!" Which erupted the room into chaos, the volume surpassing the previous level from when I'd first entered the room.

"I thought you said I was gonna be announced," I grated through clenched teeth at Khol.

"And you are."

He led me up to the front of the room where I was forced to acknowledge the crowd. I dug my nails into Khol's arm, pretty sure I was going to draw blood, but he didn't make any protests. The room was stuffed from wall to wall with dragons, more than I thought still existed from the impressions Khol had given me. And yet there they all were, the red, black, silver, and gold factions, mixed together in one intimidating group, their eyes all on me.

"Behold, our new queen," Khol's voice washed over the crowd and one by one, they began to drop to their knees to show deference to me.

Once everyone had taken the plunge, even Khol himself dropped to one knee in front of me, clasping my hand to his forehead. I trembled, not knowing what to do. My gaze skimmed over the crowd—most of the dragons' eyes were facing the floor, but I immediately caught the gaze of one dragon who was not studying the marble, or maybe I should say half dragon. *Bryn.* He was staring at me, anguish swirling in his sea storm eyes. When he realized I was looking right at him, he flicked his eyes to the floor as well. My chest constricted, and I fought to keep my composure. It shouldn't be this way, Bryn should be standing beside me, like he always has, not kneeling before me like everyone else in the crowd. And Jenna? Where was Jenna? I hadn't spotted her anywhere. Despite our recent argument, I still wanted her beside me as well. It was if I was suddenly losing everyone I held dear from my old life.

"Tell them they can rise," Khol rumbled low for my ears only.

"Oh," I said. "Right." I was in so over my head. "You

may all rise." My audience slowly lumbered to their feet and Khol repositioned himself beside me, intertwining my fingers with his again. I tightened my grip on his hand as if he were my only lifeline. "What should I do now?" I hissed under my breath, while still staring straight ahead.

"If you wish, I will speak for you. It is not unheard of to have a trusted advisor do so."

"Yeah, do that." I sighed with relief.

Khol stepped forward, dropping my hand. I fought back the urge to reach for it, to cling to him like a small child. *Ugh. Pathetic. Some queen I am.*

"Our queen wishes me to speak on her behalf." Khol delivered the crowd a relaxed smile, full of charm and self-deprecation. "She is a little overwhelmed by all of this. As I'm sure you all can understand."

A few chuckles rang out in response and a low buzz of conversation resumed in the room. I took that as a good sign. "I'm sure all of you are wondering how this came about, and I will tell you…"

A LITTLE WHILE later I found myself back in my own room, much to Khol's dismay, and sprawled out across my bed. I couldn't help but feel small in it since it still hadn't been that long since I shared it with Bryn.

Yep, here I am, a friggin' dragon queen, and I've never felt so tiny and alone in my entire life. But I didn't want to begin relying on Khol the way that I'd relied on Bryn. I would take a mate, and in him I wanted a partner, not a caretaker. Even if it seemed as if Bryn and Khol wanted nothing more than to take care of me in all things. Was it because of their dragon nature? And if that was the case, then would I have to continually fight my own nature to let them? *Being a full-blooded dragon with human sensibilities is hard.*

A knock on my door made me scramble up into a sitting position. "Come in," I called, hoping it was either Khol or Bryn. Or maybe even Jenna. I really needed to fix things with her. I just didn't have the energy to make the first move at the moment. I heaved a sigh of disappointment when a small female dragon with short-cropped silver hair stepped into view. I inclined my head inquisitively at her and she bowed down in front of me, which was pretty low because I was sitting.

"My queen," she greeted.

I studied the top of her head for a moment, jealously spiking through my system that she got to have silver hair, which was so prettier than the white I was stuck with. *Alright, P.J. don't be a petty bitch, what happened is what happened. No use being a baby about it because it won't change a damn thing.*

"Yes," I responded, neutrally.

She raised her face to meet my gaze with violet eyes. "My name is Tatiana, my queen, and I belong to the silver dragon faction."

"Yeah, I kind of figured that," I said, motioning to her hair.

A slight smile curled her lips. "Yes, well I know you are relatively new to our world. I just wanted to clarify."

"Look, I don't mean to be rude or anything, but could you please get to the point?"

"No need to apologize, my queen, you are still young, patience will come to you in time."

I barked a harsh laugh at her. "Doubtful, but please continue."

She produced a white envelope about the size and shape as the one I had received from the old queen, my biological mother, when I had been in the Smokey Mountains. A feeling of foreboding washed over me. "My clan has been holding onto this for a very long time. Our instructions were to give it to you today, after the announcement."

"And how long is a very long time?" I whispered.

"Since before your birth," Tatiana responded.

"Oh. Well then, I already know who it's from. Thank you." I took the letter from her with a shaking hand, wishing it would simply disappear. Because whatever was on the inside was certain to complicate my life further.

"It was our pleasure to serve both the old and new queen," she said, rising and heading for the door.

"Thank you again," I said without looking up at her. My attention was riveted on the small white envelope resting in the palm of my hand. Guess my birth mother thought she could still shake up my life even from beyond the grave. I tore the envelope open, kind of wondering in the back of my mind, how the silver dragon faction had resisted the temptation to open it themselves. I personally would never have been able to withstand the temptation.

Inside was a letter written in the same scrawling handwriting that had adorned my previous message from my birth mother.

My Dear Child,

It is imperative that you do exactly as I'm about to tell you. If you deviate at all, thinking you can find a better way, it will result in your death. And therefore, also the deaths of the ones you love. I have foreseen it. Please trust in my powers, which are now yours, for one day you will need to rely on them. But, for the time being, while those powers grow and change within you—you lack the skill to control them the way that's it's taken me many decades to learn how to do so myself.

This evening there will be an attempt on your life by someone you thought you could trust. She has let a Rider slip into her, for all humans carry some darkness in them, and it will convince her you have caused all of her problems. She will try to end your life by poisoning you. Do not accept any nourishment from anyone this evening. It will save your life. But do not fear. Eventually, if you follow the path I have laid out for you, you will be able to save her. That should offer you some small comfort.

Once the commotion steals everyone's attention, you are to strike out on your own. I've had a trusted subject place a package in the back of your closet behind a loose panel with everything you will need, including a way to keep Khol from tracking you. You must do this next part on your own, and

I'm sorry for that my daughter. But I will help you whenever I can. Find the strength that already exists within you.

~M

My hands shook as I struggled to process what I just read. *Jenna is going to try and kill me and she has a Rider in her.* It had to be her because there were no other female humans that I trusted left alive. But I could save her if I followed the path my birth mother had laid out for me. And then I'd have to strike out on my own on some unknown mission.

Shit. I knew that stupid letter was going to make my life more complicated.

"I HOPE you have good news for me this time," his master snapped as Terrance entered the room.

"Yes. One of our most trusted is in place. The girl will be dead by week's end, as promised."

A smile slowly spread across his master's face. "Excellent. Most excellent indeed. Let me know when it is done." He flicked his hand in a dismissive motion. "You may go now."

Terrance breathed a sigh of relief as he exited his master's office. By the end of the week the girl would be dead, and all would be well once more.

THE CARE PACKAGE was exactly where my birth mother had indicated, hidden in the back of my closet. Although it would have been nice if she could have warned me about the huge spider lying in wait. I almost knocked myself out cold when it crawled over my hand, and I slammed the side of my head into the closet door in my haste to escape it. Once I made it past that obstacle, the rest went smoothly.

My birth mother had thought of everything: wigs, colored contacts, fake I.D., credit cards, and even some sort of magically charmed bracelet to dampen Khol's connection to me. She left more instructions, which directed me not to put it on until later, when Khol was distracted, or he would notice something was wrong before I could make a break for it.

Once I was away from Khol's watchful eyes, the plan was for me to enroll under my fake name with the false documents at a high school to which I had been given directions, and I was informed that I would know what to do past that point instinctually. I was also assured that I could pass for a senior, despite my own doubts on the matter.

And then there was the letter she had left for Khol, which I was not to open, that had directions inside for him to follow. I won't lie, the not opening the letter to Khol was proving to be the most difficult part of the plan.

Sighing, I pushed my duffle bag full of my secret mission necessities into the back of my closet. I couldn't risk anyone seeing it since they'd undoubtably ask questions. At this point, questions were bad. The fact was, it seemed like I was running away, and in some ways that felt easier than anything I'd done in a long time. I just hoped I wasn't playing at high school too long because my baby bump would eventually make an appearance.

I brought my hand up to my stomach protectively. My birth mother wouldn't put my baby in danger, would she? I doubted it, but I couldn't seem to push the worry aside completely.

"Hey," Jeremy's voice startled me back to the present and I looked up to see him carrying a tray with milk and cookies on it.

I clutched at my chest as my heart eased off the gas. "God, you scared me."

"Sorry. But the good news is that I bring a peace offering from Jenna. She wanted me to drop these off on my way to workout. She even made me promise not to steal any for myself." He smiled at me, setting the tray on my nightstand. "I'll come by on my way back, okay? To talk—"

"Yeah, okay," I interjected, adrenaline spiking my system. *This is it. This is how Jenna, or rather the Rider in Jenna, is going to try to kill me. Death my cookies and milk.*

Jeremy's brow furrowed slightly, probably picking up on my nervous energy. "Jenna also said to tell you she'd be down to check on you in a bit, and if you wanted to talk, then she'd be ready."

Yeah, I bet she'll be down to check on me—to make sure I'm dead. I fought back hysterical laughter. "Yep, I'll be here... ready to talk."

Jeremy gave me one last curious glance before ducking out of my room. "Okay, I'll see you in a bit."

I didn't know what was weirder, the fact that Jeremy seemed so cavalier about how I tried to fry his lady love earlier, like we'd had a normal fight, or that my best female friend was trying to kill me. Or maybe the weirdest thing of all was how I was now taking all of these things in stride, like they were totally normal.

"Khol," I called out on shaky breath. "I need you."

Khol appeared almost before the last syllable of my request had left my mouth, and he rushed to me with worry etched into the lines of his face. "What is it? What's wrong?"

I stared at him, trying to mentally record every last detail about him, from his long auburn hair, to his high strong cheekbones that flowed up to his dragon green eyes. When I was with Khol I always felt so tiny in comparison to his large proportions, something I'd always liked. He made me feel safe and protected, like I was the most precious thing in the world to him. I was going to miss him—more than I wanted to admit. Khol became a constant in my life from the first day he had literally popped into it. I loved Bryn too, but he had been ripped away from me when I needed him the most. I knew it wasn't his fault, and I could never blame him, but he didn't have an excuse for walking away from me now. Because he had done just that...walked away from me. His intentions might be sincere, and he might be doing it out of love for me, but that still didn't change the fact that he'd abandoned me and I couldn't trust him to always be there for me anymore.

I knew emphatically that Khol would never ever walk away from me, no matter the circumstances. He'd proved it time and time again, and truth be told, that was very important to me, especially with a baby on the way. I wished I wasn't going to have to leave him behind soon. It wasn't like I had a choice if I wanted to live, according to my birth mother, but it still didn't make me feel any better about the situation. How would Khol react when I was gone and he couldn't find me? My chest tightened as I thought about what he might do. I shook myself internally. I had to deal with the task at hand. "Jenna is trying to kill me. I mean not Jenna really…but a Rider got into her."

Khol's gaze sharpened. "Are you sure?"

I swallowed around the lump in my throat. "Yes, my birth mother left me a letter. She told me a Rider slipped into her and she was gonna try and poison me and not to accept anything to eat or drink from anyone tonight."

My lower lip trembled. "And sure enough Jenna sent Jeremy down with milk and cookies for me. She had to send him because…" Tears tracked down my cheeks, much to my chagrin. I had told myself I wouldn't get emotional over this. It wasn't Jenna, not really, and I would find a way to save her just like my birth mother said I could.

"Because if you saw her, you would see the Rider within her," Khol completed my sentence for me.

"Yeah," I whispered.

"Then I must—"

"Don't hurt her!" I said in a rush. "I mean I know you're gonna have to lock her up or something but don't hurt her—please! Promise me you won't! I can save her! I know I can! Just not now!"

Khol came to me, wrapping his comforting frame around me. "I know what she means to you. I promise not to hurt her."

"Thank you," I croaked.

"Drake," Khol called, his arms still around me.

"Yes, my lord," Drake's low voice rumbled in response a moment later.

"Go to the little Speaker, escort her to a cell, a Rider has taken up residence in her, so expect a fight."

"Should I just not kill her then?" Drake asked as if he was inquiring about the weather.

"No!" I exclaimed, pulling free of Khol. "Don't hurt her!" I met Khol's sympathetic eyes. "You go—please. I trust you."

Khol nodded. "I will see to it myself then. Drake, get rid of those—" He motioned briefly to the tray. "They are poison." He then turned back to me, brushing his lips gently across mine. "I will be back shortly."

Sadness washed over me. *I won't be here when you get back. I'm sorry.* I knew he could feel my sadness, but I was hoping he thought it was connected with the Jenna situation. Soon I wouldn't have to worry about him reading my emotions at all though, and for the first time ever I was not okay with that. "All right," I said.

Both Khol and Drake disappeared, Drake taking the milk and cookies with him and Khol off to imprison one of my best friends.

Heart aflutter, I raced to my closet, yanking the duffle bag out of its hiding place. *It's now or never, life or death, and I have to do this to save my world—and the people I love.* I set the letter my birth mother intended for Khol on my bed where I knew he would see it when he returned. Again, my chest tightened thinking about how he would react when he discovered I was gone and realized he couldn't track me. *There's no time to think about his stuff now.*

I inhaled and exhaled a few shaky breaths and snapped the shiny bronze bracelet onto my left wrist. It was a perfect fit, of course. Steeling my nerves at last, I set out on my way ... alone.

No pressure though, it's only the fate of the world that's depending on me to be successful with all of this.

Chapter 11

"**Y**our transcripts have already been sent over from your previous school. You'll need you to fill out a couple of forms and I'll need to see some identification from you."

"Yeah, sure." I bit the insides of my cheeks as I dug into my bag, producing my fake ID for the elderly office lady. As I handed it to her, I tried to keep my hand from shaking. My birth mom seemed to have thought of everything, but I couldn't shake the feeling that at any minute someone would see me for what I really was…a fraud.

The office lady looked over my ID and copied down a few things before handing it back to me with a smile. "Here you go. You can sit over there and fill out these forms." She slid some papers attached to a clipboard in my direction. "And when you're done just bring them back to me and I'll give you your class schedule."

"Okay. Thanks," I said numbly, sliding the clipboard off the counter and making my way over to the greenish couch she had indicated to me. The forms were standard stuff, asking for some information that I'm pretty sure they already had, but I filled them out anyways. When I was finished, I made my way back up to the counter, sliding the clipboard to the office lady. She looked over the forms briefly and then motioned for me to wait a minute with her finger.

"Here you are," she said after digging around in a file to produce my class schedule. "If you have any problems, let me know." And with a smile and a nod she dismissed me.

Of all the things I could have been faced with, going back to high school was definitely one of the worst. Not to mention that I found myself in the unfamiliar territory of being enrolled in a high school in Spring Hill, Tennessee. I'd never been to the South, unless I counted the vision I'd had about the Rider taking over Senator Bill Wexington. I wasn't even sure what the plan was beyond me enrolling here and pretending to be a normal high school senior. Supposedly, I would instinctively know what to do.

I snorted. *Yeah, okaaay.*

I was already doubting my ability to blend in with my white hair and rainbow- colored hairpieces that I'd clipped in to try and make me less old lady and more punk rock. I was currently channeling Jenna's old look, which I was worried might be a bit much for the South, even if I didn't have any other good options. If I'd gone the wig route, I was positive I would have stuck out even more, so multicolored hair and brown contact lenses it was.

As soon as I left the office, I beelined it directly to the girl's room. I already missed homeroom and part of first period, so I figured I'd just jump right into my schedule starting with my second class and hide out in the bathroom until then.

Letting my bag drop from my shoulder, I gripped the sides of a sink, glaring at my own reflection. "You can do this," I told my punk rock reflection. "You don't need Bryn, or Khol, or Jenna, or even Jeremy. You got this." My eyes slid down to the chain on my ruby dragon pendant. I tugged it free from my shirt, wrapping my hand around it.

"Then let me put it on you." Khol's voice echoed in my mind, the ghost of his lips on the back of my neck.

Shaking my head to dislodge the memory, I dropped the pendant back inside my black t-shirt. I wouldn't let myself grow morose over thoughts of either Khol or Bryn. They were a different problem that I didn't have time to deal with now, and yet without thinking I brought my hand up to my stomach, the motion still comforting me for some reason. "We'll get through this," I whispered to my unborn child and reflection.

"Your stomach givin' you trouble?" a feminine voice drawled from behind me. Her accent wasn't quite southern but there was a definite twangy undertone.

Dropping my hand quickly, I turned towards the owner of the voice. She was about 5'1" with long blonde hair that hung almost to her waist. She had the glowing stereotypical tan that I usually associated with girls from the south. Even though she was a petite thing, she had some traffic stopping curves that made envy spike for a brief second. She wore a light pink t-shirt over a short jean skirt and cowboy boots. *Wow actual cowboy boots. I didn't think people actually wore those anywhere but on a farm. Toto, we're definitely not in Kansas anymore. Or maybe I should say Pittsburgh?*

I fidgeted nervously as I watched her give my appearance a thorough once over. If she represented the typical style for my new school then I had even less hope of fitting in than I originally thought. "I guess I'm a little nervous," I muttered. "It's my first day."

"I'm Laila," she said with a smile. "You're not from around here, are ya?" She then laughed. "Of course you're not, with the way you're dressed and all."

"That bad?" I said, grimacing. "I was kind of hoping to blend in."

"You'll do fine. The guys around here will probably fall all over the new Yankee girl. They get all excited when they see somethin' new and different. The girls on the other hand might be a different story."

Figured. I needed more guy attention like I needed another hole in my head. "Yeah, well I have a boyfriend… from back home. I'm not currently shopping for more trouble."

Laila threw her head back, laughing. "Ain't that the truth? Boys are nothin' but trouble most of the time."

Considering all the drama that Khol and Bryn had caused in my life, despite my love for them, I couldn't help the wry grin that spread across my face. "Most of the time? How about all of the time?"

She stepped forward and linked her arm with mine. "Oh honey, you and I are gonna get along famously." She pulled my class schedule out of my other hand and began reading it. "We have almost the exact same schedule." She started walking, tugging me along beside her. "You can start countin' your blessings, 'cause I got your back now, hun."

Some of my tension eased. Laila was like a smaller, peppier, southern version of Jenna. It would be nice to feel like I had a friend while I was off on my own trying to save the world.

"I DON'T THINK I can take much more of this," I grumbled to Laila as I tried to unsuccessfully ignore all the stares I was receiving at lunch. I suddenly wasn't very hungry, and I dropped the French fry I was about to eat back down on my tray. "This school isn't very big. You think everyone would have seen me by now so that they could all stop staring."

The other thing that was bothering me, which I couldn't tell Laila, was that her school was completely infested with Riders. It skeeved me completely out at first, but I seemed relatively safe as long as I didn't let on to them that I could see them. In that case, my first day nerves covered up my 'holy crap my lab partner has an alien parasite inside of him' nerves very nicely.

"They'll get over it in a day or two," Laila replied cheerfully. "Besides gettin' stared at isn't always a bad thing."

"It is to me," I grumbled. The whole situation was bringing up bad memories of my last couple of weeks at community college where I had been shunned and persecuted for things that I hadn't actually done. The girls had hated me there too, and the guys all wanted to hook up with me. The one explained the other. But at least I'd had Jenna and Jeremy there.

"So, how attached are you to your boyfriend back home?" Laila asked with false nonchalance.

I lifted my gaze and narrowed my eyes at her. "Very. Why?"

"Well, I don't know, it's just that only the hottest boy in all of Spring Hill High School is on his way over here right now."

And he had a Rider inside of him. "Shit," I swore under my breath, freezing in my seat as I watched the tall slender and yet completely ripped boy walk over to me. I tried to focus on his outer features and not on the dual imagery that usually freaked me out, but I was struggling. My breathing was coming in short little erratic bursts, and by the time he slid into the seat beside me, I was on the verge of hyperventilating.

"Hey, I'm Cliff, what's your name?" Cliff and the Rider

both smiled at me, or well I guess they were sort of one in the same, but either way the thing was grinning at me.

"I'm P—Paige," I stammered. And now I knew why my birth mother had used my real first name on my fake ID. With my nerves, I started to say P.J., and Paige was an easy save after that.

"Well, Paige," the thing said with a slight southern draw. "What do you think of our little school? Prolly a ton different than what you're used to, I bet." An easy grin settled onto its face as he looked at me expectantly.

I swallowed around the huge lump that had taken up residence in my throat. First, I had to stop thinking of the Rider as an *it*. I had to think of Cliff as a normal, non-alien hosting, teenage boy. I tried to meet his eyes but cringed away at the dual imagery again. I was so screwed. "I… umm…" I stammered.

"Well, look at you, Cliff. You got Paige all flustered. She's kind of shy, you know?" Laila interjected, obviously trying to save me from myself. If only she knew the real reason behind my nerves.

"No need to be shy around me," Cliff responded directly to me. He then reached out and patted my bare arm in what he surely meant as a reassuring gesture.

I stood abruptly, as if a current of electricity had been shot through my body, my chair toppling noisily to the floor. I'd been in close quarters with one of the Riders before, namely the emo boy from hell when he had tried to kill me, but I'd never had skin-to-skin contact with one before. It was wrong, so very wrong. I began to shake as a vision threatened to force its way into me. What would happen if I passed out right here and now? Would any of the Riders be suspicious of me or would they merely think I was sick or something? *Too late for the what if*, I thought numbly as I crumpled to the floor.

I focused in on Cliff, who was standing in front of a bathroom mirror wearing nothing but a towel. His dark blond hair appeared darker from his recent shower, and moisture glistened on his well-toned, tanned body. If not for the dual imagery of the alien Rider inside of him, plus the fact that he was two years younger than me and still in High school, I might have taken the time to appreciate his vast hotness. As it was, I was fighting the urge to not dry heave at the wrongness of it all.

I noticed Cliff was staring at himself with a grimace etched into his chiseled features. "What's wrong with you?" he muttered to his own image. Although I was sure Cliff couldn't see the Rider that was currently residing inside his body, the Rider frowned out from inside him, obviously not liking Cliff's reaction to it. The Rider's face then contorted into what could have passed for it being in pain. "Get out of my head," Cliff grated between clenched teeth as he raised his hands to press against the side of his temples. "This isn't who you are."

It was then I realized I was witnessing a battle of wills between Cliff and the Rider inside of him. Cliff began to shake, a trickle of blood slowly slipping from one nostril and oozing down his face. "I said to get out," he whispered, his voice raspy and low.

And then something wondrous happened. The Rider just kind of poured out of him, not much more than smoke, reforming in the shape of the alien standing behind Cliff. Unfortunately for Cliff, that was right about the time his eyes rolled into the back of his head and he collapsed to the ground with a loud thud. The Rider looked at him with rage, letting out a silent scream before it disappeared.

I gasped, waking up in the confines of someone's arms. Someone's arms that were not either Bryn or Khol's. "Stop," I croaked before my eyes even managed to flutter open. "Low blood sugar."

"What?" Cliff's slight southern drawl answered me in confusion.

My eyes popped open in alarm and I stared up into Cliff's face, who still had a Rider peering at me from inside of him. *I don't understand.* I saw the Rider leave his body. I saw it disappear. What did it mean that it was back? Why was I shown the vision if it didn't mean anything?

"I have low blood sugar. I'm fine. You can put me down," I said, managing to sound much more stable.

"You're not fine. You passed out cold back there. I'm taking you to the nurse. She might need to call—"

"I said to put me down!" I demanded shrilly, trying to extradite myself from his arms. And for my effort I ended up back on the ground, on my ass. *Lovely.* My breath left me with a soft *oof* before I scrambled to my feet. I glared at my would-be savior, and host to the Rider, Cliff, who was staring at me with wide eyes.

"How did you do that? You're stronger than you look."

Shit. Not good. "Adrenaline?" I said unsurely. "Yeah,

adrenaline." I repeated with more confidence. "I don't like to be carried around like that, okay?"

My mind skittered through the many times that both Bryn and Khol had carried me in such a manner. A wave of homesickness washed over me as I longed for nothing more than to be back with them...where I belonged.

My gut clenched and I doubled over, revisiting my recent meal and depositing it right on Cliff's shoes. I wiped my mouth with the back of my hand, meeting his blue eyes with horror. "I'm so sorry I—"

I what? Apparently, my morning sickness was back with a vengeance now that Khol wasn't nearby to do his magic mojo to help me out. Any hope I had at blending in lay splattered all over Cliff's ruined kicks. But surely my birth mother would have forseen this and taken it into consideration. I mean...she'd been ready for everything else. She couldn't have missed something so potentially problematic. *Right?*

"There you are," a vaguely familiar female voice said with saccharine sweetness. Long feminine fingers wrapped around the bicep of my left arm and tugged me to a full upright position. I whirled my head around as fast as I could, meeting the dark eyes of probably the last person in the world I expected to see coming to my rescue. *Nala.*

My lips opened and closed like a guppy—and a very surprised guppy at that. Nala and I had effectively been avoiding each other since...well, since we first met. She wanted Bryn, and Bryn was mine. At least he used to be.

And wanting the same guy didn't exactly produce warm and fuzzy friendship feelings between two people.

"What are you doing here?" I demanded, trying to cover both my surprise and animosity towards her.

She gave me what best could be described as a patronizing older sister look. Loving, but with a touch of exasperation. "*Your mom* sent me over because she realized you forgot your medication. She was worried something like—well, exactly like—this would happen."

I turned my head away from Cliff, who was now shaking his feet in an attempt to dislodge my less than thoughtful gift to him. "Medication?" I mouthed.

Nala gave me a sharp look that was obviously telling me to go along with her story. Normally, just because of our mutual dislike for each other in our past, I wouldn't have trusted her, but I had a sneaking suspicion because of her choice of words that my birth mother had been meddling from beyond the grave again. "Oh, right, I forgot."

"What kind of medication?" Cliff asked. "I mean—"

"Oh, she'll be fine," Nala interjected. "She just has an ear infection that causes her to get dizzy and if she's not careful, well…" She then motioned at the second viewing of my lunch.

Ear infection. Now why didn't I think of that? "I'm sorry." I mumbled in Cliff's general direction not wanting to see his face, or rather the Rider that was hiding behind his face. "And I didn't mean to snap at you either."

"It's all right," Cliff reassured me. "It just means you're gonna have to make it up to me."

Not a chance in hell, buddy. "Oh, um...sure."

"Great," he said with cheer, as if he didn't have my puke all over his shoes. "I'll be seeing you then."

"Not if I can help it," I mumbled.

"What?" he said with a hitch in his voice.

"Oh, nothing," I said louder. "I just said thanks for helping."

The brightness in his voice returned. "No problem. I hope you feel better soon, Paige." And with that the hot boy known as Cliff exited stage left with the alien that had rode in on him.

I exhaled a huge sigh of relief as I refocused my attention on Nala. Her long black hair was pulled back in a loose French braid and her blue eyes met mine as she blinked her long inky lashes. A small smirk took began to tilt the corners of her lips up. *I really hate how pretty she is.* "So, care to share with me the real reason you're here?"

An errant thought caused fresh adrenaline course through my system. "Bryn and Khol—"

"Aren't here."

"Oh," I said, trying not to sound crestfallen. *I just miss them. It's not because I need either of them to make me feel safe with all the Riders around. I am an adult woman, and I can stand on my own two feet without any help from either of them.*

"I'll explain everything, but not here." Her bright blue eyes scanned the empty hallway as if she thought someone might jump out of a locker at any moment. *And I thought I was paranoid.*

"Yeah, okay," I agreed, eager to get the hell out of school and end my first day as a pretend student, even if it meant leaving with Nala.

WE WENT STRAIGHT to my temporary humble abode… a.k.a. the huge old creepy house that my birth mother had instructed me to take up residence in. Apparently staying in a place that gave off bodies-in-the-basement vibes was a lot safer than say…a cozy apartment or something of that ilk. I hadn't slept well since I'd been staying in the murder house. I was half convinced the ghost of some victim would attack me in my sleep. I hated to admit it, but I was kind of glad to have company, even if that company was Nala.

I'm shit on my own, aren't I?

"All right, we're safe from prying ears now. Care to explain why you're here?" I huffed, wondering if we were indeed safe from *all* varieties of prying ears. Well, at least any spirits that might be hanging around didn't frequent any gossip circles that might report pack to the Riders. I hoped.

"I brought you some tea, it's made up of a special herbal blend that will help with your morning sickness," Nala said, ignoring my question.

"How do I know you're not trying to poison me?"

She heaved a huge sigh, meeting my gaze with what reminded me of Khol's exasperated face that he reserved especially for me. "Use your powers to see where I got it from then." She lifted her arm in an invitation for me to touch her.

I worried my bottom lip between my teeth. So far I hadn't received a vision on purpose...ever. Sure, I'd asked questions and gotten the answers in the form of a vision, but even then, I hadn't done anything but muse about the subject of interest. But what would it hurt to try? Besides my fragile ego, that is.

"I'll do exactly that," I retorted with false bravado, reaching out to grasp her wrist. I closed my eyes tightly and silently pleaded with my powers. *Show me where Nala got this tea from...please.* I felt myself sliding into a vision much more smoothly than I'd ever experienced before. *It's actually working!* I mentally did a happy little jig as I was swept away.

"You know where she went." Khol's *beautifully sculpted features were twisted with a mix of anger and desperation. "Tell me," he growled, reaching out to grab Nala by her shoulders. "I'll burn you to a crisp where you stand if you don't!"*

Her eyes widened slightly with fear. "I was instructed not to tell anyone—you specifically. I was told that you would know why you can't know this information, that you wouldn't be happy but would understand."

Khol abruptly released his tight grip on her shoulders, turning away from her, his dragon green eyes glowing brighter.

"Yes, I was...informed." His voice was low and inhuman. "And no, I'm not happy."

"So—" Nala started but Khol didn't let her finish.

"Drake," he bellowed. Barely a second passed before Drake appeared in a low crouch before Khol. He didn't speak and appeared to be waiting for whatever Khol would say next. "These herbs will help her?" I'm not sure if anyone else was picking up on the slight tremble in his voice, but it made me want to go to him and to take him in my arms.

"Yes, they will help her, I swear it," Drake rumbled low, not lifting his head to meet Khol's penetrating gaze.

The muscles in Khol's jaw feathered as he studied the top of Drake's head for a moment. "Fine then. Go, before I change my mind."

I snapped back into my body where I was still gripping Nala's wrist. A single tear slid down my cheek, and I let go of her so I could wipe at it with the back of my hand. Just seeing Khol, even if it was in a vision, made my homesickness that much more acute. And what about Bryn? How was he handling the news of my disappearance?

Another vision ripped me suddenly from my body.

Bryn lay on his back, the dark sheets that covered his bed twisted around his legs. His pale muscled chest glistened with sweat, heaving in and out as he slept restlessly. "Peej—" My name slipped from his sleep-encrusted lips.

He looked bad. Or what I mean is not well somehow. Even with his eyes shut, I could almost see the torment that lurked in his unseen gaze. Dark circles marred his otherwise perfect complexion, and his skin wasn't just pale but almost sickly.

"Peej—" He repeated my name again as his brow furrowed with worry. Suddenly he was sitting up, gasping for air. He ran his hand through his sweat-dampened hair, blinking in confusion as he looked down at the empty spot beside him where I wasn't. I saw a moment of regret play across his features before it turned into cold hard determination. He reached over for a glass that had been resting on the table beside his bed, drinking the contents before sliding back down in between his sheets.

"I'll make sure you're safe Peej, no matter the cost."

"Something's wrong with Bryn!" I exclaimed, slamming back into the present for the second time within minutes. Maybe whatever was wrong with him was making him act the way that he was towards me. What if there was more than meets the eye with him and me being bitter that he'd turned away from me was completely unfair. I loved both Bryn and Khol, I'd come to terms with that truth, but no matter how much I tried to deny it, there was nothing Bryn could truly do to turn me away from him. He was my first love, my best friend…my home. What if—

"Here," Nala said, interrupting my inner turmoil over Bryn and Khol. "Drink it while it's still hot so it doesn't taste as bad."

I crinkled my nose at the pungent aroma that was wafting out of the mug. "No way that stuff is gonna make me *stop* throwing up."

"Just drink it already. It'll fix things."

"I'm not gonna drink it if I don't want to," I groused. I knew I sounded like a petulant child but I still wasn't a Nala fan, even if she seemed to be trying to help me.

Nala heaved a huge sigh. "Look, I know you don't like me, or trust me, and I can't really blame you. But let me lay it out for you. You're the queen of us all now—do you really think I want to make you my enemy?"

I narrowed my eyes at her. "Too late." She wanted Bryn and had tried to take him from me. That fact fast tracked her to the top of my enemy list as far as I was concerned.

"I didn't know you. And it's the way of the dragon. Besides, if Bryn could have been swayed that easily, I would have been doing you a favor."

"Are you kidding? I mean, are you serious right now?" My dragon magic pushed up to the surface of me. If Nala wasn't careful, *I'd* end up burning her to crisp where she stood without a second thought.

She raised her hands defensively as if she sensed the danger she was in. "He doesn't want me. He's made that crystal clear."

"But you still want him." My voice came out as a low inhuman growl, and I would have put money down that my eyes were glowing too.

"Yes, but it doesn't matter. I have pride, you know. I'm not going to chase after Bryn when he's clearly made his choice."

My anger slipped from me as quickly as it had come, my face crumpling involuntarily. "Yeah, he has. He thinks

I should mate with Khol." Much to my chagrin, tears spilled down my cheeks. *Damn pregnancy hormones!*

Nala rolled her eyes. "Young male dragons are the worst. They haven't fully come into their powers yet but they've already got the ego thing down pat." She shook her head and frowned. "He doesn't really want you to mate with Khol. He just has this idea that he should be able to protect you completely, unfortunately he doesn't have the power yet—"

"And Khol does?" I interjected.

"Precisely." She smiled at me. "Although fully matured male dragons are no better. I think you've learned that from dealing with Khol."

Laughter erupted from my chest. "Between the two of them I'm lucky I still have my sanity." I paused, looking down at my hands that glistened from the tears I'd just wiped from my face. "At least I think I do."

"I almost feel sorry for you." Nala snorted. "Almost. If not for the fact that you have two powerful, handsome male dragons fighting over you." She snorted again. "Never mind, I actually don't feel sorry for you at all."

"Bryn isn't fighting for me at all. He's given up."

"He's fighting for your safety, and sacrificing himself in the process. It's not the fight you want, but it does prove how much he loves you."

I wasn't quite sure how to respond to that. I knew on some level that she was right, and I hated it. Bryn was only trying to protect me, and my vision had shown me how much he was suffering. But I loved Khol now too. I inevitably would end up crushing one of them when I mated with the other. It was easier on some level to be angry with Bryn when I was with Khol. Because otherwise I'd have to admit to myself that maybe on some level I'd betrayed Bryn just as much as he'd betrayed me. I reached up, resting my hand on my abdomen.

"It doesn't matter," I murmured. And it didn't. Whoever the father of my child was, he would be my mate. I'd made up my mind to let fate decide, because no matter which way I looked at it...fate was going to play its hand anyways.

"You're really going to mate with whoever the father of your child is?" Nala asked.

I gave her a sad smile. "Yes."

She simply grunted and pushed the mug that contained the fowl smelling concoction closer to me. I stared at it for a moment, before deciding to just drink it despite the fact that Nala was the one giving it to me. I'd clearly seen she wasn't trying to poison me and cutting my nose off to spite my face would only result in more humiliation by way of puke.

I picked up the mug and chugged the contents as fast as I could. It burned my throat, nose, and eyes. I coughed demonstratively when I'd managed to get all of it into my stomach. "Blak! That was just as bad as I thought it would be!" A sudden wave of exhaustion swept over me. "What the hell?" I slurred, fighting to keep my eyes open.

"Oh, didn't I mention that you should only take this

before bed because it's supposed to knock you out?" Nala winked at me. "No? My bad. Nighty night, little queenie."

Adrenaline spiked, but not enough to completely counteract the effects of the tea. Although I realized that Nala wouldn't risk hurting me because she knew it would result in her own death. Wouldn't stop her from being a bitch though. A title she deserved to hear out loud.

"Bitch," I grated just before slumping down onto the kitchen table.

I KNEW it was a dream immediately, or a memory really, although it was a bit fuzzy around the edges.

I was alone with Khol in his room at his lair.

"Please," I whispered, my whole body trembling. "Don't do this to me."

"I'm sorry. I don't have a choice anymore."

"It'll be rape. Are you telling me you're okay with that?"

My dream then shifted to a different memory, and it was just as fuzzy as the last one.

"I wanna be with you, Bryn. I don't wanna be with anyone else. Ever."

"We'll find a way. Somehow—we'll find a way." And then his lips sought mine out again. That was all I needed to hear. Bryn would fight for me. Somehow we would make it work.

I jolted up in bed, a scream caught in my throat, coming face-to-face with...myself.

Dread snaked its way up my spine as I met the green

eyes of the *me* I used to be. *This is it, the sign that I've finally lost it. Padded room here I come.*

"Don't worry, you're still dreaming," the me with enviable red auburn hair said, with a wry smile.

"Okay, so what am I trying to tell myself? The symbolism, now that I know I'm dreaming, isn't lost on me."

My old self chuckled. "No, you're not exactly being very subtle at the moment." She looked at me again, all the amusement draining from her face. "You're letting your fear of being alone rule your decisions."

"No, I'm not. I'm here, aren't I? Enduring this task—alone—without Bryn and Khol. I—"

"You know that's not what I'm talking about. You know I mean with the whole Bryn and Khol situation. When Bryn broke your heart, our heart, you ran into Khol's open arms because it was easy. How can you run to him after everything he's put you through? How can you think about choosing him after you tried to end your own life for Bryn's sake?"

"I love Khol too!" My voice went up an octave as I pleaded my defense...to myself. Perhaps I actually was ready for a padded room, even if it was a dream. "Since you're a part of my subconscious, I shouldn't need to tell you that I love him too! You know I do!"

"Not like Bryn. And you know that's true. Bryn is our home. He always will be, no matter how he's hurt us. Don't let your fears rule you. You need to grow up. Your insecurities and fear of being alone have ruled you from the beginning. For all your constant declarations of love for Bryn, you didn't waste any time with Khol or with Jeremy the last time Bryn wasn't by your side."

"That's not fair. That's not—"

"The truth hurts sometimes. Stop with all the teenage angst and drama. You're gonna have a child of your own soon. Fight for Bryn and stop making excuses to hide behind your own insecurities, because if you're not careful, you really will end up the with the wrong person because it's easier."

"But he doesn't want me!" I screeched, choosing to ignore what else I'd just said to myself. "And Khol wouldn't be the wrong choice. At least not a bad one. He—"

"You would be settling and you know it." I quirked an eyebrow at myself. "And are you so sure Bryn doesn't want you? Or is something else going on?"

"What do you mean?" My mind flashed to how bad Bryn had looked in the last vision I'd had about him. "Tell me."

"Well, the problem with me being you is that I only know what you know. But we both know that something isn't right. Bryn would never walk away from you the way he has without some outside force coming into play— especially with the possibility that you're carrying his child. We've known Bryn since we were both five years old. You know he isn't acting like himself. "

And if that was true then maybe I'd been the one to betray Bryn and not the other way around. *I'm an immature hypocrite.* Maybe I didn't deserve Bryn. The truth really did hurt. "So what do we—I mean *I* do?"

"How should I know? I'm just your subconscious," the old me said with annoyance. "By the way, happy twentieth birthday to us."

I really did wake up after that. I lay in the cool dark room listening to myself breath over the roar of my heart beating in my ears. This would be the first birthday I'd ever been apart from Bryn since we were five years old. No wonder it was also the first time I'd almost forgotten about it.

Yep...happy birthday to me.

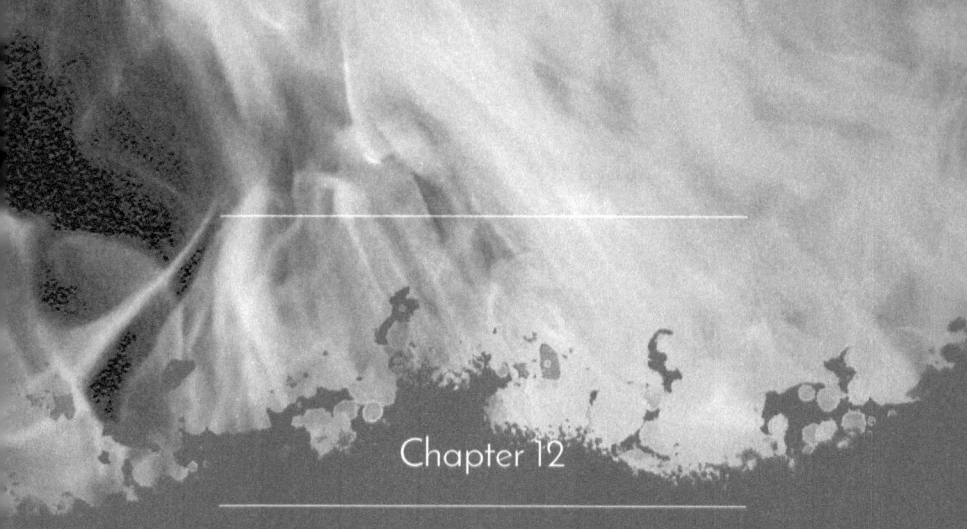

Chapter 12

Terrance's body shook with thinly veiled terror as he approached the office door where his master was currently working on business. He was always working on some kind of business. He would not be pleased with the news Terrance was bringing him this day.

"Come in," his master's voice boomed through the thick oak, before Terrance had even raised his hand to knock. He only hesitated for a moment before entering. There was only so long he could delay the inevitable. "Tell me," his master growled as he scuttled into the lush room, eyes averted towards the ground.

"She's not dead."

"And what of our operative inside the human girl?"

"No news. She is either dead or being held captive. Either way she is currently beyond our reach."

"I see." His master's voice was much too calm. "You do

realize this was your last chance, Terrance. I don't tolerate incompetence, at least not for very long."

Terrance dropped to the ground onto his knees. "No, please, my liege. I won't fail you again. I—"

"No, you *won't* fail me again." It was the last words Terrance heard before he was ripped from his host's body and pulled into the bright red stone where he would now make his new home.

Chapter 13

Eying my hair with frustration, I attempted to blend the rainbow clip-in extensions into my white hair. *I'm different, no doubt about that.* But maybe that wasn't necessarily a bad thing like I originally thought. I'd been a hypocrite when it came to Bryn, and like a child in general. A part of me had always known it but didn't want to admit it to myself.

It was time to take responsibility for my own actions and choices, and to stop hiding behind my fears and insecurities. How many times now had I declared that I would become the person I desired to be but only to backslide soon after? How many times had I blamed the actions of others for the bad choices I made? *Too many.* And the worst part was I clearly knew better.

"No more," I muttered to my scowling reflection. I let my emotions flow from chastising to hopeful in a slow trickle as I completed my morning routine and headed downstairs for some breakfast.

"You really should buy some better breakfast food," Nala complained as I entered the kitchen.

"I don't like breakfast food," I retorted. "Breakfast cookies and pastries I can tolerate though."

"The baby needs healthier stuff than sugar and carbs. It needs protein and—"

"I'll eat whatever I can keep down," I snapped. *Who the hell does Nala think she is coming in here and trying to tell me what's best for me and my unborn baby? She certainly has a lot of nerve.*

"Well, that shouldn't be a problem anymore, should it?"

"It's probably a pretty good idea if you don't remind me of the bitchy move you pulled last night," I said between clenched teeth.

Nala heaved a huge sigh. "Okay fine. I'm sorry. I just couldn't resist. I don't want you for an enemy, but I'm still not exactly your biggest fan."

I glared at her as I collapsed into a chair across the table from her. "Yeah, I get it. I guess I can kinda respect the honesty." She passed me a glass of orange juice and a breakfast cookie. "Today's my twentieth birthday," I mumbled around a mouthful of oatmeal and raison. I choked back a sob as I tried not to think again about how it'd be the first one without Bryn. And my parents. I was still in big time denial about their deaths.

"Happy birthday…I guess," Nala said automatically.

"Yeah, there's nothing happy about it." *Time to move on*

to more important things. "I had a vision about Cliff, that guy you met at my school, yesterday." She nodded her head in confirmation that she was following me. "And in it he pushed one of the Riders out of his body." I scowled down at my half-eaten cookie. "And yet he still has one inside of him. I don't know what it could mean."

She leaned towards me, her eyes gleaming a bright dragon blue. "How did he do it? How did he push it out of himself?"

"I don't know exactly. He was having some kind of battle of wills while he stood looking in the mirror, and then...bam...out the little bugger came. Of course, Cliff passed out cold afterwards, and my vision ended."

Nala slumped back in her chair, her face twisted in puzzlement. "That doesn't really tell us much."

"No shit, Sherlock," I said, picking up my glass of orange juice, and crinkling my nose. I forced myself to chug down the entire glass. *Blak!* Orange juice wasn't one of my favorite drinks, but I was trying to get something healthy in my system for the baby. Maybe I should take double the dose of the prenatal vitamins I'd picked up at the grocery store. Or maybe dragons didn't need that kind of stuff. How was I supposed to know? I'd grown up thinking I was completely human.

"I guess I'll just have to continue on with my fake schooling and hope I figure out whatever it is my birth mother sent me here to figure out." I set my empty glass back down on the table and stood. "What about you? I guess you're gonna be heading out soon?"

Nala shifted uncomfortably in her seat, flicking her gaze away from mine. "I think I'm just going to hang around here for a while. If you don't mind."

A sudden bark of laughter escaped from my chest. "Afraid to face Khol, huh? You're not fooling me."

Her cheeks flushed in embarrassment, which caused me to laugh again. "He's kind of scary if you haven't noticed. He might very well burn me to a crisp if I return without any real news about you...or with you."

"I wouldn't worry, his bark is much worse than his bite. I don't think he would actually kill you, for this anyways. I mean he let you go, didn't he?" Of course, when I first met Khol he'd scared me a little too, but that hadn't lasted long. Underneath it all he's just as human as I am...or thought I was...whatever.

She gave me a humorless laugh. "With *you* his bark might be worse than his bite, because he's a male dragon in love, but with me..." Her voice trailed off as she obviously pondered her demise at Khol's hands, shuddering. "No thanks, I'll stay here."

"Suit yourself. Even if it is...well...you. I won't lie that having someone else here with me in the Murder House is slightly comforting."

Nala tilted her head at me, much like a dog trying to understand its human owner. "Someone was murdered here?"

"Probably," I said, turning to leave. "I guess I'll just see you later then."

"Yeah, okay." Nala's voice still held some slight

confusion when I left her sitting in the kitchen, probably trying to figure out who exactly was murdered and where.

"YOU LOOK LIKE YOU'RE FEELIN' better today," Cliff's already recognizable voice stated from just behind me. When I didn't answer and continued shuffling around the contents of my locker in search of my math book, he continued on. "I hope you remembered to bring your meds today so I don't have to tote you around like yesterday. Not that I'm complaining or anything—"

"Look," I started without turning around to face him. If I could just manage to treat him like any other guy I wasn't interested in and not like an alien leper, I'd be good. "I'm sure you're real nice and all." *For an alien,* I silently added. "But I have a boyfriend from back home that I'm *very* serious about."

"Yeah, okay. Just tryin' to be friendly to the new girl is all," Cliff responded with cheer. His happy go lucky alien ass was really starting to get under my skin.

"Okay, good, just wanna make sure we're on the same page," I grated.

"Hey, Paige." I glanced over to see Laila heading my way, a friendly grin on her face. "I'm so glad you look like you're feelin' better." She paused long enough to briefly acknowledge Cliff, who I'd thought had already left. I guess the hairs on the back of my neck still standing on end should have been my first clue that he hadn't.

"Yep, I'm feeling much better." Hopefully the herbs Nala brought me would do the trick. *So far so good.* "Although I kinda wish I could have missed some more school than a couple periods."

Cliff clearing his throat from behind me caused both Laila and me to swing our heads in his direction. Even though I was mentally prepared for the dual imagery of the Rider shining out from behind his features, I still had to fight the urge to gasp in horror. "I wanted to invite you, Paige," he paused. "And you Laila, to my End of the World party this weekend."

"Y-you're what?" I sputtered, unable to contain my complete and utter shock of the party's name.

"My End of the World p—" He started to explain but Laila didn't give him a chance to finish.

"We'd absolutely looove to!" she gushed with excitement. "Just text me the details. My number is still the same."

I just stood there in stunned silence. I'd just been invited to a party themed *The End of the World* by an alien who was living inside a teenage boy, who in fact wanted to take over our world and probably end it in a roundabout manner. Were the Rider's attempting to make some sort of sick joke?

Laila elbowed me in my ribs. The pain caused me to refocus back in on the surreal reality that had become my life. "Right, Paige? We'd love to?"

"Um…yeah…sure," I said numbly.

Of course, I knew on some level it would be the

perfect opportunity to observe the Riders even closer than I was able to at school. And I knew that's the whole reason why I'd been sent here, to find out what I could about them, even if I wasn't entirely sure what I was looking for precisely. But a part of me wanted to say *hellz no* and high tail it back to Bryn as fast as I could get there.

"Great." A huge smile spread across both Cliff's handsome face and the pinched alien residing underneath his skin. Well, at least they seemed to be in accordance at the moment. Something that my body and I didn't have in common. Despite the herbs that were supposed to help me with my morning sickness, I suddenly had an overwhelming sense of nausea sweep through my system. I had no other course of action but to make a mad dash for the bathroom. Yesterday was embarrassing enough with only one Rider as a witness, but half the school was not going to be privy to what I'd eaten for breakfast.

I barely made it to the girl's room to dry heave over one of the toilets, when Laila's voice called out to me, "Hey Paige, sweetie. You okay?" The stall door squeaked open as she crowded in behind me. She gathered my hair up from my hand so I could better balance myself and locked the door behind us. "I thought you were feelin' better." There was more than one unspoken question in her voice. "You don't have an ear infection, do you?"

A feeling of ice slid over my heated skin. "What's that supposed to mean?"

"Oh, come on sweetie. I may be country but I'm not stupid. I've seen you rubbin' your belly when you think no one's lookin'." I didn't know what to say. Should I try to deny it and risk alienating the only ally I had at this school? Or should I risk telling her the truth and maybe she could help me with my secret? "Does your guy back home know? What about your parents?"

Guess there was no point in denying it when she'd already figured it out. Or was I simply letting my fear of being alone on another level rule my decisions? "Everyone knows," I mumbled. "I was just kind of hoping to finish out here before I started showing." It was a partial truth, but it would do.

"Is that why you're here? Did your parents want you away from your guy?"

"I guess." My birth mom wanted me on this mission by myself, so in a way she'd wanted me away from my guy. "It's all a bit more complicated than that," I said, pushing myself up into a standing position to lean against the stall wall.

Laila's big blue, and very innocent eyes, stared up at me with a mixture of pity and sympathy. "Does your guy want you to have the baby? Or is that part of the problem?"

I thought about how Khol had reacted when he first found out I was pregnant, as opposed to the angst Bryn had delivered me. It kind of felt like Khol wanted me to have the baby, and Bryn wasn't really sure how to react. "Which one?" I said without thinking.

Laila blinked at me and gasped as if I'd just punched her in the stomach. "You mean—you mean—"

It was too late to take back what I'd just let slip out of my mouth unintentionally. *Shiiiit.* "Yep. I don't know who the father is."

"But you said you were serious about your boyfriend back home."

"I am. Both of them." I laughed with a hysterical edge. "I'm in love with two guys, one who wants me unconditionally, and the other…well, the other I used to think did but now…I just don't know. And I also don't know which one of them is the father of my unborn child." *What about my dream conversation with myself last night?* Was the love I felt towards Khol enough to even be counted against what I felt for Bryn? Was I going to just discount what my subconscious was trying to call to my attention? I thought this morning I had made up my mind to stop with all the damn wishy-washiness of my adolescence.

I could see everything processing in Laila's eyes, and like a light being switched on, I could also see when she fully accepted what I'd just told her. "Oh, you poor thing."

I scowled at her. "I don't need or want your or anyone else's pity."

"No, of course not." She waved me off and unlocked the stall door. "My lips are sealed." She headed over towards the wall of sinks, pausing. "Do you still wanna go to Cliff's party this weekend?"

I had to bite back a laugh, but a sincere one this time. She reminded me of Jenna so much. "Sure, I just can't drink is all. But since we're spilling secrets, why are you so excited about being invited, and why are you being so nice to me? I mean you've kind of been hanging around with me, and not with a whole lot of anyone else since I've met you."

Laila's cheeks flushed briefly. "I—ah—well—most of the kids I grew up with around here...they're just different. It started happenin' sometime around middle school. At first it was just a couple of them, and I just chalked it up to people changin' as they grow up, but lately...I don't know. It's like I don't even know half of them anymore." Her shoulders slumped and she let out a huge sigh. "It sounds crazy, doesn't it? I mean some of them just creep me out somehow."

I reached out, touching her shoulder briefly, and meeting her eyes in the mirror. "I don't think it's weird at all. But if they creep you out then why do you wanna go to the party?"

She started applying lip-gloss as she talked to me. I decided to try and avoid my own appearance for as long as I could. I was getting more used to the white hair, but I still wasn't a fan. "I'm just tired of feelin' left out by the people who used to be my closest friends. They just stopped invitin' me to their parties after this one night when..." Her mouth clamped shut and she pressed her lips into a thin line, her eyes going vacant as she obviously relived the night she was referring to. "It just got really weird is all."

"Okaaay," I drew out, lifting an eyebrow in question. "Care to elaborate?"

Laila made a big production out of stuffing her lip-gloss back into her bag and fussing with her hair before answering. "Not much else to say. It was weird."

I could tell she was lying, but I also could tell that was about all I was going to get out of her for the moment, so I decided to temporarily drop it. "But you're all gung ho to go to this party now? Aren't you worried it'll…get weird again?"

She gave me a nervous smile as she turned to leave the bathroom. "It was prolly just a misunderstandin' of sorts, and I just overreacted."

I frowned at the back of her head. "Yeah, okay."

I don't have a good feeling about this.

THE NEXT COUPLE of days passed by with nothing out of the ordinary. How going to school, while pregnant with a child who I didn't know who the father was, while I tried to remain undiscovered by alien parasites hiding inside of my peers, had become ordinary was beyond me—but it had.

Nala mostly kept to herself, except when she was attempting to push healthy food down my throat or stinky tea for my morning sickness. But my nights were filled with Bryn. Some memories, some nightmares, all found when I fell into a fitful slumber. There, in my subconscious, I came face-to-face with his fathomless cobalt eyes and the man who owned them. I wasn't sure what it meant that the longer I was away from Khol, the less I thought about him and the more I was consumed by Bryn. I was starting to question how I had any romantic feelings for Khol at all after what happened between us. He'd forced himself into my bed and indirectly caused me to attempt to end my own life. Forgiving him, knowing what I did now, yes...but the rest...everything was just so mixed up in my head.

I was currently caught up in the memory of the first night Bryn and me had been together. It was so real I could almost believe I was reliving that night.

Nervous energy and excitement sizzled through my veins at the mere sight of him, and I eagerly wrapped my arms around him, fully expecting him to welcome me into his embrace. But instead, his arms remained limp at his sides, his body rigid.

Drawing away from him, I stared up at his face in confusion. "What's wrong?"

His jaw muscles feathered with tension as he stared back at me, his gaze churning with emotions I couldn't quite read. I swallowed around the sudden lump in my throat. "Bryn?"

He abruptly backed me against the wall, caging me in when his hands came to rest against the wall on either side of my head. My pulse set off at a gallop, my breath catching in my throat. "Bryn?" Uncertainty caused my voice to waver. He seemed so—so angry, and yet—yet instead of being worried or afraid a warmth simmered low in my belly.

"I couldn't stand watching you leave with him," Bryn growled. "I had to fight everything in me to not come after you."

His chest heaved as he sucked in ragged breaths. "You're mine. I won't share you."

"It's not real, Bryn. You know that. I'm yours—all yours."

He stared at me a few more seconds, his nostrils flaring. "It seemed so real, Peej—like I was losing you. It was like a nightmare I couldn't wake up from."

I slid my fingers along his arms. "I'm here now. And I'm yours. Always."

Bryn captured my lips with his, taking my mouth forcefully, dominating me like never before. I welcomed the heat of his jealousy as it morphed into fiery passion that spurred him to roughly explore me with his tongue and mouth. Our clothes fell away, and soon we were both left in nothing but our underwear.

We suddenly found ourselves suddenly in undiscovered territory, our make-out sessions previously not going beyond heavy petting, and we'd definitely never been fully naked in front of each other either. Our physical relationship was so new that we were both still in awe of the simplest things, like kissing and touching. But tonight—tonight Bryn didn't show any signs of stopping. And I sure as hell wasn't going to protest. I'd wanted to give my virginity to him since that first night in the woods. He was the one who thought it wasn't the right time or place. He kept insisting that I should have more for my first time, some deluded idea that I should expect it since I was a girl. The sentiment wasn't misplaced, even if it had left me beyond frustrated on more than one occasion.

"I need you, Peej," Bryn rumbled as his fingers deftly dipped into my underwear. I moaned, his long fingers exploring areas where no boy had ever gone before.

"Yes," I gasped into his mouth. Setting me on his bed, Bryn made quick work of removing my last scraps of clothing. He sucked in a ragged breath as his rapt gaze roamed over my exposed flesh.

"Bryn," I pleaded, reaching for him.

"You're so beautiful," Bryn whispered in reverence. He then came to rest over me, his pelvis cradled in between my thighs.

When did he manage to get his boxers off?

My heart thrashed against my ribcage. This is happening. I'm going to have sex with Bryn. Me and Bryn are going to have sex. Then my gaze locked with his, and I was pulled into the fathomless depths of his sea storm eyes, where all my trepidations seemed to drown in the abyss.

"You still taking the pill?" Bryn rasped.

Reality check. "Yeah." My mom would be absolutely furious if she knew I was using the pill for its intended purpose and not just to regulate my period. Especially if she found out I was using it with Bryn on the heels of a date with someone she had set me up with. "What about your parents—"

"Not here." He dipped his head, showering me with more kisses before pulling away again. "You ready? I don't wanna hurt you."

The way he was looking at me, the love that emanated from him—I felt like the most beautiful and special girl in the entire world. Someone who could do that for me, make me feel so cherished, deserved to have everything that I was—mind, body, and soul. So far, Bryn had only received two of those three. Tonight, he is going to have everything. "Yeah, I'm ready."

As he pushed into me, filling me in a way I'd never been able to fully imagine, I gritted my teeth and dug my nails into Bryn's shoulders. I thought I'd been prepared, since I'd heard from friends that the first time for a girl is almost always painful. But no amount of mental preparation could have readied me for what I was currently experiencing. The sharp jab deep inside my body and the burning. Thankfully, as Bryn rocked back and forth inside of me, slowly the pain ebbed into pleasure.

I finally understand why people like Jenna are so sex-crazed. This is—this is—

My entire world narrowed down to Bryn. I could no longer tell where I ended and he began.

Bliss. This is bliss.

A warmth like I'd never experienced before bloomed in my center as our powers converged. Soon it roared into a fire of need, rampaging through my system, spreading outward and erupting into spasms of ecstasy.

Holy shit, it definitely was never like that when I took care of myself.

Bryn slid his hands into my hair, forcing me to look at him. Shuddering, he pulsated within me, his muscles straining. "Fuck," he growled.

Melting into the bed, I smiled when he collapsed above me, careful not to crush me with his massive form. I ran my hands through his silky, tousled hair, then down over his sweaty back. He curled into my touch, leaning forward to kiss me with a slow languidness that spoke of shared intimacies, and unspoken promises. "I love you, Peej. More than I can even begin to explain." His voice was so low and husky it seemed to brush things on my insides, making me shudder in turn.

I sighed contentedly. "I love you, too."

If only we could stay like this forever. But our love wouldn't be enough to protect us from our parents' wrath if they found us like this.

I must have frowned because Bryn's brow furrowed. "What's wrong? Did I hurt you?"

"No, Bryn." I bit my lower lip, briefly replaying the highlights of what we'd just done. "You made my first time more amazing than I ever could have imagined." A smug grin exploded across his face. "I just wish I could stay here with you and not worry about anything else."

He rolled onto his back, tucking me into his side so my head rested on his chest. "I hate this, Peej. I just wanna be with you. I wanna be able to touch you when I want, kiss you when I want. I wanna yell from the rooftops that you belong to me." He pulled his fingers through my hair. "I don't wanna have to watch you go out on dates with other guys." His fist balled at the base of my neck.

"It wasn't so bad tonight, was it? I mean, yeah, it sucked that I had to go on that date, but" —I lifted my head so I could meet his gaze—"look at where we ended up."

He scowled. "I'm sorry, Peej. I really wanted your first time to be special, not in my bedroom because I was crazy with jealously over some guy that you're not even really dating. I just—"

"Shhh..." I brought my finger up to his lips. "I'm glad it happened. I wanna give everything that I am to you, Bryn. The rest doesn't matter. Tonight was the best night of my life so far,

because I just shared something with you that I've never shared with anyone else. You own me now—heart, soul...and body."

"You own me, too, Peej. Everything that I have—that I am—belongs to you and only you. Always." His lips sought mine, our kisses becoming feverous again.

Then my dream shifted to another night that held a first for me, but of a much different kind. It was the night that I was first been with Khol—so in actuality my dream shifted to a nightmare.

"Khol," I croaked. "Khol—I'm ready." Am I ready to die though? Can I really do this?

Khol appeared in front of me only a few inches away, pushed me back onto the bed, and covered me with his body, his mouth aggressively slanting over mine. He was obviously ready to get down to business, and maybe it was better that way, so I wouldn't have a chance to lose my nerve.

My body responded to his scorching kisses, even as my heart froze like a block of ice inside my chest. As he tore at my clothes, I found myself arching up to meet him, wanting—at least physically—what he had to offer. Too soon, or not soon enough, we were both naked, and Khol was claiming parts of my body with his touch that I had sworn only Bryn would ever know.

Clawing and biting at Khol, I was overwhelmed by the urge to hurt him as he rocked into me, hating and loving what he was doing to me at the same time. Things with him were different than they'd been with Bryn. There was no soul-deep connection. There was no feeling of being exactly where I belonged. All I found within Khol's embrace was intense physical pleasure, which maybe would have been enough, if I didn't already know what I was missing.

Sweltering heat seeped out of Khol's pores, wrapping itself around me as the back of my neck began to burn. "You belong to me now," Khol growled as he stared down at me, capturing my gaze. "Say it."

"Yes," I gasped on the tail end of a moan, wishing I could deny the words, but I felt it—I felt his magic burning me, branding me, making me his.

"And I'm yours. Say it."

"Yes. You're mine."

And then I arched up one last time before blacking out.

I LET KHOL CLAIM ME, *the words played over and over in an endless loop in my mind as I slowly fought my way back to consciousness. I was cold—empty. When I'd been with Bryn, I'd felt so good, so right, but being with Khol had been wrong—even if he had brought me pleasure. Maybe it won't be difficult to take my own life after all. Had Bryn felt our connection breaking? Surely he had to have. What must he think of me now, knowing what I'd done to make that happen?*

Shame bubbled in my gut, shoving bile up my esophagus.

Blinking my eyes open slowly, I was surprised to find that I was alone. No Khol. Well, isn't that nice? He finally got what he wanted, and he didn't bother to stick around afterwards.

Lurching from bed, I stumbled towards the bathroom, not

caring if I was naked or not. It didn't matter for what I was about to do. I shut and locked the door and started the water running for the bath. As the hot water filled the tub, I scanned the bathroom for options. My eyes stopped when they ran over a small hand mirror. I snatched it up and broke it on the counter, picking up the largest shard.

I have to do it—I have to do it now before I lose my courage.

I sank into the nearly full tub, hardly noticing when the hot water practically scalded me. I set the glass shard on the edge. When the water covered me up past my chest, I turned it off and picked up the shard, leaning back.

Passing the jagged glass back and forth between my hands, I watched the lights glint menacingly off its surface. I have to do it—there is no other way. I refused to doom Bryn to a miserable life. My death would bring him happiness—well, eventually anyways.

Besides that, the emptiness that was eating at my soul, knowing I could never have him again, was enough to make me want to end my life all in itself. But I would never make this choice for myself alone. I'd always thought suicide was the coward's way out, an easy escape from problems that would only make a person stronger if they stayed to face them. What would happen if the hero of a story died before they had a chance to become who they were really meant to be? I never thought myself capable of doing such a thing, but then again, maybe I wasn't the hero of this story, I was simply the main character in my own life.

But I wanted to live—even now as I readied myself for death

—I craved life. There was still so much to do, so much to experience, the good and the bad. I don't wanna die now. I forced air into my lungs. No—it isn't time for selfish thoughts. This is for Bryn. Everything is for Bryn.

I held the shard tightly in my right hand, drawing blood, the pain not registering in my state of mind. Dipping my hands under the water again, I pressed the glass into my left wrist, slashing along the vein with all my might, quickly switching hands to do the right wrist. But the shard slipped from my numb fingers before I could repeat the process. Blood swirled around me, diluted by the water and I leaned back, hoping what I'd managed to do was enough. It has to be enough. My head lolled as the room spun and my eyes slid shut. I love you, Bryn. I'll always love you and only you.

"No!" someone roared, but it was far away—much too far away—for me to care.

Another voice joined the first. "Peej! No, no, no, no, no. Please, no. How could you do this? Save her! You have to fucking save her!"

But I was too sleepy to care about anything anymore.

SWIMMING TO CONSCIOUSNESS SLOWLY, I found myself in bed, the sheets clinging to my sweaty body, and my hair plastered to my face. Why did my brain sistent on showing me things like that? I thought memories such as the first time I was with Khol and the night I tried to take my own life were suppressed far enough down that I wouldn't be plagued with such nightmares. What was the point? What was my mind trying to tell me this time? It had shown me my first times both with Khol and Bryn… as what…a comparison? Did I want myself to remember how I used to feel about the both of them as opposed to what I felt now? Did I want myself to remember the type of love I felt for Bryn that led to my attempted suicide solely for his happiness. *That was before he walked away from you*, a not so helpful voice offered.

No. Suddenly it was if an internal light switch had been flipped on. A feeling of resolution settled over me…*finally*.

Real love, true love…the kind of life altering love that Bryn and I share just doesn't go away that easily. That kind of love takes root in your heart, spreading throughout every fiber of your being. That kind of love leaves you half alive whenever the other person isn't around. That's what Bryn and I have, and it shouldn't matter that he walked away from me. It shouldn't matter that he was acting on some misplaced sense of duty to protect me—because he did those things out of love. He loves me just as much as he always has. He's just an idiot is all.

I laughed out loud. Of course, that part has always been true as well. It'd be different if he cheated on me, or abused me, or some other unforgivable offense. I thought Bryn had been the one to break our relationship, but maybe the truth was that we had both done that. But the kind of love that Bryn and I shared could fix anything. Had *The Princess Bride* taught me nothing?

I loved Khol, the man that he'd become for me, but I could

never love him the way I loved Bryn. I was kidding myself to think so. Bryn and I had promised each other always, and I wasn't going to let my own insecurities stand in the way of that, or his for that matter either. When I saw Khol and Bryn again, I would let them know my decision. I would let them know that it would be Bryn or no one for me...*always.*

Chapter 14

"I heard you cry out in your sleep again last night," Nala said conversationally as she stepped into the bathroom. She came to stand behind me as I worked on curling my hair. I was attempting to better blend the hair extensions into my crone-ish white hair. *Attempting* being the key word.

I shrugged without taking my eyes off of my own reflection, and the tedious task at hand. "I had a nightmare."

"Every night this week?"

"Yeah, what of it?" It wasn't like she really cared about my mental health. Sure, she seemed to care about me and my unborn child's physical health, but that was probably just to protect her own hide. We both knew what would become of her if she let anything happen to me when she could have prevented it.

Probably sensing she wasn't going to get any more out

of me about my nightmares, Nala wisely changed the subject. "Have you been drinking your tea?"

It was then I did meet her blue eyes in the reflection of the mirror. "No. And you know I haven't because it's plain to see that the supply hasn't been diminishing." Before she could say anything, I cut her off. "But the morning sickness symptoms seem to have passed, so I don't think I need it anymore." I resisted the urge to stick my tongue out at her. *How very mature of me.*

A flash of something I couldn't quite decipher crossed her face before she slumped casually against the door jam. Maybe just a little too casually. "It's probably best to be sure. You don't want to raise suspicions, do you?"

"I'm done with that heinous tea," I responded flatly.

That stuff alone could serve as a form of birth control. Just let the would-be-mom get a whiff of it and tell her she'd have to drink it every day to prevent morning sickness and she might rethink the whole wanting to have kids thing...forever.

"Damnit!" I exclaimed when I caught some hair in my bracelet for the umpteenth time. I set the curling iron down, pulling the pieces of hair out of the bracelet that were still attached to my head. Sadly, a few didn't make it and I let them fall into the sink.

"Why don't you just take that off until you're done with your hair?" Nala asked in a tone one might use to talk to a small child.

"I would if I could." I ignored her condescending attitude and set back in to finish doing my hair. It took me so much longer than when Jenna did it, and it never looked even half as good either. "If I take it off, Khol would be here probably before I even set it down." I sighed and turned the curling iron off. My hair was as good as it was going to get—with me being the stylist anyways.

Nala looked up sharply at me. "What do you mean?"

Wow. She really was afraid of Khol, wasn't she? "Don't worry, my birth mother let me know that I wasn't to take it off at all. She—"

"Is that why he can't find you?" Nala interjected, her face visibly paling.

I rolled my eyes. "Yes. But like I said, there's no reason to worry. My—"

"No," she interrupted me...again. *Rude much?* "That's not what I'm asking, entirely. *How* does it keep him from tracking you?"

I gritted my teeth and decided not to scold her for interrupting me—twice in a row. I guess she was just worried. "It breaks the connection that exists between Khol and me. He can't sense my emotions, and he can't track me. He's totally cut off."

Her eyes flared a brighter dragon blue before she looked away from me, mumbling to herself. "*All* connection to him. *Shit.*"

"What?" I said, alarmed.

"Nothing," she snapped, spinning on her heel to leave. "Don't worry about it."

Before I had a chance to say anything else, the door to

her room slammed shut. I stared after her for a moment before letting my gaze drop to the shiny bronze bracelet that was fitted perfectly on my wrist. I let the fingers of my right hand run idly over the delicate markings I was convinced meant something, I just wasn't sure what. I wondered how much longer I'd have to wear it. Not that it wasn't pretty, it was just that I hated being forced to do... well practically anything.

My phone beeped. I hit the unlock code and read the message from Laila.

Be there in 5.

K

I gave myself one last check in the mirror before heading out of the bathroom. My hair was somewhat presentable. At least it was better than the first couple of times I'd attempted to style it. My make-up also was done...adequately. I still hadn't figured out my new color palate completely, but that was only something time would fix. My black lace tee fit me snuggly, showing off the few curves I did have, and looked the right combination of dressy and casual when paired with the dark low-waisted jeans I had on. The dragon pendant from Khol sat at the perfect level to draw more attention to my cleavage than I probably wanted, but I refused to leave it behind. My outfit was completed with a pair of knee high, low heeled, black, zip-up boots.

It was warmer this time of year in Tennessee than I

was used to, but I wasn't wearing open-toes shoes going into a nest of Riders. What if I needed to run, or kick, or something? One did not wear open-toed shoes of any kind when heading into enemy territory of the alien kind. If there was a 'how-to survive a party with alien Riders' somewhere, I'm sure that rule would be in it. Once I was satisfied that I looked the best I could under the circumstances, I made my way outside to wait for Laila on the front porch of the creepy Murder House.

I was only outside for a minute or two when a big black pickup truck pulled into the driveway. The window rolled down, and Laila's blonde head peeked out. "Well, are you comin', or what?" she said, excitement laced into the tone of her voice.

I shut my mouth and shook my head. What had I expected, a Volkswagen Bug or something? She might remind me of Jenna at times, but she most certainly wasn't her, not by a long shot. I opened the door to the massive truck, and pulled myself up into it, barely managing to shut the door before Laila was burning rubber to get out of my driveway and to the party. I, for one, would have preferred a more leisurely pace since I wasn't exactly looking forward to the end of the world, even if it was only the theme of a party.

Once I had my seatbelt in place, I turned to eye Laila's outfit. She'd gone with a cute little red dress and cowboy boots. *Ugh.* It seemed to be the style here, but I cringed every time I saw a girl rocking out cowboy boots with a skirt. But then again, maybe I should have tried a little harder to blend in. I tried to picture myself in similar attire and … *Nope. Never gonna happen.*

"You look nice," Laila said, interrupting my inner fashion critic. "Just how far along are you anyways. You don't seem to be showin' at all."

I bit my lower lip. That was the million-dollar question, wasn't it? If I actually knew how far along I was then I would know who the father of my unborn child was. Well, maybe. There was still that whole dragon versus human gestation difference thing. Not that it mattered anymore though, I'd already made up my mind that I would be with Bryn, no matter who the father was. I just hoped Khol and Bryn both would go along with that, especially if Khol turned out to, in fact, be the daddy.

I decided to go with another partial truth. "I'm not exactly sure. If I knew exactly then I would also know who the father is."

Laila nodded, keeping her eyes on the road. "Yeah, I guess that makes sense."

I slumped down in my seat, hating that Laila had reminded me of my "who's the daddy" predicament. Not that it was ever entirely out of my mind lately, but even still, I didn't want to focus on something I couldn't do anything to change. "Yeah, um, talking about that doesn't really put me in the partying mood."

Laila's cheeks flushed a dark crimson that I could easily see with only the aid of the streetlights we were passing under. "Sorry," she mumbled.

"It's okay." We then sat in an awkward silence that

lasted until Laila flicked on the radio. I let out a loud groan. "Please, no. Not country. I think my morning sickness is gonna make a dramatic comeback." Laila glanced at me before turning her attention back at the road. We both laughed. I was guessing turning on the radio hadn't broken the awkward silence in the way she planned, but it had gotten the job done in the end.

"So how much longer?" I squinted at the clock on the dash, realizing we'd only been driving for five minutes. It seemed like much longer. I guess the feeling of dread that had settled over me made time seem like it was dragging on.

"We're almost there. This isn't that big of a town."

"I've noticed," I grumbled. In comparison to Pittsburgh, Spring Hill made me feel like I was practically out in the middle of nowhere. *A perfectly good place for a nest of Riders to take up residence. No one will hear you scream.*

"That's Cliff's place, up on the right," Laila said a few minutes later.

Even if she hadn't pointed it out to me, it would have been kind of hard to miss with all the cars parked out front. She pulled neatly into a spot at the end of the row and turned the truck off. As she slid from her seat and hopped down to the curb, I took a moment to gather myself. *I can do this. I have kickass powers inside of me that I don't even fully comprehend yet. Yeah, and you don't know how to use them either.*

I clenched and unclenched my fists before unbuckling my seatbelt and sliding from the truck cab. Laila was waiting for me on the sidewalk, reapplying a peachy gloss to her lips with the aid of a tiny compact. With a soft snick she closed it, dropped it into her small messenger bag and looked up at me. "You think about how you're gonna explain not drinking without sounding lame?"

"Medication?" I shrugged at her with doubt.

Her face scrunched up as she considered that option as a viable lie. "I guess it's the best you've got. And with what happened the other day, it could just work." She then fidgeted with the hem of her skirt one last time before turning to lead the way to Cliff's.

My legs seemed to protest my intentions with every step I took, my feet suddenly a thousand times heavier than normal. It felt like I should be reciting some verse from the *Bible* or something. *Yea though I walk through the valley of death, I will fear no evil... Wait...how does the rest go again?*

I brought my hand up to encircle the dragon pendant, its warmth comforting, until I actually stood at the threshold of Cliff's house. If was strange going to a party without Jenna, and without Bryn at least waiting for me inside somewhere. The last party I'd actually attended had been the night I'd nearly been raped by a guy who I didn't know, and I had finally figured out my true feelings for Bryn. It was a turning point in my life, and this party had all the signs of being another kind of turning point for me. I just hoped it would spin me in a positive direction when all was said and done.

Laila was almost as nervous as I was because she

hadn't said a word to me all the way up the front walk. *I wonder how she would feel if she knew what she was really walking into?* We both hesitated at the front door, and it was me who finally found the courage to reach for the doorknob. My breath caught in my throat as I turned the knob, pushing the door open. Just like what I associated with a normal high school party, we were greeted by loud music and even louder talking. I'm not sure what I expected, but it all seemed entirely *too* normal. Laila clutched at my arm as we entered, and damn if she wasn't latched on tight enough to draw blood.

"Hey, ladies," Cliff drawled, as if appearing out of nowhere. *Creepy much?* As if having a Rider inside of him wasn't bad enough, he had to pull that weird stalker-ish thing guys do that's only cute when you actually like them. Bryn and Khol were both very skilled at it. "Was wonderin' when you two would show up," he said while he looked at me, making it clear who he really was addressing. "You want something to drink?"

"Yes," Laila said.

"No," I said at the same exact time. When Cliff raised his eyebrows at me, I felt the need to explain. "Medication, remember? I really don't wanna get sick again."

Cliff smiled at me good-naturedly. "Right. Don't want you ruinin' any more of my shoes."

I glared at Cliff and the stupid Rider inside of him that were both seemingly amused with their little comment. "Come on, Laila. Let's go get you something to drink." I tugged her along, not really sure where I was going.

"Awe, come on, Paige. I didn't mean nothin' by that," Cliff said, following behind us. "Besides, the kitchen is the other way."

Without acknowledging him, I pivoted on my heel, taking Laila with me, heading in the opposite direction. "This is gonna be a long night," I mumbled under my breath. I sent up a silent prayer that I would find what I was looking for and that this would all be worth it.

I stumbled to an abrupt stop when we got to our destination, all the fine hairs on my body standing to attention. Every single person in the kitchen had a Rider inside of them. *Every. Single. One.* "Oh, God," I said, swiping my sweaty palm over my mouth in horror. *There is no way I'm gonna be able to handle this.*

"Are you not feelin' good again?" Laila whispered to me from the side of her mouth.

"More than you know," I whispered back through gritted teeth.

"You gonna be sick again?"

"I'm way beyond that point." I forced myself to stand up straighter, donning an air of false confidence. "Now let's get you that drink." How's that saying go? Fake it until you make it? I wasn't sure if I was that good of an actress, but I was damned sure going to try to be.

"Okaaay," Laila said, drawing the word out to let me know she didn't exactly know what was up with me. *That would make two of us.*

As we strode towards an ice chest obviously filled with various kinds of alcoholic libations by the way everyone seemed to be orbiting around it, Cliff scrambled to get ahead of us. "Hey, what can I get you then, Paige? A coke, or sweet tea, or water, or something?"

My lips turned up in a wry smile. *Oh, how sweet, the alien wants to play host to me. Too bad my whole planet had already been doing that and I am so over it.* "Nothing, thanks."

"Natty Lite? Don't you have anything left besides Natty Lite in here?" Laila said with annoyance as the sound of ice sloshing around reached my ears. I almost wanted to laugh, the more things change, the more they stay the same. Were teenagers, no matter where in the world, whether they were fully human or playing hosts to aliens, forced to drink the beer cast offs of local society?

Cliff frowned down at Laila. "You know all the good stuff always goes first. Maybe if you would have gotten here earlier you could've had something else."

Laila finished flicking the ice off a can of Natty Lite and cracked it open, lifting it to her mouth. She proceeded to chug it all down in almost one go. *Huh.* And maybe her solution was the same as mine always had been: to use quantity to make up for quality in beer. But then again look what almost happened to me the last time I'd attempted to actually apply that flawed logic as a solution.

"I need to go to the bathroom," I said to both Cliff and Laila, hoping that Laila would be a good girlfriend and offer to come with me, and Cliff would be a good host and direct me to the nearest one. Too bad neither one of them wanted to fulfill those particular roles.

"I'll wait for you here," Laila said, making goo goo eyes at a cute boy and his little friend inside of him.

"I'll show you where to go," Cliff said, a smile on his face. *Ugh.*

"Fine," I grated. I supposed Laila wouldn't be much help anyways. I was seriously outnumbered and she was a non-gifted human who had absolutely no idea what was really going on right under her nose.

"Come on." Cliff tried to link his arm with mine and I sidestepped him, not wanting to come into contact with his bare skin again. The abrupt move made him frown at me.

"Do I need to remind you again that I have a boyfriend back home?" I punctuated my sentence with the best death glare in my arsenal.

It didn't even faze him. "Can't blame a guy for tryin'," he said, chuckling.

"Actually, yes I can," I snapped.

As I trailed along behind him, I wished I could use my dragon magic to fry him to a crisp, but I knew it was just the Rider I wanted dead, and not poor Cliff, at least not the real Cliff. When we got to the top of a huge set of winding stairs, Cliff sauntered down to the end of the hallway, turning the light on in the bathroom for me.

As I moved to walk past him, he stuck his arm up to rest his hand on the edge of the doorjamb, completely blocking my way. "Aren't you gonna thank me for takin' you to this bathroom where you don't have to stand in line?"

"Ummm... Thank you," I said crisply, trying to duck under his arm, but he wasn't having any of it. Or maybe it was the Rider that wasn't having any of it.

Cliff's features were suddenly overtaken by appearance of the alien within. Stumbling back, I gasped. "Cliff has been difficult to hold on to from day one," the Rider snarled at me, grabbing a huge clump of hair at the back of my head. "But I have a feeling if we get one of us into you, and the two of you make nice with us"—he smiled a big toothy grin at me—"then Cliffy here will be a lot more easy to manage."

Riders couldn't possess dragons. I still wasn't exactly sure why, but if they tried to put a Rider in me they would know something was different and my cover would be completely blown. I couldn't allow that to happen. I twisted abruptly, managing to wrench myself out from under Cliff's tight grasp, losing a clump of hair in the process and slamming him into the wall. His head hit at a wrong angle, or just right for me as luck would have it, and he crumpled to the ground, out cold. He probably hadn't been expecting that. That made two of us...or should I say three?

Chest heaving from the adrenaline still coursing through my system, I stood there for a second, staring down at Cliff. *What the hell am I supposed to do now?* "Think, P.J., think," I whispered hoarsely to myself.

I glanced back down the dark hall just to make sure someone hadn't come up behind me when I wasn't paying attention. Much to my relief the coast was still clear. But I knew I had to do...something...fast.

Okay, first I should probably check to make sure Cliff is still sucking in oxygen. I tentatively stepped over his slumped body, my heart thrashing against my ribcage, half expecting him to suddenly sit up and attack me like some grade B horror movie villain. But he didn't, and the rise and fall of his chest let me know that I hadn't killed him. I heaved a sigh of relief, short lived, as I heard footsteps coming up the stairs. *Shit.* In a moment of panic I grabbed Cliff under the arms and dragged him into the bathroom. It was harder work than I would have thought, and as soon as he was far enough in, I shut the door behind us and locked it.

Great—now I've managed to trap myself in an even smaller space with the hostile Rider. Go me!

Swiveling around the small second story bathroom, I scanned the area for some kind of—I don't know— inspiration to help me out of my predicament, but none came. I was about one panicked second away from ripping off my Khol repelling bracelet so that I could call him for help. The only thing stopping me was that I didn't seem to be in any immediate danger...yet. Well, that and I didn't know if my pride could take that kind of blow. I was kind of attached to the idea of doing things on my own now, and besides, if I was going to be with Bryn, I couldn't keep relying on Khol for everything without killing Bryn a little more each time. I needed to learn how to rely on myself.

My pulse exploded against my eardrums when a sharp rap sounded on the door. *Sound calm. Sound normal. You can do this.* "Someone's in here," I squeaked. *Yep...I sounded like the epitome of calm. Nothing suspicious going on here... nothing at all.*

"Cliff in there with you?" a male voice asked, while I heard a decidedly masculine chuckle at his question. *Shit.* Two Riders outside the door, and me stuck in here with a third. *Think, P.J. Think.* My eyes finally settled on the window. I bit my lip with determination. There really wasn't any other way. I stepped over Cliff's prone form, pushing the medium sized frosted window open. Hoisting myself up onto the ledge, I looked around for options to climb down to the ground on. A tree, a drainpipe, a vine— something—anything. But there was absolutely nothing.

A loud groan came from the bathroom floor as Cliff started to come to. *Shit. I have to make a decision on what I'm going to do...fast.*

"Cliff man, you in there?" the Rider outside the door asked, suspicion in his tone. Cliff groaned louder in response. "Hey," the Rider said. "What's going on in there?"

The door handle rattled as he tried to turn the locked knob without any luck. It looked like I was going to have to jump. Hopefully, I'd just sprain an ankle or do something benign. I wondered briefly if I should try to tuck and roll or just jump feet first. Or maybe—

"Not so fast," an angry Rider growled from Cliff's body as he grabbed me by my shoulder. I let out a startled scream, teetering forward towards the ground. I instinctively reached back to grasp Cliff's hand. But instead of keeping me on the ledge, the sudden movement sent us both careening forward. With nothing else to do but fall, I clamped my eyes shut, wishing I had never left the house tonight. *Why, oh why, didn't I spend a nice evening at home at the Murder House? Spending time with ghosts isn't as bad as becoming one.*

Suddenly a weird—familiar—sensation of dizziness overtook me, and instead of feeling the impact of the hard ground shortly before my emanate demise, I landed with an *oof* on a bed. Of course, Cliff crashed into me half a second later.

"What the fuck?" Cliff exclaimed.

I opened my eyes to find the purple and white pattern of my bedspread that I had been using at the Murder House under my nose. I quickly reeled around, picked up the lamp from my nightstand, and knocked Cliff out cold again. As he slumped down to the ground, I found myself wondering for the second time in one evening if I had killed him.

My bedroom door slammed open, hitting the wall behind it to reveal a battle ready Nala. She paused to take in the scene of Cliff unconscious on the floor, and a freaked out me standing over him with what was left of my lamp and relaxed a bit. "Who's he, and what happened?" she asked a little too calmly.

"That," I started, surprising myself with how normal I sounded, "is the Rider who was going to blow my cover by trying to force one of his buddies into me because his host has some kind of thing for me." I inhaled and exhaled a couple of times trying to get fresh oxygen to my brain. "And I have absolutely no idea what happened. One minute I'm hurtling towards the ground to my death, and the next I'm here."

Nala's pursed into an O of surprise. "You transported yourself and him here? You're too young to have that kind of control."

"Hey! I'm the same age as Bryn and he can already do it."

And then everything sank in. I had—finally—been able to use the super cool dragon power I'd been drooling over since I first found out what I really was. Too bad I had absolutely no idea what I'd done to access it, besides having a near death experience. And cool or not, that wasn't something I was willing to replicate, even for a power that awesome.

"All right. Fine. I really don't want to get into to it with you about your powers right now. The more important issue is, what exactly do you plan on doing with your new little friend, now that we have him here?"

That was a good question...a very good question indeed.

Chapter 15

"**S**o what are you going to do with me?" the Rider inside of Cliff asked in an exasperated tone.

"I don't know yet," I gritted out as I resumed my pacing from one corner of my room to the other. Cliff, and the alien leech inside of him, was currently tied to a wooden chair that Nala had brought up from the kitchen. We'd used rope and duct tape to secure him there...lots and lots of duct tape. *I guess that goes to prove that duct tape really is all-purpose.*

"Aren't you going to question me or something?"

"Look," I said, coming to stop directly in front of him, "if this is so hard on you, then why don't you just ooze on out of Cliff's body and leave him alone?"

The Rider made Cliff's handsome face grimace at me in response, "It's not that simple."

I crouched down in front of him, peering up with curiosity at the Rider inside of Cliff. The alien seemed to have almost eclipsed him completely since the moment he came to in my room. "So why don't you try and explain it to me then."

He narrowed his eyes at me with hatred. "No."

This is all a bit surreal. Was this actually happening or was I having some kind of weird dream? It felt real —it felt like I was awake. And yet the fact that I was having this conversation with the Rider inside of Cliff while he was duct taped to one of my kitchen chairs in my room, seemed a bit...ridiculous. I guess I had to stop repeatedly questioning that my life had turned into one surreal moment after another. "Really? You just asked me if I was gonna ask you questions, and—"

"I didn't say I was going to answer them," he snapped with more irritation, like I was an annoying little gnat circling his head.

"Fine. If that's the way you wanna play it, then I'm about ready to enroll you in Torture Class 101." But could I actually torture Cliff's poor body? I had no doubt my conscious would have no problem letting me cause some major damage to just the Rider, but he wasn't just the Rider at the moment. "Why are you still in Cliff anyways? I saw him push you out. I saw you leave."

"How do you know that?" The Rider's jaw dropped, or I guess Cliff's jaw dropped. Everyone kept telling me to think of a host and the Rider within as one and the same, to which I used to be able to do pretty easily. But with one currently residing inside of Jenna, and with having the vision of Cliff pushing this Rider out, it was beginning to be more and more difficult.

I let a slow smile creep across my face. It was obvious the Rider had figured out that I was a dragon, but I was obviously under the mistaken impression that he had also come to the conclusion of who I was specifically. Guess I was wrong. Time to fill him in. "I *saw* it in a vision."

He stared at me, shock playing across his features. "Impossible. You're a dragon."

I flopped into a reclining position on the floor in front of him, crossing my legs casually. "Yes, I'm a dragon." I smiled brightly at him. "But I'm also a Seer, and a very powerful one at that."

"The dragons only have one Seer, and she's a gifted human. And she should be dead by now," he blurted out, seemingly unable to stop himself.

All amusement drained from me. "I am that Seer. And clearly I'm neither human nor dead." Of course, until recently even I had thought I was human, at least partly, so I couldn't really expect the Riders to be privy to any information that said differently. I rose from my sitting position, and came to stand as close as I would dare to the Rider. "But I'm hoping you'll be soon…dead that is."

"What are you doing here?" the Rider demanded, clearly trying to hide the fear in its eyes. "Did you come here for me? Because of who I am?"

Huh? "Who you are? I don't know who you are, besides Cliff that is."

He let out a dark laugh. "Well, isn't this perfect." He

paused and I could tell he was trying to weigh what he should say next. "Okay. If you let me go, I'll get my father to back off of you guys, to leave you alone. I mean a lot to him...in both my forms. And he doesn't care about you guys, not really, just the threat you pose. If you promise to leave us alone, we'll do the same."

My jaw slackened as I stared at him. *Is he kidding? There's no way he actually thinks I'll go along with that.* "You can't be serious. You killed our families, slaughtered my people, are trying to destroy our world—and you want us to simply look the other way from this point on? Maybe I hit you on the head too hard," I muttered. *Can Riders suffer brain damage if their host does?*

"My father felt threatened, and we're not trying to destroy your world. We like it, actually."

"No. You've destroyed worlds before. Decimated them for their resources like the parasites you are and then moved on to the next world you planned to victimize. And how you've been treating our world—*my world*— definitely proves you plan on doing the same here."

"Mistakes," the Rider pleaded. "We didn't know any better. We were just trying to survive. But we like it here —want to stay."

"Well you're not!" I bellowed, finally losing control of my temper. I could feel my dragon fire magic spark to life just under my skin, practically begging for me to release it on the Rider. But I fought the urge because I knew, even through the haze of red that was tinting my vision, that I didn't want to hurt Cliff.

The Rider's eyes widened to the size of saucers when he finally realized how much danger he was really in. "We can make a bargain. I swear. Just don't hurt me."

"How many have begged for your mercy? How many of my people begged before you slaughtered them in cold blood? Men, women, and children, all of the same, just because of who we are. This is our planet and you can't have it!" Flames crept up into my fingertips, and I stretched out my palms in Cliff's direction.

"That was my father! Not me! We're not all the same! Some of us just want to stay—to live!" Sweat trickled down Cliff's terrified face. "Please…"

"Tell me," I growled. "Tell me who your father is, and what his end game is."

"Sena—Senat—Senator Bill Wexington is my father's human host…and my real father is the one inside him… our leader," the Rider stammered.

What were the chances? I had both Senator Bill Wexington's son, and the son of the lead Rider both as my prisoner. Actually—I chuckled darkly to myself—I knew none of this had happened by chance. My birth mother had seen it all and planned for it to happen. There was no other explanation.

"Senator Bill Wexington is your father?" He seemed to be the center of all of this from the beginning. One of my first big visions had been of the alien Rider taking possession of him. He also seemed to be the one leading the charge that was anti-American citizen's rights—or anti-human rights, if I really wanted to be accurate.

Maybe if I could take him out, then the rest of the Riders wouldn't be as difficult to manage.

"Yes." The alien made Cliff's head bob in affirmation. "He'll make a deal for me—trade—"

"Tell me," I growled, my throat feeling raw. "Tell me what he's planning."

Cliff's crystal blue eyes blinked at me slowly a few times before the Rider began to speak again. "He wants control. He wants the humans as slaves. We won't kill off your world. We want to stay, to live, like I said, but we want—"

"To rule," I finished for him. It was a story as old as time itself. The struggle for power. *How cliché.* Couldn't they at least come up with something new? I never quite understood it myself, but then again, I've heard that those with power usually didn't pay much mind to it, and those without, or with a little, made it their focus, or sometimes obsession. I clearly have always had power, and now I had more than I'd ever dreamed of, and more than I'd ever wanted.

"Yes," Cliff's full lips responded with the fowl sound of the Rider's voice. "So you see, it doesn't have to involve you, if you don't want it to. We'll leave you alone to do whatever it is that you do, and we'll do our thing. The humans are no concern of yours, not really."

A low animalistic growl erupted from my chest. "Until not too long ago I thought I was human. I was raised to think I was human. I still *feel* human." I tried to keep my fire from jumping to him, from burning him alive, because I didn't want to hurt Cliff. Beyond that I knew that keeping this particular Rider alive for the moment would do our cause more good than if he was dead. *He's full of information, useful information*, I reminded myself.

"The people who raised me, who were the only real parents I ever knew...were human." But it was hard—harder than I thought to not act on my murderous impulse. I had to leave—leave the room. Now. Or he would die. They both would die.

Slamming out of my room, I darted down the hallway, fire dripping from my fingertips. "Nala!" I screamed. I needed help. I couldn't handle my emotions and all of my new raw power at the same time. "Nala, please!" But she didn't come. I knew she was afraid. Afraid because she was a water dragon—afraid that my fire would consume all of her and leave nothing but ash.

I dropped to my knees as things around me blackened and burned—the carpet, the wall, my clothes. I had two choices: I could somehow find the strength of will to get myself under control, or I could rip the small—hot—very, very hot, blackening bracelet from my wrist to call on Khol for help. The latter was more appealing, easier, but...

Bryn. His name swam through my mind as I struggled to come to a decision before I burned everyone and everything down around me. If I wanted him, wanted to be with him the way I truly desired, I was going to have to stop relying on Khol. I needed to trust in myself, in my own strength of will. The old dragon queen, my birth mother, wouldn't have given me her powers if she didn't think I could handle them. I had the strength in me somewhere. I just had to find it. For Bryn. *Always for Bryn.*

Conjuring an image of Bryn in my mind's eye for focus, I pictured his dark blue eyes glittering with amusement as he laughed at something silly I'd done. His full firm lips would curve up slightly at first, and then his patented smile, complete with dimples would spread across his perfectly chiseled jaw. I wanted him to look at me like that again, to laugh easily in my presence like he used to. I wanted to banish the new, hardened Bryn from my life forever, because I'd made him that way. I had changed him. *Me.* I wanted *us* back, and I would do anything—anything, including burn down this world to have a chance with him again.

And just like that, my magic pulled back into me, taking all of the fires it had started with it. I was surrounded by blackened and still crackling…well, everything…but nothing was actually burning anymore. I laughed hoarsely. I'd somehow actually done it, and all by myself to boot. *No.* That wasn't exactly true. I'd done it with Bryn, because he was as much a part of me as my own soul. I could never let myself forget that again, never let anyone or anything come between us. Or maybe I'd done if for Bryn. But I was too tired to care at the moment, all that mattered was that I *had* done it. Somehow. I'd stopped my fire from burning the creepy Murder House down around me.

A contented smile spread across my face as I collapsed

to the ground, my mind going as black as the carpet my face pushed into.

"SO THIRSTY," I rasped.

"Using your fire magic will do that. It won't ever burn you though, but I guess you found that out the hard way," a familiar voice rumbled from nearby. "Here, drink this."

My eyes snapped open, alighting on Khol. "Wha—what —how did you find me?" It was then I noticed that I was not, in fact, in the Murder House any longer, but lying in Khol's large bed.

He handed me a glass of chilled water, and I took it with shaky hands. I watched him with wide eyes over the rim as I greedily gulped down the best glass of water I'd ever had. When I finished, I lowered the empty glass to my lap, gripping it tightly. What would Khol's reaction be now that I was back? Would he be angry that I'd gone? Or would he be ready to pull me back into his arms to pick up where we left off? I was hoping the former because he'd be easier to deal with in that mood when I told him I'd chosen Bryn.

He eyed me warily, his green eyes blazing with unreadable emotions. "I don't know what you're feeling," he said, his mouth dipping into a frown.

"It's the bracelet." I tapped the tiny intricately made bronze bracelet on my left wrist. "My birth mother gave it to me to wear so you couldn't track me."

Khol's nostrils flared. "I see. Will you be taking it off now that you're back then?"

I bit my lip, glancing down at my hands that still gripped the empty glass in my lap. "No. I'm not ready to take it off just yet."

Deafening silence engulfed the room, and I didn't need to be able to read Khol's emotions to know he was not happy. I decided to change the subject and quickly. "So how did you find me?"

"You used enough magic to announce your presence to all of dragon kind."

"Oh." I hadn't considered that. Of course, with all the magic I'd used, Khol probably zeroed in on me in seconds.

"What did you do with the Rider? The one I had at the house—the one—"

"We have him here," Khol interjected. "He's important then, like I thought?"

I did meet Khol's electric green eyes then. "Oh yes," I breathed. "Very important."

Khol leaned forward, his expression growing more intense. "Tell me."

"His father is the lead Rider, and his host is none other than Senator Bill Wexington. He's the son of both the lead Rider and the Senator."

A tight smile turned Khol's lips up. "He is very important indeed." He abruptly came to me in a burst of speed almost too fast to track with my eyes, and took me in his arms, inhaling sharply as if in pain as he crushed me to him. "I went out of my mind not knowing where you were, not being able to sense you." He pushed his nose into my hair, inhaling. "I've missed you so much."

"Khol—I…" This was going to be harder than I originally thought. I loved Khol, I really did. He just wasn't Bryn. Despite that, my body responded to Khol's, and a liquid heat bloomed inside of me. But the difference now was that I wouldn't let myself get swept away in those urges. I wouldn't let the ease of our relationship rule my decisions. No one ever said love was easy.

Khol's body tensed around me and he pulled back from our embrace enough to meet my eyes. His gaze bore into mine, and after a moment's time, what seemed like forever to me, he backed away from me completely. "I see."

"Khol—I—please—I'm sorry. You know I love you—I do. And you've got to believe me. I never would have done…" My voice caught in my throat as my mind skidded over the memories of the intimate moments Khol and me had shared. "I never would have…" I tried again, but this time was stopped short by the look on Khol's face. It was a mixture of hurt and anger. And my heart cracked just a little for him. Why did he ever have to fall for me? Why did things have to be so complicated?

"So, you're back to wanting Bryn again," he said without question. "And if he still doesn't want you?"

"He wants me," I whispered. "He's just afraid that being with me will result in my death."

Khol stared at me with a mask of neutrality, all hurt

tucked away behind it. "And if it does? Result in your death?"

"Then it'll be my fault, and none of yours. I should be able to protect myself." And that was the truth of the matter. No one was ever truly safe, not really. And relying on someone else for security would result in my suffering no matter which way I looked at it. I had to rely on myself for my own protection.

"So my little Seer has finally become our little queen." Khol gave me a smile that didn't touch the sadness in his eyes. "I told you that you'd find the strength in youself one day."

I stood and went to him, cupping the side of his face. "Thanks to you."

He brought his large hand up to cover mine, leaning into my touch, and meeting my eyes with uncertainty. A familiar feeling of electricity shot through my system. I always felt sparks when Khol touched me. "I can't lose you again," he rasped gutturally. "He doesn't deserve you."

I tried to pull away from him then, but he held me to him with his strong fingers. "I don't care what you think," I said, anger building in me. "I can't help that I've loved him practically all of my life. I need him almost as much as the oxygen I breathe! I loved him before I even met you!"

The muscles in Khol's jaw spasmed as he ground his teeth together. "Yet you came to my bed willingly. And you trembled so sweetly under my fingers and tongue." His words were soft but there was no mistaking the underlying cruelty that they meant to inflict on me. "You had no need of him to help you breathe when I let you do the same to me."

My lower lip trembled as tears gathered in my eyes. I knew this wasn't going to be easy, but I hadn't expected Khol to be cruel, to use all of my fears against me. He knew I felt ashamed for doing what I did with him, and for still being involved with Bryn. There was no way he didn't know with his close emotional connection to me. He was just trying to hurt me like I was hurting him...and it was working. "Don't," I squeaked. "Please don't say those things to me."

"You mean the truth?"

I opened and closed my mouth not knowing how to respond. He was right. Of course, nothing he was saying to me was a lie, not really. It was then he captured my lips with his, and as I gasped in surprise, he swallowed down all the air in my lungs. I struggled against him, even as his body made mine hum with excitement. I was attracted to him, even now. Just because I loved Bryn more didn't change the fact that I loved Khol too.

He shoved me back onto the bed, pushing my arms up over my head, and holding me in place as he continued his assault on my senses. I couldn't help but moan when he ground himself into me. Even when he had essentially blackmailed his way into my pants by threatening Bryn's life, Khol had always brought me pleasure. Why would now be any different?

"Khol—stop—please," I begged when he freed my

mouth only to begin kissing a trail of fire down my neck and other more sensitive areas.

"I won't lose you again," he growled.

It was with those words I knew how truly desperate he'd become to have me for keeps. He was about to do what he swore he would never do to me again. He was going to take from me without asking—he was going to claim me against my will. As in the past with Khol, it wouldn't be rape, not really, but it wasn't exactly what I wanted either. *At least not mentally, or in my heart.* Or maybe this is what it means when someone says another person seduced them? Was Khol seducing me? As my body arched up into his touch, I was pretty sure I had the answer, and I was not happy.

"Don't do this to me, Khol," I hissed. "You promised."

"And you promised to wait—to wait until the child was born. We all agreed." He freed me from my shirt and bra, and while he still held my arms over my head with one hand, his callused palm skimmed roughly over my naked flesh, eliciting a moan from me. And I hated him for it.

"You were gonna cheat. You admitted it—and I changed my mind," I grated, my fire magic pushing up through me as my anger began to heighten. How dare he pull this crap with me again. Maybe he hadn't changed as much as I thought he had. "Khol, stop, before I make you." My voice had changed, dropped to a low animalistic growl. "I don't wanna hurt you."

Paying no mind to my words, Khol tugged at my pants, tearing them from my body. I lay before him now, with only a tiny lace thong keeping me from being completely naked—something in the past that would have been sexy, but now—*I was pissed.*

An inhuman scream erupted from my chest as I summoned the strength from somewhere deep down to shove Khol off of me. In fact, not only did I manage to dislodge him from me, but I threw him clear across the room. He landed in a heap on his ass, a dazed expression on his face. I pulled myself up to my full height, letting my fire magic explode from my palms.

Khol, with almost no effort at all, captured my magic in his own palms, smiling at me. "This little display of power—it only makes me want you more," Khol rumbled, his eyes raking over my nearly naked self, causing goose bumps to erupt all over my flesh. "You're acting more and more dragon with every passing moment, and that means I'm the one you belong with."

"I belong with Bryn."

"He's too human. And beyond that, he's a black dragon. Your powers clash. Your flames would consume him and leave nothing behind. Even weaker red dragons are no match for you." Khol paused and offered three words to me in a hushed voice, "Think of Drake."

I knew what he was referring to—when I first discovered my dragon fire magic I'd nearly killed Drake—a red dragon. "I would never hurt Bryn. I love him too much."

Khol raised one of his eyebrows at me in question. "Like Jenna."

"That was different. That was—"

"Over me." Khol's voice held a note of triumph, like making that point alone would win me over. All it did was make me angrier.

"Maybe you're too dragon for me. What if I need someone with more human-like emotions?" I retorted, knowing it would bother Khol deep down. He'd never loved anyone the way that he loved me before, and there was a vulnerability he wasn't used to inside of him because of it. He wasn't absolutely sure he knew how to treat me, not really.

"Enough," he seethed. He locked his fire backlit eyes with me briefly before he leapt through the air with lightning speed, pinning me against the wall with his rock solid body. He dipped his head to whisper in my ear as I turned my face away. "He doesn't have a second form. You do." My whole body shook with fear. Khol knew how much I was afraid of being able to shift into a dragon. He'd been very careful to not show me his other form, or to let anyone else for that matter, as to not freak me out now that I knew I was fully dragon. I guess this meant we were playing for keeps, pushing an entire elevator's worth of each other's buttons.

"No. It doesn't mean I have to change, not ever. Not if I don't want to." Yep, that's right, I fully intended to rely on complete denial when it came to shifting into a dragon. I refused to lose that part of the illusion of my humanity.

Khol chuckled low and dark in response. "You won't have a choice. It *will* happen. It's just a matter of when."

His words sank in slowly and when they finally hit home, I cried out, "No! Why didn't you tell me that before? Why should I believe you now?"

"Because I didn't want to scare you. But now it's obvious you need more than just a simple dose of reality. Things won't work with him. I don't understand why you insist on trying." Khol's voice had dropped down to a barely audible level, and I could hear the pain that had been hiding under his anger. I'd hurt him deeper than I ever had before, because this time he had dared to hope for it all.

My own anger slipped away, causing a dull ache in my chest. "I can't help the way that I feel," I croaked. "I'm sorry."

"What changed? What changed while you were away?" Khol's voice sounded so small and brittle.

I squeezed my eyes shut, letting the fresh tears that had been gathering in the corners spill down my over my heated cheeks. "I don't know. Things just seemed to become clearer to me somehow when I was away."

"It's that damn bracelet. It keeps me from you, and you from me. Your birth mother has clearly been meddling in our lives. I should have known from that letter. I should have known from…everything." He reached up with one hand and started to bend the bracelet off.

A chill ran down my spine. He was right. My birth mother had been meddling in everything since before I was even born. What if the bracelet did more than just make me untraceable and unreadable to Khol? What if it was messing with my head somehow? "What did the letter say?" I asked on a shaky exhalation. But Khol ignored me, focusing on removing the bracelet. "Khol, tell me please. I deserve to know."

"She wanted me to be prepared for a change in you when you returned. She wanted me to give you some space," he growled, still struggled with the piece of jewelry. "I thought she meant—I don't know—not that you would come back and suddenly not want me any longer." He abruptly released me, turning away. "It's welded on. We're going to need a special tool to get it off," he said, frustration oozing through his entire body as he stood perfectly still.

"What? What the hell?" How did it become—wait—it was my fire magic. I distinctly remembered the bracelet growing really, really hot back at the creepy Murder House. I reached up, clutching at the dragon pendant Khol had gifted to me. It was perfectly fine. "Why didn't the pendant—"

"It's been charmed to be fire magic proof. It was made for our kind specifically," Khol answered before I could finish my question.

"Oh." *So why didn't my birth mother fire proof the bracelet?*

"Get dressed. We have more important things to worry about right now." I didn't know how to react. One minute Khol was ready to force himself on me, and the next he was acting like I was the one who was focusing on our little love triangle to the detriment of everything else. "I'll be outside when you're ready." He stalked out of the room without so much as a backward glance at me.

"Okaaaay," I mumbled to myself. Not that I wasn't ecstatic for the reprieve from Khol, but I wasn't exactly sure what just happened. Had Khol accepted that I wanted Bryn and not him? I highly doubted it, and yet he had walked away...literally. Maybe he'd just realized we *did* have more important things to worry about at the moment and the rest could wait.

I harrumphed to myself as I located my discarded clothes and pulled them back on. I for one was ready to get back to dealing with the Rider inside of Cliff instead of focusing on my screwed up love life. Because screwed wasn't even a good enough word to describe my situation with Bryn and Khol...not by a long shot.

Chapter 16

Terrance blinked his human host's eyes in complete disbelief as he settled back into the familiar body. When he was ripped from it, he had thought it would be the last time he would exist outside the red stone that imprisoned him. He knew many others that had been placed there by his master to never return. He questioningly looked up at his master and immediately averted his gaze in submission.

"They have my son," his master growled with restrained fury. "Consider this your last and second chance at this life." There was a long pause before he spoke again and Terrance didn't dare so much as to twitch a single muscle. "Get him back no matter the cost."

Terrance rose and left the room without a word. He didn't need to say anything. His master knew that he understood what was truly at stake. And he had no intention of losing his freedom again.

~

I KNEW how important it was to get any and all information that we could from the Rider inside of Cliff. The opportunity we had was priceless, and yet all I wanted to do was to find Bryn. So much had changed since the last time I'd seen him. Well, at least from my perspective. After all, I was still pregnant and didn't know whether Bryn or Khol was the father, but none of that seemed to matter in regards to wanting to be with Bryn anymore.

But what could I say to him that I hadn't already said before? Love wasn't the issue to him. Love, in fact was what he claimed was his motivation to give me up—for my own protection. There had to be some way to make him understand—make him see that it wasn't his job to protect me.

I needed to talk to Jenna—the real Jenna. I hadn't allowed myself to think in much detail about her being possessed by a Rider. I had too many other things to deal with while I was away and it was just easier to pretend what happened with her was all a bad dream. *Yep, I'm not only the new dragon queen but the Queen of Denial as well.*

I was suddenly overcome with the irresistible urge to visit her. I missed her more than I ever thought possible. Sure, she was completely self-absorbed at times, sex obsessed, and utterly annoying but—she was Jenna and I loved her. Plus, I was well aware that I lived in a glass house and certainly was nowhere close to perfect.

Now...where would I stash her if I was Khol?

An undetermined amount of time later, I huffed and puffed down yet another hallway with annoyance, still no closer to locating Jenna. I didn't bother to ask Khol because I knew he would keep me from her under the circumstances. *Stupid overprotective dragons!* Maybe if I could find Jeremy, I could force it out of him. I wondered if having a Rider in Jenna had dampened his newfound devotion to her? He had to know it wasn't really her that had sent him to deliver her cookies of death to me.

I heaved another huge sigh, close to giving up, when I spied Jeremy, *speak of the devil*, coming down the hallway. *Isn't that the way it always is? You only luck into something just when you're ready to throw in the cards?*

"Jeremy!" I called out, hurrying towards him with excitement.

A sudden grin spread across his face. "I'm glad you're back." He swept me up in a bear hug, swinging me around in a circle. I giggled despite myself. *Yep...I missed Jeremy too.* Even though he started out as just another guy trying to play tonsil hockey with me, since his feelings for Jenna had developed, we'd been able to relax into a real friendship. "Have you figured out a way to fix Jenna?" he asked, hope filling his caramel-colored eyes as he set me back down on my feet.

All feelings of elation instantaneously drained out of me. "Not yet." I paused to study the ground, gathering the courage to meet his eyes. When I finally lifted my gaze, I cringed at the disappointment in his expression. "But I know I will. My birth mother said I could, and she's never wrong, apparently."

He nodded, letting some fresh hope settle into his tense features. "Okay. So what's the plan then?"

"I wanna see her Jeremy. I know you're probably gonna say it's a bad idea but I just miss her so much, and I just—"

"Yeah. Okay," Jeremy interjected.

Huh. I'd been prepared to argue with him about getting to see her. I definitely wasn't expecting him to cave so easily.

Reading the surprise in my expression, he said, "She can't hurt you, and she knows she has a Rider inside of her. It's almost like she has a split personality or something. Jenna—the real Jenna—there aren't even words to explain how awful she feels about—"

"Trying to kill me."

"Yeah." He grimaced.

I touched his arm. "But she's okay besides that? I mean no one is mistreating her, right? Khol promised he'd protect her." And yet another instance of me turning to Khol for aid. But then again he was the red dragon lord, and I was the dragon queen. Technically, I could ask any dragon for assistance and expect them to give to me.

"She's safe but…" His brow furrowed with concern. "She's not doing well. The animals…well, they won't talk to her and she's just—"

I gasped. "Oh God, no. I never thought about that part —either way." A Rider with the ability to talk to and in a minor manner control animals—we could have all been so screwed. "I'm sure once the Rider's gone, they'll talk to her again."

"That's what I keep telling her," Jeremy mumbled, studying the floor. His head jerked up to look at me as if he forgot for a moment he wasn't alone. He gave me a weak smile. "Come on, we'll go see her now before anyone else…" He raised his fist up to his mouth, forcing a cough. "Khol," he said, smirking, and turned to start walking back down the wall in the direction I had seen him coming from, "tries to stop you."

I couldn't help but laugh as I fell into step beside him. "He is a bit controlling, isn't he?"

Jeremy stopped in his tracks, raising his eyebrows up to practically his hairline. "A bit?"

I rolled my eyes. "You know what I mean."

We finished our trek in silence, coming to a halt in front of a huge wooden door. As Jeremy pulled it open, I only hesitated for a second before following him in. Much to my surprise, I found myself looking at a bedroom with prison bars in front of it. It was like someone had just installed bars as an afterthought. And I supposed, that's probably exactly what happened. *Talk about a whole new definition to being sent to your room.*

I trailed along behind Jeremy, scanning the room for Jenna. Only when we were standing right up next to the bars, did I notice her sprawled out on the bed, staring up at the ceiling. She looked so tiny and lost, laying there with black messy hair and light brown roots. I was overcome by the urge to run to her and hug her, but of course, I couldn't for obvious reasons.

"Jenna," Jeremy said in a soft tone. "Someone's here to see you."

Jenna heaved a huge sigh. "I told you, I don't want any visitors. Please just go away." Her voice was so flat and utterly hopeless sounding, lacking all of the usual vibrance that Jenna always seemed to have in her. It was if someone had sucked out her very essence. My stomach knotted immediately, bile pushing up into my throat.

"Jenna," I said. "I needed to see you. Please, won't you talk to me?"

She sat up suddenly, her eyes locking onto me, and the next thing I knew, she was running towards the bars with a huge smile on her face. She was still, in that moment, the best female friend I'd ever known. But as she got closer, the dual imagery of the Rider inside of her, shining out from behind her pixie face, caused me to involuntarily take a step back, letting out a strangled scream. My reaction halted her dead in her tracks, her face going ashen. She blinked back tears that were gathering in her deep brown eyes as she stared at me.

"I'm sorry!" I blurted out, desperately wanting a do-over. "I knew what to expect, it's just that…" What could I say? Seeing an alien living inside of you kind of freaked me out? Well of course—duh. "I—I'm sorry." Maybe I shouldn't have come to see her after all. I thought I could handle it, but maybe I was wrong.

Jenna's eyes finally filled to the brim, the tears spilling

out and rolling down her cheeks, her lower lip trembling. "You know I would never try to kill you. I mean—*I* would never try to kill you. And the animals—they won't talk to me anymore. I know it's in there—I can feel it but I can't see it! Can't control it when it starts implanting things in my head!" She wailed the last part, dropping to her knees.

Tears of my own began to flow freely down my face and I desperately tried to think of something comforting to say. "I'm gonna find a way to get it out of you—I promise."

"What if you can't? Or what if even when it's gone it leaves some kind of—I don't know—darkness behind?" Her body quivered shook as she sobbed. "I tried to kill you. It made sense at the time. It convinced me that you were to blame for all of my problems...losing my family... being here...just everything." More huge sobs wracked her body. "It made total sense—to kill you—my *best* friend."

"Jenna—I..."

As I peered into her beseeching gaze, I began to wonder if it was so easy to convince her I was to blame... because I was. I swallowed to try and combat the burning in my chest and throat, more bile bubbling up.

Turning to Jeremy, I shook my head rapidly, panic oozing through my system. "I'm sorry—I thought I could —but I can't." Those were the only words of explanation I managed to get out before I bolted from the room—ran from Jenna, one of my best friends who had an alien inside her.

Once outside of the room I continued my mad dash,

not sure where I was going, letting my feet lead me blindly. Where could I go? Not to Khol. I knew I could find comfort in his arms, but that would be the easy fix, and short lived at that. Not to Bryn either. I wasn't sure how he would receive me at the moment, and I didn't think I could handle being turned away from him in the state I was in. So I continued to blindly run, tears smearing the world into bright water colors before my eyes, until I found myself outside in one of the many gardens surrounding the compound where I collapsed under a huge tree.

As I brought my knees up to my chest, hugging them to me, I realized that I'd never been so utterly alone in my life. Sure, I might have felt this alone in the past, but I was just being overly dramatic—a truth that I felt down to my core in that moment. Now—now I actually was alone. I had no one to turn to—no one who understood me the way I needed to be understood. Because that's what I really wanted...understanding. Isn't that what everyone wants on some level? That's why sometimes love just isn't enough, because if there's no understanding, then a lack in communication will drag the relationship down. Look at what happened between Bryn and me.

I lingered beneath that tree until no more tears would come, and the air began to grow chilly with the onset of dusk. Eventually I found sleep.

Chapter 17

I dreamt I was lost in a maze. As I rounded a corner, one identical to the last, my gaze alighted on Bryn. He grinned, showcasing his dimples, before turning to lope in the opposite direction. He glanced over his shoulder, calling out, "This way, Peej." As if it was a given that I would follow him.

And of course I did. Or at least I tried. Steel bands wrapped around my waist, anchoring me in place. I screamed at him to wait, but he didn't seem to hear me. I struggled to loosen the bands, belatedly realizing that they were in fact arms. Whirling around in a panic to find out who was keeping me from Bryn, shock rolled over me when I found my capture to be Drake. Smirking, he leaned close to my ear to whisper, "You belong with my lord. And I'll make sure he gets you."

I screamed.

"Everything's okay. It was just a nightmare," a

heartbreakingly familiar voice murmured from underneath me. My eyes snapped open, and I inhaled sharply. *Bryn!* His hands sifted through my hair, smoothing it back from my face.

"Peej," he whispered my name with reverence as I swept my gaze up the line of his chest to meet his fathomless blue eyes. My entire body instantly tightened with need, and I surged up to slant my lips over his. I needed him, needed to taste him, needed to feel his skin underneath mine. I'd never been so singularly driven to possess Bryn so desperately before. It was all-consuming, as in, if I couldn't have him, all of him, immediately, I would shrivel up and die.

As I pushed my tongue into his mouth, demanding to be accepted, I maneuvered myself to straddle him. A low growl rumbled in the back of his throat, his hands threading into my hair, pulling me tighter against him. I frantically undulated my hips, grinding myself against him, wishing there were no clothes separating us. *Maybe I can burn them off without hurting him?*

"I need you—now," I gasped into Bryn's mouth as he thrust his hips to meet me while I continued my frantic gyrating rhythm. I'd sworn to never need anyone again. Especially a man. Obviously I'd been deluding myself. I needed Bryn in that moment more than I needed oxygen in my lungs. It's exactly what I'd told Khol, and it was true. I was empty without Bryn and I needed him to fill me up, and not just physically. I needed him to make me feel—to feel...*more.*

He abruptly froze, halting everything. "No. Peej. We can't do this." His chest heaved, breathing ragged as he grabbed my wrists. He then slid out from under me.

"I need you, Bryn. Please." *Apparently I'm not too proud to beg anymore.* "I don't wanna be with anyone but you. It's been you, and only you for as far back as I can remember. It'll be you—always."

His sea storm eyes churned with anger as he regarded me. "You never seem to have a problem getting cozy with Khol. It seems to me you want him plenty."

Any sort of reply stuck in my throat.

Bryn's lips turned up into a cruel smile. "Even the first time when I was sent away, you couldn't seem to keep your hands off him."

White-hot fury coupled with adrenaline shot through my system. "Nala—that's all I have to say about when you were sent away—Nala." I ground my teeth together. "And as for the rest"—unbidden and unwanted images of the intimacies I'd shared with Khol played across my mind's eye—"you practically put a bow around me and handed me to him." It was true, if Bryn hadn't walked away like he did from me, and he had just let our—even if it was semi-permanent—mate bond reform then I never would have so much as kissed Khol again.

"A willing gift," Bryn growled.

I rose to my knees so I could reach him, swinging my arm through the air, my palm connecting with the side of his face with as much force as I could muster. I love you— you stupid asshole!"

Bryn blinked dark lashes over shocked blue eyes at me, all anger draining from his face. "You hit me." He brought his hand up to cover the small red splotch blooming on his perfectly chiseled jaw. "I can't believe you just hit me," he mumbled numbly as he continued to stare at me.

"You deserved it."

Bryn shook his head slowly, the shock turning into some unreadable emotion. "I think you should leave."

I raised my chin at him petulantly. "No."

"No?" Bryn said incredulously.

"No."

"Then I guess I'll just have to make you." Bryn's face morphed into a mask of Zen, all cold clean lines, and no emotions, at least none I could read. Which was beyond frustrating because he used to be an open book to me.

As he reached for me, I dove under his arms and popped back up, smacking him across his other cheek.

Fresh shock playing across his features. "You—you hit me again."

Thanks, Captain Obvious. Next, would you like to tell me that the sky is blue?

"Yeah, I did hit you again. And I'm gonna keep hitting you until I smack some sense into that thick skull of yours."

Did I really just say that? When did I become so violent? *Since Bryn started refusing to see reason,* that helpful little voice whispered in my brain. As if to punctuate my point, I reached up and slapped Bryn again. This time he just stood there as still as a statue, his big blue eyes blinking in confusion at me. His lack of reaction only angered me more. So of course, I hit him again…and again…and again. He continued to just stand there. *What the hell?* The sharp crack of my palm meeting his flesh, first on one side and then the other was the only sound in the room besides our harsh breathing. I just couldn't seem to stop myself. *Crack, crack, crack*…a steady rhythm was taking shape, and I seemed to be a slave to the dance.

Finally Bryn reacted. He moved with the speed of a dragon and Guardian combined as one, and I abruptly found myself pinned under his body on his bed. His eyes blazed the fiercest dragon blue, and even though I couldn't see them, I was positive mine glowed just as brightly. *What will he do?* I absentmindedly wondered, too focused on his perfectly formed face, and how even contorted with anger, it was the most beautiful one I'd ever laid eyes on.

"You may be quick to try and give me away Bryn Aries O'Bannon, but make no mistake—you always have been and always will be mine," I spat.

A low growl erupted from his chest and before I could register what was happening, his lips came crashing down on mine. He covered me with his entire body, pinning me with his weight into his mattress. I moaned my approval as his tongue plunged into my mouth, hot and wanting.

This is what I need. This is what I've been waiting for.

As he ground himself into me with wild abandon, I lifted my hips to meet him. Tearing at his clothes with a desperation he seemed to match, within what seemed like the blink of an eye, Bryn loomed over me, naked and ready to finally give me what I needed. *Him.*

Despite the raw hunger in his eyes, he hesitated. "Peej —we shouldn't—why won't you just—"

"Let you go?" I snarled. "Never. I'll never let you go. You promised always and I'm here to collect."

Bryn's pupils noticeably dilated farther as he stared at me with wonder. "Always," he murmured, and as the word left his mouth, I could almost see the acceptance wash over him. He finally understood. He finally realized he belonged to me and when he promised always, there would never be any going back. We didn't need to be mated as dragons for that to be the truth between us. Being mated to him would merely be an added bonus.

He brought his lips back down to mine in another onslaught of need, and in one quick motion he came to find his home inside me. I cried out as the pleasure of feeling him again rippled through my system. "I love you, Peej. Always." Bryn's voice was a guttural sob as he began to build a blistering pace.

My magic—my new stronger magic, flowed up to wrap around us in a sweltering embrace. I instinctively knew that this time, our mate bond would be complete… the real deal. No words were needed between us like when Khol had claimed me. Bryn's soul and mine were linked together on a much deeper level.

I cried out at the pure joy of knowing he was finally and completely mine. Our session was much quicker than normal, but then again we hadn't been together in quite some time and our current need was raw and primal. Even still, the familiar feeling of ecstasy began in my center, pushing its way out through my body before I fell to pieces in his arms, shouting his name for the world to hear. Bryn called out my name with his own release just before I slipped into darkness.

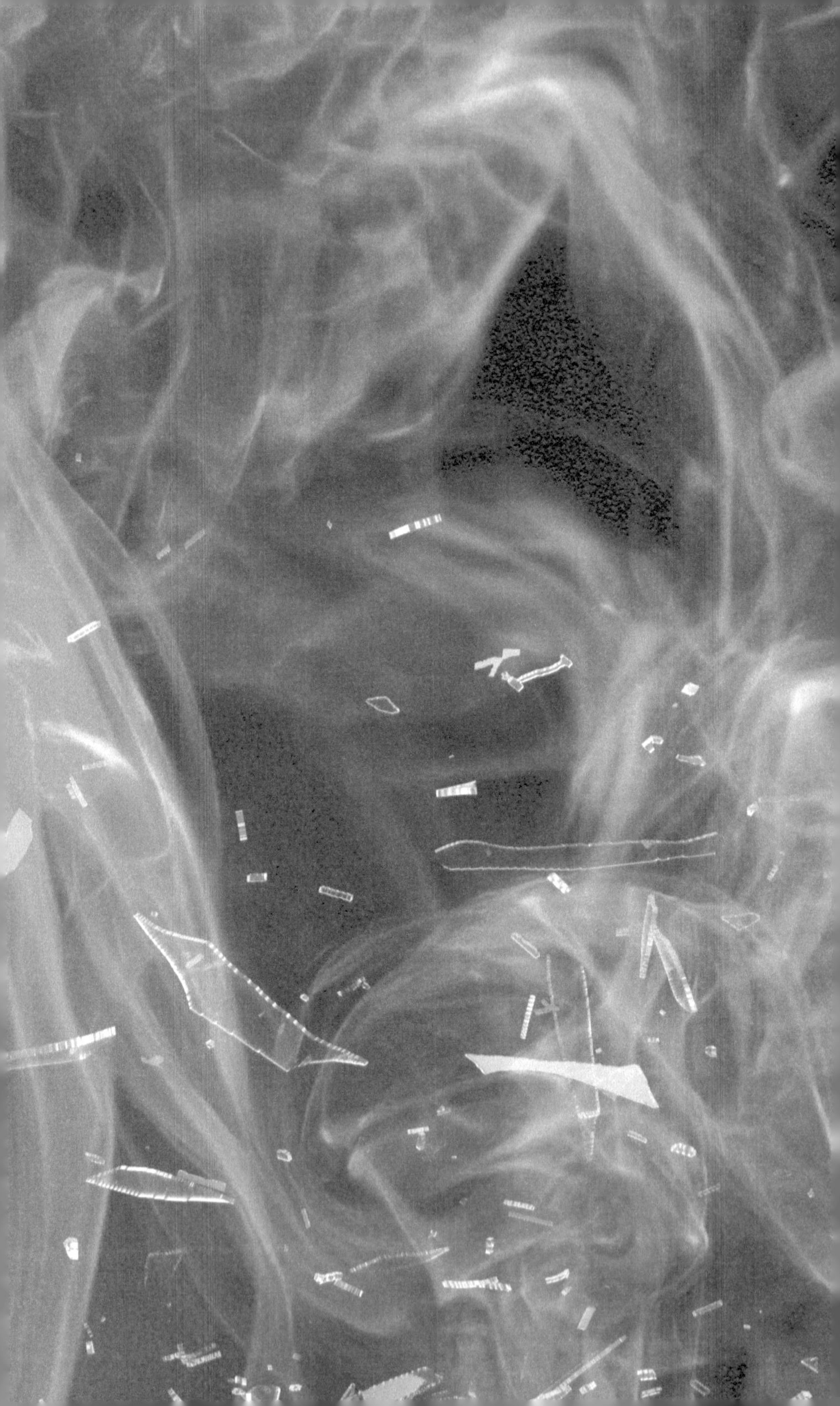

Chapter 18

"You don't look well," I said, knowing there was no way to tell Bryn that tactfully. "Were you sick or something?" I considered the vision that had me so worried about him, the one when he woke up as if from a nightmare covered in a sickly sweat.

"I haven't been sleeping very well," Bryn replied, running the tips of his fingers down my naked back, eliciting a pleasant shudder from me. "But I have a feeling that's all gonna change soon." I didn't have to look at him to know he was smiling.

I inhaled deeply, letting his delicious scent overwhelm my senses as I lay with my head on his chest, my hand making lazy circles across his skin. "I had a vision about you. I was worried."

"I'm fine. Now."

I snorted. "So sex is the cure-all for you then?"

"With you it is," he rumbled.

I ignored the sensations his voice alone did to my insides, persisting with my line of questioning instead. "Are you sure? It just feels like something else is going on."

He blew out an exasperated breath. "Like what?" He knew I wasn't going to let it go until I got some real answers.

"I don't know. I just feel..." Very conspiracy theory-ish is what I wanted to say. But about what? It all seemed to start when the Riders broke into the compound and shot me. How did they find me so quickly and without any resistance? I just couldn't shake the underlying idea that there was a traitor amongst us. *But who?* "I don't know. Maybe I'm just being paranoid."

"Who could blame you if you were being paranoid? With everything that's been going on lately—how the hell did a Rider get into Jenna anyways?" Bryn added one more thing to my list that had me bouncing back to conspiracy theory territory again. There was something else going on right under my nose, I knew it. If only I could get my powers to work the way I wanted them to, then I'd be able to figure it out.

"Let's go," I said, pushing myself up and out of bed. "We have a Rider to question."

As I bent to pick up what was left of my clothes, Bryn's body heat seeped into my back me as he lifted my hair up to kiss the nape of my neck where his mate mark had finally sunk all the way into my skin. "Mine," he murmured, wrapping his arms around my middle, pulling me flush against him.

"Bryn," I chastised, even though I wanted nothing more than to lose myself in his intimate embrace for just a little bit longer.

"Yes, my queen," he said, his smirk evident against my bare skin. His tongue then darted out to lick the back of my neck.

"Bryn, I mean it. I—we have responsibilities. To our world." My words seemed to sober him up and he released me, leaving me bereft without his warming touch.

Just as I finished pulling my shirt over my head, Bryn's door flew open, the heavy wood slamming off the wall to reveal, not Khol as I half expected, but his second in command, Drake. His face was contorted into a mask of rage as he looked back and forth between Bryn and me. "You just couldn't stay away from him, could you?" he growled, his eyes flaring brighter.

He then looked at me with bewilderment. "Why? Why would you choose him over my lord? You're our queen, you deserve better than a baby dragon."

I was still processing what he said, when Drake rushed across the room, pinning Bryn against the wall. "My lord won't kill you—but I will."

"NO!" I screamed, moving with speed I didn't realize I possessed. But before I could reach Bryn and Drake, Khol appeared.

"What the hell is going on?" he bellowed.

Drake immediately released Bryn, dropping to the ground in front of Khol. "I was protecting my lord's interests," Drake said, not sounding the least bit sorry. If anything he sounded proud of his actions.

Khol took in Bryn's half-undressed state as he leaned against the wall gasping for air, and he met my wide eyes with question. "Tell me," he whispered.

"I—I've chosen," I stammered, my voice not sounding even half as confident as I wanted it to.

"I see," he responded with absolutely no emotion whatsoever.

A huge lump formed in my throat, my stomach knotting up as I waited for his reaction. I wasn't worried for Bryn's safety, not with Khol anyways, because I knew Khol would never do that to me. He would never try to kill Bryn like he had once threatened, because ultimately it had resulted in my near death.

"Drake," Khol said between gritted teeth. "Explain yourself."

"I believe I already have," Drake spoke with his head bowed and his eyes averted to the ground. "I was protecting my lord's interests." His head then snapped up to meet Khol's dark gaze head on. "Even when my lord wouldn't do it himself."

Khol took a step back, shock playing across his features. "What have you done?"

"Khol?" I said with uncertainty, my stomach cramping.

I knew I was missing something vital. What did Drake do besides just try to choke Bryn to death? I had to know. I moved quickly to Drake's side before anyone could protest and reached out to touch him. I silently willed my powers to cooperate with me. I needed them to show me what I was missing—what Drake had done. I gasped as I was thrown head long into a vision as soon as my skin made contact with his.

There was so much information, and one revelation after another played out in front of me in quick secession. Some of the minor details escaped my notice, only the major ones registering as images whizzed across my brain:

Drake arranging for the Riders to kill Bryn. I wasn't their target at all. Bryn was the one they were aiming for. It seemed Drake was enraged when I had almost lost my life in the process. He knew how it would affect Khol. The herbs Nala was giving me for my morning sickness had a little something extra added in, courtesy of none other than Drake. Before I left he had been putting that little extra something into my food. It was meant to strengthen the bond between Khol and me—Nala knew, of course. She hadn't given up on having Bryn for herself at all. And Bryn was being...poisoned. Slowly, very slowly by Drake as a back-up plan. Not only that, but Drake had been giving Bryn herbs in an effort to foster some kind of connection between him and Nala. He planned to stop the poison as soon as Nala could manage to bed him and gain him as a mate. Nala was not privy to that part of the plan. She never would have gone along with Bryn being poisoned. Bottom line: Drake was determined that Khol would have me for his mate. But nowhere did I see that Khol had anything to do with it, or any knowledge even hinting of what Drake was up to.

As the visions faded away, I let go of Drake, dropping to my knees. "We trusted you."

Khol slid his arms around me, lifting me up before I crumpled fully to the ground. He turned me to face him, his eyes beseeching mine. "What did you see?"

I closed my eyes before responding, knowing what I was about to tell him would only cause him more pain. "Drake is the traitor. He arranged for the Riders to kill Bryn in the shooting that nearly ended my life instead. He's been putting poison into Bryn's food, and he's been giving me herbs to strengthen the bond between us—so I would choose you."

I thought back to the visions I had about Khol after my attempted suicide and when he had been with the female dragon Shannon. How could I have been so stupid? Those visions were showing me Drake's reaction to those events. I was focusing on the wrong parts within them. They were a foreshadowing of events to come. "Nala helped."

I opened my eyes and focused on Khol. His face constricted into harsh lines with the force of his agony. I had just informed him that his most trusted dragon—his second in command—had betrayed him—and to top it all off—my feelings for him had been helped along—pushed by magic. That's why when I donned the bracelet from my birth mother, cutting off my connection with Khol, my feelings for Bryn had pushed back to the forefront of my heart.

Khol let me go and I crumpled to the ground, my eyes tracking his every move as he stalked towards Drake with deadly intent. Drake raised his chin defiantly at Khol as he came to stand in front of him. "I did it all out of love," Drake said softly, his voice the only indication of his true fear.

"I know," Khol said, reaching out with lightning speed to snap Drake's neck. I screamed as Drake's lifeless body fell to the floor in what seemed to be slow motion. And before I could even blink, Khol had ignited his fire magic to burn the remains of Drake.

"Macon," Khol called out as he stood watching Drake burn. Almost instantly, Macon appeared beside Khol, his expression showing shock of his own as he looked down to see Drake's burning body. He dropped to one knee, bowing deeply before Khol. "You are my second now, Macon. Don't disappoint me as Drake did." Khol then turned to me. "I'm sorry." Pain played across his features briefly before he disappeared before my eyes.

As soon as he was gone, a dam within me broke, sobs wracking my body. I never betrayed Bryn willingly. Magic was used on me. How did I not sense it at all? And Bryn... he hadn't so much as touched Nala despite the magic that had been used on him. He was stronger than I'd been with Khol. I'd come close...sp very close to letting Khol have me before I was sent away on my mission to Tennessee. And then it would have been too late. I would have never had another chance with Bryn. I lifted my gaze to meet

Bryn's burning blue eyes and he came to me, sweeping me into his comforting embrace.

My Bryn...my mate...my home. "Bryn," I murmured. "I'm—"

"Shhh..." he rumbled. "I know." I wanted to ask him if all was forgiven. I knew we were finally mated but that wouldn't change the fact that he might continue to be bitter about my seeming eagerness to hook up with Khol. And okay, I had definitely been eager, but as it turned out, it hadn't been entirely my fault.

"Why didn't you sleep with Nala? How did you resist?" Another topic probably best left for another time, but I had to know, even if it made me a hypocrate.

Bryn tilted my head back towards him with the aid of his long index finger. "Because I love you. Not her."

It was both the most perfect and worst thing he could have responded with. The most perfect because him telling me he loved me so unconditionally was something I was worried I'd never hear. It was the worst because I hadn't treated him the same in kind. I hadn't loved him unconditionally at all.

I slipped my chin off of his finger, crushing the side of my face to his chest. "I don't deserve you." And in that moment I knew that I didn't, that Bryn was more than I ever deserved to have.

"No, you don't. But I guess we're stuck with each other from now on." I could hear the smile in his voice as he teased me like he used to. *God, I've missed him.* I clutched him to me even harder, pushing my nose into his chest so the only thing I could smell was him, and not the lingering scent of burnt flesh.

"Let's get out of here," Bryn murmured as he tightened his arms around me. "I don't want a reminder of what just happened." And with that, a familiar feeling of weightlessness surrounded me as Bryn transported us out of his room. *Not that he needs that room anymore*, I thought smugly, because he was mine and he would be back in *our* room, with *me*…where he belonged.

"Peej," Bryn rumbled. "I'll never leave you again—I swear—I'm here—always." Tears began to freefall down my face. I couldn't believe I'd almost lost him…again. And in some way, even though Drake had manipulated me, I'd willingly participated in the destruction of our relationship. "Hey," Bryn tried to console me as he continued to hold me tightly to his chest, tenderly stroking my hair. "Don't. Don't think about what could have happened."

I pulled away from Bryn reluctantly, gazing up into the face of the man I loved, the face of a fallen angel—*my fallen angel*. "We thought everything had been settled before, both in the dragon realm and after. Who's to say something won't rip us apart again?" Another huge sob escaped from my constricted chest as I allowed myself to say my worst fears out loud. Who was to say if Bryn was really and truly mine? I'd dared to believe it before and look where that had gotten me. I'd been shattered into a billion pieces.

"We'll be more careful. Trust no one but each other. It's

the only way to survive this apparently." He pulled me back into his arms. "I don't care if that baby is mine or not, I'll love it like it is."

I didn't think it was possible but I started to cry harder. I'd wanted to hear those words from Bryn from the beginning, to hear him say he'd never really walk away from me, that it had all been one huge mistake—and it had been. Thanks to Drake. "I love you, Peej."

"I love you, too," I croaked.

He tilted my head back, claiming my lips with a tenderness that spoke of a forever kind of love. Our kind of love. *Always.*

Chapter 19

Bryn was mine again, something that only in my wildest dreams had I dared to hope for. And we finally had the answers to what ultimately caused our relationship to crumble. Despite the current chaos: me becoming the next dragon queen, Jenna getting possessed by a Rider, me going to Tennessee on a solo mission, me hooking up with Khol, me finding out I was pregnant—well, somehow Bryn and my relationship felt stronger than ever. We weathered the storm and came out on the other side better for it.

Bryn was my true mate now, *my Anam Cara*, our marks wouldn't be disappearing anytime soon, unless one of us died, and I wasn't about to let myself consider the possibility of that grim reality. With Bryn by my side, I could make everything else right again. Because I had also learned that the person I needed to depend on the most was me. Bryn was my partner—my mate—but it wasn't his job to take care of me, even though he certainly seemed to want to.

"Do you feel okay?" Bryn tried to hide the worry in his voice. "You still don't have morning sickness, do you?"

I laughed into his chest, where I was currently splayed across. We decided to have just a little bit more alone time before facing the real world again. Both of us had been dealing with a little too much of that lately. "No, I'm fine."

"God, Peej, you have no idea how much it was tearing me up knowing you were pregnant and me not being there for you. At least not in the way I wanted to be."

It was almost weird how easily I was moving on from everything now that I had Bryn back. He made me feel anchored to reality in a way that no one else probably ever could. Sometimes it felt like if I didn't share things with Bryn, they really didn't happen, or didn't mean anything. I guess that's because he'd been the most important person in my life since I was five years old. "I don't wanna think about any of it, Bryn. Let's just pretend none of it happened."

"Peej—that's just not realistic."

"Fine. If you can't pretend, then lets at least not talk about it." I frowned into his chest. Why rehash all the unpleasant things that happened between us lately when we could simply be enjoying what was between us now?

Bryn didn't say anything for a few minutes, and I knew he was thinking about if he should just go along or argue with me. He heaved a huge sigh, causing my head to move up and down with his chest. "All right. You might have a point."

"I always have a point." I sat up, grinning at him.

"Yeah, but I didn't say it was a good one." Bryn gave me his patented lop sided grin complete with dimples, his eyes glinting at me with mischief.

My insides melted. I'd dreamt about that smile, combined with that gleam in his eyes, quite literally. I was suddenly hit with an overwhelming desire to have my unborn child wear that exact same smile. "I want the baby to be yours. So badly, Bryn," I said around the huge lump that had formed in my throat.

Bryn's face clouded over. "Yeah, me too." He then guffawed. "Us parents...at twenty...who would have thunk it?"

"Certainly not me. I always thought if anyone, Jenna would be the one to get pregnant this young."

"Yeah, you and me both."

Not wanting to let our conversation turn anywhere darker when it came to my pregnancy, I knew it was time for us to get back to reality. *I always hate this part. Reality bites.* "We have a Rider to question." I pulled myself out of his embrace with reluctance and began getting dressed.

"You mean *you* do," Bryn grumbled as he too started pulling his clothes on. I stopped and stared at his chiseled body. Even though Drake had been poisoning him, Bryn still looked mighty fine...mighty fine indeed.

I gnawed on my bottom lip. "Are you sure you feel okay? I mean Drake was poisoning you. I think that maybe we should have Khol use his healing powers on you or something." Would Khol have to touch Bryn, kiss him? That would be veeerry interesting, I smirked to myself.

"You've got to be kidding me," Bryn growled. "Khol's done enough. I'll be fine. The poison will pass out of my system. Besides"—he grinned at me mischievously—"I can think of plenty of ways to *work* it out of my body and none of them require anyone but you."

I chose to ignore his remark about Khol, laughing. "That doesn't even make sense, Bryn. I'm gonna label that innuendo as failed."

"It's not failed because you got what I was going for," Bryn protested with false indignance.

"Yeah, okay, whatever." I rolled my eyes, turning to leave the room. It felt so good—beyond good—to be able to talk to Bryn like this again. I'd missed him so much. He might be more, but he was still my best friend—my best friend with tons of extra benefits. "By the way"—I stopped and met Bryn's gaze with narrowed eyes—"if you ever try to leave me again." I paused for dramatic effect. "I'll more than just slap you." I don't know why I felt the need to tell him that at that moment, but I did. Maybe on some level I felt most things we could move on and not talk about... bury our heads in the sand...but not that.

Bryn gave me a tight-lipped smile. "We're mated now. Nothing to worry about."

I bared my teeth at him. "If something happens—like

before—if you walk away from me—I'll make you regret it."

Bryn's brows furrowed as he studied me. "Are you threatening me, Peej?"

"Yeah, I guess I am."

Bryn's full lips turned up slightly at the corners, showcasing his dimples. "I wonder if it's the whole being mated thing, but I kind of think it's hot, how you're reacting to the thought of me leaving."

I quirked one bemused eyebrow at him. "Seriously?"

"Yeah." His eyes darkened to show the sudden heat in them that was burning for me. "I know I was stupid, Peej —beyond stupid. But you know I did it all out of love for you."

I flicked my gaze to the floor, not wanting to get caught in the magnetic pull of his sea storm eyes. "That almost makes it worse," I mumbled.

Macon appeared in front of me, causing me to jump. One would think I'd be used to dragons popping in and out around me by now, but I wasn't. And I could only sense the ripple of power letting me know someone was about to appear if I was paying attention, and not fully focused on Bryn. "My lord sent me to bring you to question the Rider known as Cliff. He wanted to remind you that you also have queenly duties that go beyond seeing to your mate, Bryn." *Harsh.* But then again, I guess Khol reserved the right to be a little mean to me after everything we'd been through together.

"Lead the way," I said, somehow managing to curb my sarcastic tongue.

Bryn and I trailed along behind Macon silently, hand in hand. The tension between Macon and us was palpable. I sensed Macon wanted to say something to me but just couldn't bring himself to broach whatever subject it was. I was sure it either had to do with Jenna, or the fact that Bryn and me were mated...again. Either way, I was glad he was keeping his mouth shut.

When we came to a huge wooden door, much like the one that Jenna was stashed behind, Macon pushed it open, stepping back to allow us entrance. We both slid past him, and I for one didn't make eye contact.

"It's about time," Khol's snapped as soon as I crossed the threshold. I looked up to meet his eyes and beyond his annoyance was a world of pain. I had completely crushed him by choosing Bryn. I knew that on some level, but seeing it was something else entirely. I dropped Bryn's hand as my face heated. *How can I be so callous?* I didn't have to rub it in Khol's face, did I?

"Hey," I said, my face flushing. *I'm a horrible, horrible person.* But then again I couldn't really be considered a person so... *I'm a horrible, horrible dragon.*

I glanced to my right, spotting a tied up and bloodied Cliff. "What the hell? What did you do?" *Oh, please don't tell me that Khol has been taking out his anger on Cliff.* I was still holding onto the hope that we could return him to his normal life once we figured out a way to get the Rider out of him.

"What needed to be done," Khol responded coldly.

Yeah, okay. I could tell by Khol's expression that there would be no arguing with him over this. If I had wanted it to go differently then maybe I shouldn't have stayed in bed with Bryn and been there to protect Cliff's body instead. "Did you get any useful information at least?"

"Nothing exceptionally useful." Khol strode over to stand inches away from Cliff, who flinched away from him with fear. "The time for questioning is over."

"Okaaay," I drawled out. "So why am I here then?"

"We need to figure out how to remove a Rider from its host." Khol waved his hand over Cliff's head as if I should have known that. "Here is the perfect candidate for us to experiment on."

"What?" I was so not using poor Cliff as a guinea pig.

Khol's mouth flattening into a thin line. "Would you rather use Jenna?"

"No! Of course not. It's just…" I shook my head. "Poor Cliff."

"Every war has collateral damage. You, as a queen, should get used to that fact."

"And I guess Cliff is a better choice than Jenna for that," I mumbled to myself. I lifted my head, meeting his steely gaze square on. "What do I need to do?"

"WHAT ELSE CAN WE TRY?" I ground out, beyond frustrated. We had spent—Khol, Bryn, and myself—the last couple of hours trying to force the Rider out of Cliff's body with everything we could think of. I just didn't understand it. My birth mother said it was possible, and she said I was the one to do it. But how? When neither Bryn nor Khol responded to my question, I repeated it with more vehemence. "What else can we try?"

"I don't know." Khol scrubbed a hand down his face, exhaustion marring his features. "I just don't know." Bryn remained silent as he stared at Cliff, his dragon blue eyes blazing brightly.

"Well, we can't just give up!" My voice climbed a few octaves.

"No one's giving up," Khol grumbled. "Maybe we just need a break, to take some time to think about this.

"I want that thing out of Jenna now!" *I will not cry again. I will not cry again.*

Bryn put his arm around my shoulders, pulling me into his side. "I know," he murmured, brushing his soft lips against my temple. "I know."

"Fine. We'll take a break." I pulled myself away from Bryn and stalked towards the door. I was letting my anger take hold in me so I wouldn't feel the anguish of not having the answer to save Jenna yet. *But I will find it if it's the last thing I do.*

"My lord!" Macon burst through the door, nearly knocking me over. "We're under attack!"

"The Riders?" Khol growled.

"Yes."

"How did they breach our wards?" Khol swore under his breath. "Someone had to have led them here."

I was supposed to be queen, but I didn't have the experience and scope of knowledge to deal with this kind of thing, so I looked to Khol for answers, as usual. "What should we do?" I tried to hide the panic in my voice, failing miserably.

Khol was already leaning down to untie an unconscious Cliff when he responded, "We retreat, and re-gather ourselves. We have something they obviously want very badly, but we're not in a position to use it to our full advantage when we're on the defensive."

"So we run away?"

Khol grimaced. "I would prefer a different choice of words, but yes."

"We need to bring Jenna with us!" I sprinted from the room, not waiting for anyone.

"Peej!" Bryn was close at my heels. "I'll help you!"

I nodded but didn't turn to acknowledge him. I was on a mission. I had to get to Jenna before the skeevy Riders did. Just as I made it to the door of Jenna's prison, Jeremy came barreling out with her slung over his shoulder, unconscious. "What's the plan?" he blurted out as soon as he saw us.

"Well, you already have the first part covered. I guess the next step is to get the hell out of Dodge," Bryn answered for me.

"We'll use a gate," Jeremy said, turning to lead the way down the long corridor.

Anxiety sparked to life in my mind. *What if we don't make it? What will happen if—* Shoving my worry aside, I sped along quickly behind Jeremy, hand-in-hand with Bryn. I only stumbled a few times trying to keep up before Bryn scooped me up in his arms. I didn't bother to protest because I knew he was right. We'd move faster with him carrying me.

We finally made it out of one of the back exits and scurried towards the forest, where Jeremy would open the gate, a.k.a. escape route. *Strange how we haven't seen one single Rider on the way out.* In fact, we hadn't spotted anyone on the way out. I hardly had time to register the wrongness of the situation when we burst into the clearing, coming face-to-face with a horde of Riders.

We skidded to a stop just as Khol appeared beside us with Macon, who was carrying a still unconscious Cliff. It was evident in that moment that our little crew had run straight into a trap.

"Give me my son," Senator Bill Wexington snarled.

"Nala," Bryn growled. And sure enough she was standing a little bit behind our dear Senator, arms crossed.

"You set us up," Macon chimed in angrily. "We were never under attack."

Nala sneered at Macon. "No. But I convinced everyone that we were, and all your allies high tailed it out of there. You're alone now."

"Why?" Bryn demanded, his question obviously directed at Nala.

Her face softened when she shifted her gaze to his.

"We belong together, can't you see that? I knew it from the first moment I laid eyes on you."

"She's our queen. You can't kill her," Khol snarled at Nala.

"Why not? We've gone all these years without a queen, we can manage without one again. I would have been happy to let her live, but she couldn't keep her hands off of him."

I tightened my arms around Bryn possessively, too shocked to feel the full strength of my anger at Nala for what she'd done.

"Enough!" the Rider that was Senator Bill Wexington interjected. "You can work through all of your ridiculous drama after I get my son back."

"Not going to happen," Khol growled. "Not unless you agree to leave our world."

The Senator's lips curled up in what was supposed to be a smile, at least that's what I thought he was going for. "We'll see."

He waved his hand and a tall figure stepped forward into the light. *Holy shit! It's Evan Thompson.* He was the Gatekeeper who had starred in my long-ago fantasies, back before all of this had begun. Now a Rider's silhouette blazed from inside of him.

Evan began moving in a similar fashion to what I'd seen Jeremy do to open a gate. Although in my opinion, Jeremy did it with much more confidence and grace. *Yep... because that matters right now.* When Evan finished and a gate shimmered open to the right of us, more Riders stepped through.

"As you were saying?" the Senator asked, tilting his head at Khol.

Khol's power snapped through the air as he readied for attack. It hummed against my skin, spiking my system with adrenaline, and ratcheting up my nerves. Bryn set me on my feet, tensing for what would happen next. I didn't have to look at Macon and Jeremy to know that they were doing the same. We wouldn't go down without a fight.

"Just give me my son and we'll leave you in peace." The Senator tried using a more placating tone. "We have no interest in the affairs of dragons. Just the humans."

"I want Bryn," Nala demanded. "You promised if I helped you that you would get rid of her." She raised her index finger, pointing directly at me.

Bryn bared his teeth. "I'll never be yours, Nala. You're not the type of woman I could ever want. Besides, you think after I've had a queen, I'd want you?"

I couldn't help the smile that tugged at my lips. *That's right! He's mine bitch!*

The Senator sighed demonstratively. "All right. Let's see what else I have in my little bag of tricks that might convince you to see things my way." He motioned again with his hand and some dragons, a few from every faction appeared on their side. The effect of the battle lines being drawn was not lost on me. And before the shock of him having additional dragons on his side could fully sink in, the Mac Daddy of surprises stepped forward. Bryn's father walked into the mix.

"Dad?" Bryn's voice wavered in question. "I thought you were dead."

The Senator spoke up. "Seers and Speakers are useless with one of us in them, but Gatekeepers and Guardians— oh yes—they work quite nicely. So, I decided to keep a few of them around, just in case."

"Don't worry, Bryn," I whispered under my breath. "We'll save him and Jenna both."

"It's time you found out the truth, Bryn. You're not my son." Bryn's father's lips curled up into a sneer. "Your mother couldn't conceive, and then we were given a gift. At least we thought it was a gift at the time. I never thought you'd shame me the way that you did by taking up with P.J. when it's against our laws. But I guess you're not even fully human. No wonder whoever left you for us didn't want you."

What? My mind immediately went to when my birth mother had revealed that Bryn, another dragon, at least half dragon, growing up so close to me hadn't happened by chance. She told me that he was there for a reason. At the time I hadn't considered the true implications.

"I'll enjoy taking you out myself just for the heartbreak you caused your mother. She was so ashamed of how you disregarded the most important law of being a Guardian. May she rest in peace. It's your fault she's dead after all. Yours and hers," he hissed, his eyes briefly darting to mine.

Everything seemed to happen at once. Bryn's father

launch himself at Bryn, but I couldn't track anything else that was going on after Nala slammed into me, causing me to hit to the ground. She scrambled to get on top of me, placing all of her body weight on my chest while choking me. I desperately reached for my fire magic, but black stars danced in front of my eyes, stealing my focus. Water trickled over my face, covering it, and I sputtered for air.

Dazed, I registered that Nala was using some kind of water-power to suffocate me faster. I gasped for air again, my lungs on fire, and came back with a mouth full of water. My vision grew darker and my thoughts slower. I knew she was drowning me—killing me.

Suddenly the pressure released, and I jolted up, gasping lungful after lungful of fresh air. I clutched at my throat, my vision returning in time to witness Khol shove his fire magic into Nala. She let out an ear-shattering scream, and then she was gone, nothing but a pile of ashes. *Good*, I numbly thought.

I stumbled to my feet, scanning the clearing for Bryn, who was currently rolling around on the ground with his father. Bryn was at a huge disadvantage because it was obvious he didn't really want to hurt him. His father clearly didn't feel the same way. "Help him!" I screeched at Khol.

"Enough!" Senator Bill Wexington's voice rolled over everyone like a clap of thunder. "Hold him," he ordered Bryn's father, who stood with Bryn, bringing him into a headlock. The Senator met my eyes. "Him for my son."

It wasn't even a decision. "Okay. Just don't hurt him."

The Senator nodded at one of the Riders standing beside him who walked slowly over to Cliff's prone, unconscious figure, picking him up. Khol came to stand behind him so he couldn't make his way back to the Senator just yet.

"Now let Bryn go," I said with false calmness. My insides were finding a new definition for panic.

Bryn's father released him, and Bryn walked steadily back towards me. Khol then gave the Rider holding Cliff a rough push to get him going. I reached my shaky hand out to Bryn, needing to feel his skin under my fingertips. He gave me a tight smile, and I knew he was thinking it was his fault we were losing Cliff as a bargaining chip—that he should have been able to best his father—that he couldn't even protect himself—how would he protect me and my unborn child? I could read all of his tormented thoughts in his eyes but I couldn't bring myself to care as long as he was safe.

As soon as my hand gripped his, I heaved a sigh of relief. "I love you," I mouthed to him. None of the rest mattered. We might be down, but we weren't out just yet. I would make him understand that eventually. We were finally bonded as *Anam Caras* and together we could take on the world.

Bryn's father abruptly appeared directly behind him. The Rider inside of him shone so brightly it eclipsed his host's features. He met my gaze, grinning down at me. In that instant, understanding slammed into me.

"No!" I screamed, my heart fisting painfully in my chest. I reached for my fire magic, but it was too late—all too late. I watched, completely helpless to stop it, as Bryn's father gripped his head and twisted, snapping the neck of his only son. The sharp crack shot through my skull and pierced my eardrums. "No!" I heard myself scream again as Bryn's hand slipped from my grasp, his body collapsing lifelessly to the ground.

Life over. My Life is over.

"Like I said, he wasn't really my son."

Silence swallowed me whole.

My entire being aware of nothing but Bryn, I threw myself at him, wanting nothing more than to curl up and die right alongside him. But someone caught me around the waist and began to run towards the pulsating gate with me in tow.

Sound came back to me in a rush, someone's hysterical screams pounding against my head. *Is that me? I don't know and don't care.*

When whoever was carrying me reached the gate, they jumped in without pause. My gaze remained riveted on Bryn's crumpled body even as my skin iced over, and the oxygen was sucked from my lungs. I didn't stay conscious for much more than a moment as the magic of the gate pulled me down into welcome oblivion.

Acknowledgments

I have a whole list of people that deserve to be thanked here, and with that in mind, I was going to simply use my original acknowledgments from the first version of Broken Gates buuuut …I'm currently in the process of moving and all of my books are in boxes. I would rip all those bad boys all open to find my copy of the old Broken Gates but let's face it, that seems like entirely too much work and I'm already stressed from all the packing as it is.

I would rather list no one here than risk accidentally leaving someone out. So to avoid such a catastrophe, I'm simply going to thank all of the readers out there that have given my books a chance. You mean the world to me. Thank you.

About the Author

Ava Wixx escaped into books at a young age and decided to stay there. It was only a matter of time before she was driven to create her own fantasy worlds from fear of running out of places to explore.

Reader, writer, dreamer … Ava only toils in reality when absolutely necessary. She lives in North Carolina with her husband, and spoiled mini-poodle.

(If you want up-to-date info on book-y things then visit Avawixx.com and don't bother with the social media. Because let's face it, Ava is an online slacker and she signed up for some accounts but never actually posts.)